# WARRIOR'S REDEMPTION

## TRIALS OF THE AEGIS
### BOOK THREE

## AARON HODGES

# ABOUT THE AUTHOR

Aaron Hodges was born in 1989 in the small town of Whakatane, New Zealand. He studied for five years at the University of Auckland, completing a Bachelors of Science in Biology and Geography, and a Masters of Environmental Engineering. After working as an environmental consultant for two years, he grew tired of office work and decided to quit his job in 2014 and see the world. One year later, he published his first novel - Stormwielder.

**FOLLOW AARON HODGES…**

And receive TWO FREE novels and a short story!

https://aaronhodgesauthor.com/newsletter

Book 1: Warbringer

Book 2: Wrath of the Forgotten

Book 3: Age of Gods

Book 4: Dreams of Fury

## *The Alfurian Chronicles*

Book 1: Defiant

Book 2: Guardian

Book 3: Conquest

## *The Swords of Heaven and Hell*

Book 1: Darkstrider

Book 2: Voidlight

## *The Four Circles*

Book 1: Help! My Wizard Mentor Had A Heart Attack And Now I'm Being Chased By A Horde Of Giant Spiders!

## *The Untamed Isles*

The Path Awakens

# The Kingdom of Fresia

# 1

Crouched in the shadows of a narrow alley, Kaila Dwyn waited.

Tah'raus was restless tonight, as if the city held its breath. Somewhere in the distance, a dog barked once, then fell silent. Wooden shutters banged against stone walls and a newborn's cry carried through the dark. Above, laundry stirred in the ocean breeze.

Old wheels creaked closer. Kaila let the cart and its driver pass, untouched—unaware of the monster crouched just a few feet away.

Elysian. That's what she was—what she would always be to the people of this city. One of the monsters that had warred with humanity for a thousand years. But she would not hold their prejudice against them. At least, not tonight. Tonight, Kaila Dwyn had more important prey.

The squeaking faded as the cart turned a corner. Then came the rhythmic thump of boots on stone. Holding her breath, Kaila glanced out from her hiding place. A heavy fog had rolled off the harbour as the hour struck midnight, curling through the streets. The agimet-powered streetlamps struggled to pierce the mist…

*There!*

She pressed her back against the crumbling wall as silhouettes emerged from the mists. The soldiers were close—close enough to make out the murmur of their voices and muted clink of armour beneath heavy cloaks.

The patrols had begun three months ago, shortly after the coronation of the new Matron. The people of Tah'raus were afraid after the brutal murder of their monarchs. Fresia had withstood a thousand years of war with their Elysian enemy, but it had been many decades—if not centuries—since that violence had touched the capital. The soldiers were meant to reassure the people that all was well.

But then those soldiers started dying.

It was a shame it had come to this. At first, she and Ambrose and the others in the Elysian resistance had been hopeful when they'd learned about the death of the old Matron—and that Jenna Frye would be crowned in her place. Because they knew something no one in the Magisterium knew: Jenna was one of them. Elysian. Born to the assassin known only as the Reaper.

An Elysian sitting on the Fresian throne could have changed everything.

But of course, the world wouldn't change just because you hoped it would. And there was one thing Kaila Dwyn had learned in her short life—people always act in their own best interests.

Jenna Frye had betrayed the people of her blood and pinned the deaths of her mother and father on the Elysian. More specifically, the individual known as Kaila Dwyn.

Well, if the new Matron wanted to make her a monster, Kaila was happy to oblige.

She shifted her weight, boots silent on the stone. Her fingers itched for the crystal in her pocket, but she hesitated. Lately, her Gift had been…off. Sometimes she heard strange noises when she drew *atar* from the crystals—odd, almost musical notes that set her teeth on edge.

More than once, the distraction had broken her concentration, sending whatever object she was moving crashing to the ground. Usually, those were just rocks she used as projectiles; but once, it'd been Ambrose himself.

The tailor had *not* been impressed.

It was just stress. Too much pressure, not enough sleep. She had hardly paused since the night of the Summer Gala, when she'd lost everyone and everything that had still mattered to her.

But what else could she do? This war was all she had left.

Kaila hesitated a second longer, then drew her knife instead. Turning her attention to the patrol, she counted their number as they marched past. One, two…six silhouettes emerged from the mists—twice the usual number. Apparently, someone high in the Magisterium was growing cautious. Finally.

There was still no Warden, however, from what she could tell. They were the Magisterium's only true weapon against the Gift of the Elysian. Yet the armour-clad soldiers had hardly been seen since the inauguration. There were whispers in the underground about disagreement within the order, but nothing solid. For now, Kaila and the other Elysian took the Trickster's blessings where they could.

Exhaling, Kaila adjusted her scarf, careful not to let her fingers graze her throat. The burns had almost healed, but the skin was still thin and itched like the devil when she thought about it. The scar, however, would be with her forever—a final parting gift from her time as a Daughter of the Magisterium

It was also a reminder of their so-called *mercy*.

A tremor shook Kaila's soul. Every night, she revisited that night atop the Sanctum and watched Rohan fall. Again and again, she tore the collar from her neck and suffered its searing kiss to save him.

And again and again, she saw him spurn her.

He was the only man Kaila had ever met that had made her believe things could get better. That maybe there was a way forward for human and Elysian, a path without violence or fear or…

*Get away from me!*

It was as though he'd torn a chunk from her soul, leaving a gaping wound that would not mend. Every day she woke was pain, every moment a waking nightmare from which she could not escape.

The crunch of stone beneath heavy boots snapped Kaila back to the present. It was time. She tensed as the first of the soldiers passed her hiding place—then froze as he paused, turning in her direction. Blood pulsing in her ears, Kaila watched him from the darkness, even as her fingers crept again towards the crystal. Agimet would reveal her, but if she was seen now, a knife wouldn't be enough for six men…

The soldier grunted something unintelligible to his companions and continued walking, footsteps muffled by the mist. Kaila exhaled her relief, waiting as the other five continued past. Only then did she slip from the alleyway and start after them.

The soldier in the back was obviously a veteran; the way his head moved, eyes constantly scanning the shadows. One hand rested on the hilt of his sword, ready for the slightest hint of danger.

He would be the first.

Kaila slipped through the mists. She wouldn't have used her Gift for this one anyway. Her power tended to be noisy. Instead, the rasp of steel against leather was the soldier's only warning. Then she was on him. Her blade flashed, a wicked, pointed thing that tore through the leather of his armour, deep into his flesh.

Garrick had taught her to aim for the kidney, and as her target stiffened in a silent scream, Kaila knew she'd found her mark. Clamping a hand over his mouth, she dragged him into the mist, then lowered his body carefully to the ground. He twitched once, then stilled.

She held her breath, listening for any hint the others had noticed—but the fog was her ally tonight. The steady rhythm of boots ahead didn't so much as falter.

A second soldier met his end in the same manner. Unfortunately, this one carried a lantern. Kaila tried to catch it before it fell, but the handle was slick with dew and it slipped through her fingers. Crystal shattered as it struck the cobbles, sending shards of glowing agimet skittering across the street.

"Ambush!"

The cry went up from the remaining soldiers as they spun and saw her standing alone in the street.

*So much for traditional weapons,* Kaila thought as she reached into her pocket and drew out the agimet.

Unlike the crystals used by the Magisterium, her crystal was raw and unpolished, untouched by any blade or chisel. The Elysian needed uncut agimet for their magic; crystals that had been fractured or shaped became dangerous to them, even addictive if used to fuel their Gift.

*Atar* flooded Kaila's veins as she drew on the crystal's power. Silver light spilled from her eyes, flooding the street with its glow. The sight was enough to give even a grizzled veteran pause. Without a Warden, these men had no protection against her magic—and they knew it.

But they were also soldiers of Fresia, indoctrinated from birth to stand tall in the face of the evil Elysian. So while the colour drained from their faces, one wearing the badge of a captain drew his blade.

"Come on, lads!" he bellowed. "Let's show this beast what Fresian men are made of!"

Kaila suppressed a sigh. It was always the same. At least it made things simpler. As the four advanced, she spun a thread of *atar* from her soul and directed it at the captain. She was what Theron called a 'Mover', and as her thread connected with the man's soul, he discovered exactly what that entailed.

Before the captain could take two steps, she had him wrapped in her power. With a swipe of her hand, she sent him hurtling into a nearby wall. The gesture was entirely showmanship, but it served to make a point—don't mess with an Elysian.

The captain left a bloody mark on the stone as he slumped to the ground. Silence followed as Kaila turned to the remaining soldiers, a faint smile on her lips. This was usually the point where they fled.

But the Sisters must have been giving some particularly vigorous sermons lately, because instead, all three charged at her, screaming.

*Well, that complicates things…*

The world shimmered as Kaila activated her *atarsight*. Concentrating on their *soullights*, she spun three fresh threads of *atar* into existence. The more she connected with at a time, the more difficult it was to use her Gift—but she didn't have time to deal with them one by one.

The largest of the soldiers was already swinging at her as

she connected. No time to think—she pushed him aside with her Gift and the blow went wide.

Unfortunately, her concentration failed as the others lunged at her, breaking the connection before she could strike a mortal blow. Cursing, she ducked, narrowly avoiding a sword slicing through the fog. A second blade grazed her shoulder, but the heavy cloth of her cloak deflected most of the blow. She dived, sliding across the slick cobblestones with a grace that would have made her father proud.

A bellow rang out behind her.

She came to her feet as the captain charged again, sword raised high, teeth bared. No time for her Gift—Kaila hurled her dagger and prayed her aim was true.

*Thunk.*

The brute stumbled as the blade plunged into his eye socket. His momentum carried him forwards, however, and Kaila had to duck aside to avoid being crushed as he fell.

Another was on her before she could recover. This one was smart enough not to announce his attack with a shout. His sword swept towards her and this time Kaila was too slow. The blade tore across her shoulder, and she stumbled back, biting back a scream.

Grinning, the soldier chased her. He had a mean look about him, with cruel eyes and a jagged birthmark on his cheek. He offered no respite for Kaila to recover—but she was angry now. Snarling, she sent a thread of *atar* hurtling in his direction.

His *soullight* jerked like a marionette on a string, before the force of her Gift launched him into a pile of crates lying in the mouth of the alley. Splinters flew as they crumpled beneath his weight. He didn't rise again.

Gritting her teeth, Kaila swung around, searching for the remaining soldiers. Only the captain and one other remained now. The mists swirled around her, obscuring the street, but Kaila had an advantage. Opening her *atarsight*, she spotted their *soullights* immediately. They were trying to use the mist as cover to creep up on her.

*Finally, a break.*

Hot blood trickled down her shoulder. She pressed a hand to the wound, trying to slow the bleeding, and centred herself in her Gift. The *atar* in her crystal was nearly gone, but unlike other Elysian, Kaila had the power to recharge agimet crystals—instead of waiting hours while it did so naturally. Her only limitation was that she needed at least some ambient *atar* to draw from. With Tah'raus being built over a powerful nexus, that wasn't a problem here, but over the past few months she'd been experimenting outside the city. The further she went from the nexus, the more difficult recharging the crystals became.

For now, the *atar* in her crystal was enough for what she had planned. A thread of silver shot through the night, connecting to the pair of soldiers as they emerged from the mist. They stumbled as Kaila raised her hand, suddenly finding themselves immobilised.

Kaila allowed herself a smile. It was over. She could feel their fear—the kind that made knees buckle and bowels clench. It was a terror only the truly helpless could know; the kind so many Elysian had felt in their final moments, before the agents of the Magisterium dragged them away—

*SCREECH!*

A shriek like tearing metal slammed into Kaila's senses. She staggered, clapping her hands to her ears, but it didn't help. The noise only grew louder, redoubling in force, drilling into her skull. A scream tore from her lips—and strangely, it wasn't alone. Other voices joined her own, their shared agony echoing through the streets…

*There was a man in the darkness. Oberon. The fallen king of the Elysian. He loomed in the sky above her, his face shaded by the dark of night, eyes aglow with moonlight. There was anger on his face.*

*"Is this what has become of my children?" His words thundered. "Too weak to claim their birthright?" He turned from her.*

*"Wait!" Kaila cried, stretching out a hand. "Wait, please, I don't—"*

Something jerked Kaila back to the freezing streets of Tah'raus. She awoke face down, cheek pressed to the damp stone, her entire body radiating pain. Groaning, she forced her eyes to open—and almost lost the contents of her stomach as the world swam. Her vision flickered from white to red to black, and distantly she was aware of where she was, of danger…

*The soldiers!*

Heart palpitating, she sat bolt upright, already scrambling for a weapon—but her hands came up empty.

Leather scraped on stone. Something shifted in the mist. The soldier with the birthmark lurched into sight. Snarling, eyes full of hatred, he thrust his blade at her midsection.

Still on the ground, Kaila scrambled for her agimet—but as her fingers closed around the precious crystal, she found it empty. Every drop of *atar* had been drained, as if an inferno had raged through her *soullight*, consuming all it touched.

She had nothing left.

*Clang!*

Steel rang on steel as a blade appeared from the mist, deflecting the blow. Kaila flinched as sparks scattered across the cobblestones—and then a giant of a man stepped between her and the soldier. His eyes glowed with *atar*, muscles rippling with the impossible power of a Bruiser.

*Garrick.*

Kaila sagged to the ground as he squared off against the

Fresian soldier. Steel clashed again, hard and violent, but *atar* made Garrick as strong as ten men—and twice as durable. He wasn't the kind of Gifted you went up against in a physical contest. Within a few heartbeats, he decapitated the soldier with a backhanded swing of his greatsword.

Still aching from whatever she'd done with her Gift, Kaila propped herself up on one elbow as the Bruiser approached and offered her his hand. Reluctantly, she accepted the aid, and pain redoubled as he hauled her upright.

"You alright, kid?" the big man asked. His nose was misshapen and mean-looking scars crisscrossed his face, but she knew from Theron this face was only an illusion woven by Ambrose, their leader.

"I think so," she muttered, before turning a frown on the Bruiser. "What are you doing here? Weren't you supposed to be clearing out the Chapman warehouse?"

A frown creased the big man's forehead. "We finished that an hour ago. I came looking for you when you didn't show at the rendezvous." He hesitated, glancing around at the bodies in the street. "What the hell happened here?"

*An hour?* Kaila hesitated. Had she really been out that long?

"I'm...not sure," she said hesitantly.

*Something* had happened with her Gift. The last thing she remembered was reaching out for the remaining soldiers, ready to hurl them into the nearest wall. Instead, she'd blacked out. Why? And if she'd been out so long, what had happened to those last two soldiers?

Shards from the broken lantern still lit the street. She counted the bodies—all six were here. Clutching her wounded arm, Kaila stumbled towards a pair that had fallen together, and froze.

It was the last two soldiers alright, but...

*What in the Trickster's name happened to them?*

Kaila couldn't look away. Their bodies were twisted, limbs bent at unnatural angles, and their eyes were still open and staring, the whites stained scarlet. Blood had run as tears down their cheeks, bubbling from their lips. Her gaze lingered on their faces. The way their lips curled back and theirs mouths twisted…

It looked like they had died screaming.

*Whatever* had killed them, the pair had died in agony.

Kaila staggered back, horror rising in her throat to choke her. This hadn't been her, had it? A Mover couldn't do this to a person. This wasn't what her Gift did.

*Was it?*

"Kaila?" Stones crunched as Garrick approached. "What…" He trailed off, finally noticing the pair of fallen soldiers.

"I connected to them with my Gift," she croaked. "I heard a noise, some kind of ringing. Next I knew, I was waking up on the ground…"

Could this really have been her? If so, this was nothing like what had happened before. It terrified her, thinking there might be something wrong with her power. Especially now she didn't have Theron to guide her.

No one had seen him since that night atop the Sanctum. It was like he had just…disappeared. Most Elysian believed he had died that night, vanished into the bowels of the black dome like so many of their kind. Strangest of all though, they didn't talk about him. It was like a taboo had been placed on his name, as if just to speak it might invite the same fate upon them.

For a while, Kaila had held out hope. He'd been alive when she fled that night, suffering, in agony from the aftereffects of agimet withdrawal. But *alive.* And when she'd heard about the death of the old Matron, how her only daughter Jenna had been elected to take her place…

But that had been three months ago.

"Kaila, if something is happening with your Gift, we need to tell Ambrose."

Kaila startled at Garrick's voice and finally tore her eyes from the bodies. Slowly, she nodded. Ambrose might not be a Mover, but he was still one of the most powerful Elysian in the city. If anyone could understand what had happened with her power, it would be him.

If he had time for her problems, of course.

Since their failed attempt to steal the Aegis and undermine the Magisterium's leadership, the tailor had thrown himself into resisting the new Matron's reign. He wouldn't get another chance at the Aegis—not in his lifetime, at least—but as he'd told her the night after their failed heist: life didn't wait for you to catch your breath. You either stood back up and kept fighting, or the world stayed exactly as it was.

Kaila closed her eyes, thinking of everyone and everything she had lost in this fight. Just a year ago, her days had been spent in the classroom, labouring under the watchful gaze of Sister Eurador. Kaila had loved the woman like the mother she had never known. The old woman's betrayal had been the first cut in her soul. If only she'd known how many more would follow.

Her father. Rohan. *Theron.*

And now even the very magic that had led her down this road might be changing—*failing.*

"We'd better get moving," Garrick said quietly. "Suns coming up—won't be long until someone stumbles across these men…"

Nodding, Kaila cast one final glance over the street. The first light of day had touched the horizon and the mist was beginning to clear. The six dead men lay where she had left them. She felt a pang in her stomach. A piece of her regretted the bloodshed. A very *small* piece these days, admittedly, but a piece all the same.

Maybe, if they won this fight, her children would get to live a different life.

For now, she hoped Jenna Frye enjoyed the message. The new Matron could turn her back on their people all she liked, but that didn't mean the Elysian would lie down quietly. If Jenna wasn't willing to change the world, then the Elysian would do it without her.

There was no turning back now.

For too long, the Elysian had lived in the shadows, hunted by the Magisterium, painted as monsters. Humanity had been taught this war was a necessity—that if they didn't fight, the enemy would slaughter them in their homes, their villages, their cities. Fear and lies had been the Magisterium's chosen tool to keep their power intact.

No more.

This time, the war wouldn't be fought in a distant land—it would be fought here, in the streets of Tah'raus.

And this time, the Elysian would win.

# 2

Jenna rubbed her eyes as the words on the page blurred. She blinked, willing her vision to clear before the lines floated away entirely. This was her fifth meeting of the day, and there was still no end in sight. With a quiet sigh, she gritted her teeth and forced herself to focus.

Things were escalating out in the streets. There'd been three separate attacks last night. The first—a jewellers—had been looted, its shelves overturned, the owner left bruised but alive. At least the losses were limited to nonessential items.

In the second attack, a month's worth of grain had just up and vanished from one of their warehouses. With the growing unrest, that grain had been badly needed to pacify the people.

Worst, however, was the attack on the patrol. Six soldiers, butchered in the street. A bystander, watching through the shutters of a nearby home, had provided a Sister of the Magisterium with the report now in Jenna's hands.

*A single young woman, maybe twenty, with long black hair…silver eyes…cut down the sergeant first…*

Exhaling through her nose, Jenna set it aside. It was *her* again.

More than a few witnesses had seen her true face the night of the attack on the Sanctum as the Elysian illusion failed, flickering between the false Eliza and the raven-haired woman. Given Eliza's past, it hadn't been difficult to trace the Elysian back to Elgoss and ascertain her real name.

*Kaila Dwyn.*

Her name had spread like wildfire since that night. That was Jenna's fault, in part. She'd needed a scapegoat after the death of her mother and father—and the Elysian girl had been neck deep in the entire affair.

It had cost her brother dearly, ruined his reputation. But after what Kaila had done to him, he hadn't needed much convincing to go along with the story. Anything that might hasten the Elysian's appointment with justice.

Jenna had assumed the girl would realise her newfound notoriety and disappear. But her response had been quite the opposite. Instead, she'd struck back, launching attacks on warehouses and marketplaces; now she even dared assault the soldiers of the Magisterium.

These new deaths only fuelled the rumours. The capital was alive with talk of the rogue Elysian, an assassin maddened by bloodlust, striking at humanity itself—driven by hatred, or hunger, or some other monstrous instinct of the Elysian.

If only it were so simple.

Because it was clear Kaila wasn't working alone. The attacks were too coordinated, too precise for one person to be behind them. The attacks last night had been almost simultaneous—Kaila had only been involved with the attack on the patrol. She certainly had a talent for dealing death.

"Ahem."

The man seated across the table cleared his throat, dragging Jenna back to the present.

"Your Royal Matron," he said, his voice pinched, "as you can see, we are in desperate straits. Are you certain the Wardens cannot be spared to aid us in this matter?"

Jenna let out a long breath. "As I have told you many times, Lord Chapman, with the dangers we are facing on the frontier, that is quite impossible."

He hesitated. "Then…perhaps your personal guard?"

Jenna allowed her face to darken—even as she resisted glancing over her shoulder. She didn't need to look to sense the presence of the black-armoured soldiers arrayed at her back. She understood the man's frustration. Here she sat, flanked by no less than *three* Wardens, while his warehouses went unguarded and her soldiers died in the streets, powerless against the dark magics of the Elysian.

She should send them; Jenna knew it in her soul. Her duty was to the kingdom now, to her people. And yet, she hesitated. Her father had never trusted the Wardens, had warned her about them before his death. Their order loathed change— they would see everything he had created burned if they had their way.

But that wasn't why Jenna Frye hesitated.

*"It's because you're Elysian, Jenna. Like me, and Theron. She's not your mother."*

Her stomach twisted. Kaila's words from that night atop the Sanctum haunted her still. In a twisted sort of way, she owed the girl a debt, for revealing the truth about her mother. If she hadn't, the woman would have dealt with Jenna once and for all after that disastrous night.

Instead, Jenna had struck first.

But now she was caught between a kingdom she'd sworn

to protect—and a heritage she had only discovered on that terrible night.

Returning her gaze to the merchant, Jenna lifted the papers and crushed them into a ball. It was somewhat galling to see the disappointment on his face, but he'd dared question her authority. A new Matron couldn't afford to show any weakness.

"You have your answer, Lord Chapman," she said, her voice sharpened steel. "I have already doubled our patrols. Perhaps it is time the nobility began heeding my warnings and took charge of their own security. Now," she continued, rising to her feet, "if you'll excuse me, I have other appointments to attend to." She gestured toward the door in dismissal.

Chapman hesitated. He obviously wanted to say more, but a glance at her Wardens seemed enough to make him reconsider. He bowed stiffly and turned to go.

Her bodyguards waited until he'd departed before offering their opinion.

"We could cleanse these vermin from your streets, Matron." The Warden's voice was like ice. "You need only give the command."

Jenna shivered despite herself. Sucking in a breath, she turned to face the three Wardens. Encased in identical black armour, it was impossible to distinguish one from another. She knew one was a woman from her voice—but even that was so distorted by the iron visor as to seem almost inhuman. She studied them in silence, then stepped forward.

"Have you rooted out the traitors in your ranks?"

There was a pause, then one stepped forward. "We are sworn to the defence of Fresia—"

"I asked you a question, Warden," Jenna interrupted, her voice low. "Under my father's reign, your order stirred unrest in these streets. You undermined the will of the crown. I do not see why I should trust your order to bring peace now."

She raised her arm and light spilled from the silvery armlet that covered her forearm.

*The Aegis.*

For thousand years, ever since the passing of the First Matron, T'iana, its power had been shared between the Matron and her king. Jenna, however, didn't have a king—as far as any living soul was concerned, Theron Falkenrath had died the same night as her mother and father. And so the other half of the Aegis had been locked away.

Fortunately, even a divided Aegis had power over these creatures. So long as she didn't have to test it…

"Matron," the Warden pressed, "given the danger posed by this creature, we Wardens are willing to set aside our grievances."

"I am not so quick to forgive," Jenna retorted. "Your order failed to defend my predecessors from a single Elysian assassin." She advanced a step, fist clenched, the shining light of the Aegis bathing her face. "Now you think I would trust you with defending our entire city?" She sniffed and turned her back. "Kaila Dwyn is but one girl. I am confident the soldiers of Fresia will deal with her. In the meantime, should the Wardens wish to restore my faith in your order, you will bring me the traitors that started the riots under my father's watch."

Her demand, as always, was met with a stony silence. That didn't bother Jenna. Not even her father had been able to convince the Wardens to give up one of their own. But so long as they refused, she could delay the decision she knew she had to make.

*Are you one of us, or one of them?*

The question chased itself through Jenna's mind as she

started for the exit—but she barely made it around the briefing table before the chamber doors burst open. Immediately, steel rattled behind her as the Wardens snapped to alert. Jenna sensed a strange pressure in her ears, followed by a *popping* sensation as three black blades materialised in outstretched hands.

They needn't have bothered. The newcomer was only Rohan, her brother, though by the look on his face, the young man had violence on his mind.

"It was her again, wasn't it?" he demanded, marching up to her table and slamming down his hands.

Jenna grimaced at his lack of decorum. Turning to the Wardens, she gestured for them to leave. There was a moment of hesitation, before they obeyed, filing out in icy silence.

"Rohan, *please*," she hissed when they were finally alone. "This is *not* the time for one of your outbursts."

Rohan hadn't been himself since that night atop the Sanctum. He'd lost the woman he loved on that barren dome of concrete—and the loss had hollowed him out. Left him broken, scrambling for meaning in a world that didn't care who it hurt.

"Outbursts?" he growled. "Eliza is still out there. I can *feel* it—and that *thing* knows where she is!"

Jenna gritted her teeth, stifling her anger. She had tried —First Matron, she had tried—to explain it to him. The Eliza he'd known had never existed—the woman he loved had always been an illusion, a mask worn by an Elysian infiltrator. But Rohan refused to believe it. Instead, he clung to the hope the real Eliza was still out there somewhere—imprisoned by the creature that had replaced her the night of the ceremony. The creature now wreaking havoc on the streets of Tah'raus.

*Kaila Dwyn.*

Jenna had to give the girl credit. She certainly knew how to make a Matron's life difficult.

"Rohan, I swear to you, I'm doing everything I can to find her," she said quietly, "but please, I cannot have this conversation with you again. Not today."

His face darkened. "Not today," he hissed. "Not *ever!*" He gestured at the doorway where the Wardens had departed. "Why aren't they out there, *hunting the Elysian?*"

*Because I'm one of them,* Jenna wanted to scream at him.

Once, he would have been the first she would have gone to with her secret. She desperately needed someone to talk to about all of this; about the night their mother had tried to kill her and the strange power that shone from her eyes when she held the forbidden crystals…

…but she could almost *feel* Rohan's anger. His hands shook, his entire body seeming to vibrate with the strength of his rage. If she told him, he wouldn't listen. He would only see another betrayal—or worse, think she too had been replaced by the enemy.

"Because Eliza is dead, Rohan," she said instead. If he wouldn't believe the truth, she would force him to accept the lie.

The words struck him like a blow. He reeled away from her, breath coming in ragged gasps, shaking his head.

"Don't say that," he croaked. "She's out there, Jenna, I know it." Straightening, he stepped closer and took her hands in his. "Please, I know you think it saved me, but it was only trying to save their own scheme." He drew in a breath, his eyes growing hard. "They're evil, Jenna. After what they did to us…they're not capable of good. You have to send in the Wardens. Its…" His eyes flickered closed. "Whether she's alive or…or dead, it's the only way to avenge her memory."

Swallowing, Jenna found herself nodding. "I…I'll think about it, Rohan," she said quietly, "but please, you must go now. My next appointment…"

"Okay." There was still pain in the young man's eyes, but this time he went, turning and fleeing through the big double doors at the end of the chamber.

Slumping into her chair, Jenna watched him go. There was a hollow feeling in her chest, like his words had carved a piece out of her.

*They're evil, Jenna. After what they did to us…they're not capable of good.*

Her eyes flickered closed. What was she going to do?

"Excuse me, ma'am, but I was told I could find the Matron here?"

Stuffing her pain deep down inside, Jenna made a mask of her face and lifted her head to greet the newcomer—and the breath caught in her throat. A man with a familiar face strode towards her.

It was Theron.

No, that wasn't possible. He was locked away, imprisoned deep beneath the Sanctum where no one could ever find him. Her heart raced as she rose, blood pulsing, the brilliance of the Aegis filling the room. It wouldn't save her. Not if this was really the man she had married, the Elysian imposter…

…but no, no something was wrong. As the newcomer reached the table, he fell to one knee and bowed his head.

"Matron, I beg your forgiveness. I came as soon as I could, but I fear I have arrived too late."

Realisation struck Jenna like a blow. It did nothing to slow her pounding heart. The man had the same mocking smile as Theron, the same blond hair and blue eyes. But there was a hint of grey at his temples and lines on his forehead.

This *wasn't* Theron. It was someone much, *much* worse.

The man kneeling before her was General Leonardo Falkenrath, the man they called Iron Hands.

He was also Theron's father—and the only person alive who knew the truth about what that meant.

That Jenna Frye had married an Elysian.

# 3

"I'm sorry, Kaila, but I'm removing you from active duty."

Kaila's head jerked up as Ambrose strode into the room. "*What?*"

She sat behind the bar of a dilapidated tavern known as *The Rusty Gull,* where Garrick was carefully preparing the stitches for her arm. The tavern was one of Ambrose's safehouses—deep in the port district of Tah'raus, where only the roughest of citizens dared tread and a uniformed soldier hadn't been seen in years. After Theron's disappearance, Ambrose had gone underground—officially, he was away at his ranch in the south, taking a well-earned vacation.

So far though, the precaution had proven unnecessary. There hadn't been so much as a whisper about the famous tailor operating a secret Elysian crime syndicate in the capital. But Ambrose was nothing if not cautious. He still had people all over the city watching his official ventures, to alert him if word finally leaked out.

Ambrose himself wore another face whenever he left the hideout. Being a Weaver, that came as easy as breathing to the man. Today though, he wore the one Kaila had first known him by: a man with harsh obsidian eyes and jet-black hair, the silver streaks of age just beginning to show at the temples. His suit was one of his own, a midnight blue jacket that hugged his narrow frame.

He and Kaila had clashed frequently at the beginning of all this, when she'd seen him as a puffed-up noble who thought he was too good for his own kind. Now she knew how much he had suffered at the hands of the Magisterium, she understood him a little better.

They still clashed frequently.

"I had a surgeon check the bodies before they were found," Ambrose explained as he pulled out a chair. Sitting alongside her, he nodded at her arm. "That looks nasty."

"She was lucky," Garrick commented. Threading his needle, he leaned in close, then picked up a bottle of clear liquid the barkeep referred to as the *Good Stuff*. "Ready?"

"Just do it," Kaila said through clenched teeth.

She promptly sucked in a breath as Garrick poured half the bottle over the wound. It *burned*.

"Well…?" she grunted, turning to Ambrose—more as a distraction from the pain than in any real hope the tailor would have a satisfactory explanation.

"As you reported, four died by either a weapon or blunt-force-trauma. But the last two…" He grimaced. "I'm told their internal organs had been…liquified."

Kaila felt the blood drain from her face. "What…what could have done that?"

"That's just the thing." The tailor's eyes didn't so much as flicker from hers. "I have no idea."

She swallowed—then winced as Garrick pulled a stitch tight in her arm. Even that wasn't enough to divert her growing panic, however. Ambrose's answer was exactly what she'd feared. Her power had always been different. When she'd first held agimet, Kaila hadn't been able to use the *atar* inside—unlike every other Elysian tested before her.

Then, when she *had* discovered her powers, she'd *also* learned she had the ability to recharge agimet crystals from the nexus itself—acting like a catalyst to speed up the process. Just as the Wardens were able to do.

And now…this.

"You can't take me off the streets," she said quietly, steeling herself against the pain. "The patrols are getting larger. You need every Elysian you have out there fighting."

"I do," Ambrose said. Kaila's heart rose, until he sighed and stood. Walking around the table, he took out a pair of cups and set them on the bar. "Equally, I cannot afford to lose one of my most powerful Elysian because some…anomaly left you helpless."

Kaila flashed Garrick a glare. He was meant to have kept his mouth shut about that part. The Bruiser averted his gaze but said nothing. Ambrose returned with the glasses and poured a measure from the bottle of *Good Stuff* into each.

"Did you think I wouldn't find out about that part?" he asked, offering Kaila one of the mugs.

She accepted it with a grimace. "I don't care if it puts me at risk." She stared at the liquid inside the cup, then downed it in a single swallow. It burned almost as bad going down as it had on her wound. "If I die, at least I'll die doing something *worthwhile.*"

Ambrose said nothing, just watched her with those obsidian eyes.

"And if you hurt one of *us?*" he said at last.

The words were like a punch to her gut. "I would never —*gah!* Garrick, *what the hell*, I'm not a pincushion!"

"Sorry," the Bruiser muttered, looking sheepish.

With fingers the size of sausages, he probably wasn't the best choice of medic to be fair, but everyone else was out on assignment or sleeping off the night's activities. Feeling the weight of her eyelids, Kaila would need to do the same soon.

"You don't know how or why it happened, Kaila," Ambrose pressed. "So how can you be sure it won't happen to your friends?"

His tone was reasonable, but Kaila wasn't having any of it. He could use sense all he liked, she wasn't about to accept a demotion without a fight.

"It was *one time*," she snarled, pain and the spirits giving her the courage to confront the crime lord. "One little anomaly—and I *still* beat those men."

She didn't mention the strange music she'd been hearing the last few times she used her power. That was irrelevant, probably.

"You melted their *brains*, Kaila!"

Kaila's scalp prickled. As she looked into the tailor's eyes and saw no give in the man, something shifted inside her. A crack, a fissure in the wall of her soul. It was happening again. Her power was all she had left—*and now she was going to lose it*. Just like she had lost everything else. The world shimmered and it took all her will to keep herself from falling apart right then and there.

Clenching her fists, she drew in a breath. "They worked for the Magisterium," she insisted, refusing to surrender to the tailor's logic, "they got what they deserved."

"*No one* deserves to go like that, Kaila!"

The glass in Ambrose's hand made a *thud* as he slammed it onto the bar. For a second, the harsh glow of *atar* burned through his illusions, filling his eyes with light.

"Honestly, I can't even *begin* to understand how that could have happened," he hissed, "but I know I don't want it ever happening again. *Not unless you can control it.*"

There it was. He was afraid of her. Her own kind. The despair rose within her again, threatening to consume her. The worst of it was, she couldn't even deny it. Not really. She had no idea whether it would happen again, if the next time it did, who she might hurt.

"You know I'm right about this, Kaila," Ambrose said, his voice became soft again as he knelt beside her chair. "These Gifts we have, they're dangerous. Even those of us who have been using them for decades barely understand a fraction of what we should."

"But I'm the only Mover you've got," she whispered, still not quite ready to surrender. "And if a Warden shows up, I'm the only one with the power to counter them."

"Kaila, for all we know, it's your Warden's power that caused this anomaly." Ambrose drew in a breath. "As for Movers, you're right. But we have other Elysian with firepower." He seemed to consider for a moment. "Garrick, how would you feel about bringing in a Binder?"

Kaila glanced at the Bruiser, who finished the last stitch and sat back. "Not great, boss," he muttered. "They're noisy…but until Kaila gets her head on straight, yeah, I suppose one would certainly leave an impression." His eyes darted in her direction, then away again. "Sorry, Kaila."

She said nothing, but her shoulders slumped. That had been her last hope. A sharp pain began in her chest as her heart began to palpitate. The thought of being unable to go out, to use her power, *to fight…*

*Darkness.*

The breath caught in her throat as she imagined herself locked away where she could do no harm to anyone. Somewhere dark and silent where all she could do was think about what she had lost, the people she had loved, who she had failed. Her father and Theron and Rohan.

"Please, Ambrose…" she managed a little gasp as, trembling, she wrapped her arms around her chest. "Please, I need to be out there—"

"No, you don't, Kaila" Ambrose said, not unkindly. "You haven't stopped since we lost Theron." He laid a hand on her good shoulder. "The truth is, I should have brought you in long before this. Maybe that's why this happened—because we pushed you too hard. But now it has, I'm *ordering* you to rest. You need a chance to heal." He paused, those grey eyes examining her. "This war is only just beginning, Kaila, and when the real battle arrives, I'm going to need my best Mover in fighting shape—not dead in some pointless skirmish, okay?"

Kaila swallowed. She could feel the tears gathering in her eyes. Raising an angry hand, she batted them away. She wouldn't cry. Not anymore. There was no room left in her for that.

"I don't know what happened," she whispered, finally addressing the real problem. "My Gift was working *fine*, but when I connected to them…it wasn't like what Theron taught me."

Ambrose frowned. "I will ask around. There *are* other Movers in the city. Maybe one of them can help you figure this out."

He left the other part unspoken—that *Theron* might have known. He was the best Mover anyone had ever known. But Theron was gone. And Kaila was alone.

"Thank you," she rasped, rising.

"Kaila…" Ambrose's voice called her back. He held out his hand. "Your agimet, please."

*Darkness…*

She stood, trembling, staring at the tailor's outstretched palm. "But…"

"I'm sorry," he said softly, "but until we know more, I can't take any chances. Besides, our stocks are running low…"

Blood pounded in Kaila's ears. Taking her off duty was one thing, but this…she hadn't gone without agimet since Theron had given her that first crystal. She was helpless without it, without her Gift, unable to so much as lift a pebble…

But one glance into Ambrose's eyes told her there was no fighting this. She could feel the emotion washing through her, the tears threatening again, so in a rush Kaila pulled her pair of crystals from her pockets and thrust them into his hand.

Then, her soul feeling suddenly empty, she turned and marched into the rear of the tavern, where those in Ambrose's employ had their quarters.

———

Back in the Rusty Gull, Ambrose watched the young woman disappear into the dark corridor. He knew that fury in her eyes. He had felt it himself in his youth, that burning, uncontrollable need to lash out. It was like an old friend, reflected in the eyes of every young rebel that passed through his organisation.

But in Kaila, it was different. Until recently, that fury had been tempered by something precious amongst the Elysian.

Hope.

But of course, hope couldn't last in this world. Not for the likes of his people. He had seen Kaila's hope die the night the boy had betrayed her, when Theron had been lost.

Now her fury was uncontained, a wildfire that threated to burn this city to the ground. Little wonder Kaila had lost control of her power. He should have intervened sooner, but the number of powerful Elysian at his disposal was limited…

…and he'd needed her Gift.

The doors to the kitchen swung open with a squeal of old hinges, followed by soft footsteps. He turned as Eliza Wrenn appeared at his side. He offered his latest apprentice a smile. "You heard?"

Eliza nodded, concern wrinkling her brow. "What's wrong with her?"

Ambrose sighed. "Truthfully? I don't know. I've never heard of anything even *close* to what happened to those men. I don't know what to make of it."

Eliza nodded, blonde locks bouncing as she undid her hair tie. Her eyes drifted to the corridor where Kaila had disappeared. The two women had been childhood friends, until Eliza's parents had decided she would become a Daughter of the Magisterium. If not for Kaila, Eliza would have still been living that life of privilege.

Instead, Kaila had attacked her in a rage and abducted her, bringing her to Ambrose and Theron—who had concocted a plan to have Kaila impersonate her as a Daughter of the Magisterium.

The plan had worked…until it hadn't. Instead, it had ended in the loss of Theron and the ruination of Eliza's entire life—or her liberation from the Magisterium, depending on how you looked at it. Eliza, ever the pragmatist, had ultimately chosen the later.

"Could it have something to do with the Aegis?" Eliza asked. She'd read the reports Ambrose had gathered about that night—including Kaila's own eyewitness recount. "Didn't she say it felt like something inside her had changed when she touched it?"

Ambrose pursed his lips. "We know so little about its

power—*any* of our powers, really." It was the unfortunate consequence to spending centuries at war; those who might have once known these secrets had died long ago, and too few lived to an age where they could pass their knowledge to the next generation. "Until Kaila appeared, we didn't even know that Wardens had the ability to charge agimet crystals."

"Will she be okay, though?"

"I hope so," he said, avoiding answering the question directly. He had spoken reassurance to Kaila, because that was what she needed. But truthfully, this was one of the rare times in his life he wasn't sure of the next steps. "I wasn't lying —we're going to need her. She's the only living Elysian who's ever defeated a Warden—even if she had help from Theron. They *will* come after us, eventually." The past few months, the black armoured warriors had remained out of the war, but that couldn't last. He glanced at Eliza, a thought coming to him. "Perhaps you could help?"

"Me? I don't know anything about Elysian magics."

"No, but maybe this isn't about the *magic*. Maybe this is about the girl. You've known her longer than anyone else."

Eliza arched an eyebrow. "What exactly are you proposing?"

# 4

"General Iron Hands, this is most…unexpected."

Jenna was proud the words came out steady, without so much as a tremor in her voice. She'd had a lot of practice with dangerous situations as of late, though this might yet prove the most perilous.

*Iron Hands was here!*

Not only was he the most powerful general in the realm—commanding over five thousand battle-hardened soldiers—he was also the father of Theron Falkenrath, the man she had married on the night of the Summer Gala.

The same Theron Falkenrath, it turned out, the General had secretly banished for his Elysian blood—and who was currently locked in the bowels of the Sanctum, kept secret from everyone but Jenna herself.

They had exchanged the official council chambers for a sitting room at her suggestion—ostensibly out of respect for a man of his title. Really, it had given Jenna time to compose her thoughts. Now, she stepped aside, gesturing for the general to enter, before following him inside and closing the door behind them. The Wardens she left outside—this was definitely not a conversation she wanted them listening in on.

The room she had chosen for them was the Matron's personal solar, where her mother had once dined with the most powerful nobles of the realm…

…and where the old woman had died three months ago by Jenna's hand.

*Murderer, assassin, killer!*

The words whispered in her ears as she turned to face the one man who might know her secret.

Leonardo Falkenrath stood at ease, arms clasped behind his back and shoulders straight. His face remained an iron mask as she approached, a smile plastered on her face.

"General, the journey must have been long. Could I interest you in a drink?"

She slid past him without waiting for a response. She'd sent her servants ahead to prepare a decanter for her special visitor. Jenna poured herself two fingers of brandy, before glancing at the general, her hand hovering above a second glass.

"Fifteen years aged in an oak barrel," she said. "My mother always kept a bottle for important guests."

The general's sapphire eyes studied her before inclining his head. The gesture sent a shiver down Jenna's spine. It was disturbing how similar those eyes were to his son's. No wonder Iron Hands hadn't wanted the world to know what Theron was—seen together, there would be no denying the pair shared blood.

Though, there was a softness in Theron that was absent in the elder Falkenrath. Looking into that icy gaze, she could well believe this was a man who could order the execution of his wife and daughter without losing a moment of sleep.

Forcing herself to breathe, Jenna poured the second glass and extended it to the general.

"You've grown," he said as he accepted, his voice deep, measured. "I remember when you were just a child hiding behind your father's trousers."

"My father always spoke highly of you, General," she replied, finding herself a spot in the lounger. She gestured the general towards the sofa.

"I prefer to stand, thank you," he grunted. He swirled his glass, studying the amber liquid, before taking a sip. "Your father and I were comrades in arms," he continued. "He was a great man, though he and I did not always agree on the path he chose for Fresia."

Jenna's heart pulsed, pressure gathering against her ribcage. If her father had ever let slip the truth about her heritage…

*No, if this man knew what I was, he would have come with an army, not diplomacy,* she reassured herself.

Whatever her father had told this man, the truth of her own bloodline remained safe. For now.

"General," she began, her tone growing cool. "It has been a long day, as you might imagine. I assume you didn't ride all this way just to speak of the past. What is it you came here for?"

That earned a flicker of something in the old man's face. His eyes grew sharp, focusing on the woman seated before him.

"My apologies for the secrecy, Matron, but in a way, the past is *exactly* why I came," he spoke quietly, sipping his brandy. "You see, several months ago, shortly before her death as I understand it, I received a letter from your mother."

The words sent a chill through Jenna's stomach. *Damn you, mother!*

Surely, the bitter woman wouldn't have risked putting her secret to paper? It had the power to destroy them both, after all. Her fingers twitched, but Jenna resisted the urge to search for an escape. Instead, she channelled calm. The situation hadn't changed. Whatever her mother had put in that letter, this man wouldn't be standing here if he knew what she was.

"She was a disturbed woman, at the end," Jenna replied after a moment. "Seeing assassins in every shadow—except the one under her own nose."

"The Daughter Eliza?"

"Kaila Dwyn," Jenna corrected. "The imposter that wore her face."

The general pursed his lips. "I saw your brother leaving the meeting room earlier." His eyes found Jenna's. "His rage is understandable. It is a great shame for a man to be made a fool by Elysian magic.

A lump lodged in Jenna's throat, but she swallowed it down. Crossing her legs, she pressed a finger to her chin.

"Perhaps we should be candid, General Falkenrath?"

"Perhaps we should."

"Then let me say this," she said, sitting back in her chair. "I know your son was Elysian."

"So you know my shame," he replied. Downing his glass in a single gulp, he crossed to the cabinet and poured himself a new measure.

"I must admit to a certain…panic upon receiving your mother's letter," the general continued when a fresh drink was in his hand. "My son was always a devious child. When I discovered his mother's corruption…well, perhaps you understand better than most the pain of that deception."

Meeting her eyes, he lifted the glass to his lips and took a sip. Jenna just watched him, not trusting herself to speak. She needed to learn exactly what this man knew.

"The thought of that creature wearing the crown of Fresia…" The general shook his head. "I came as quickly as I could, expecting disaster. So imagine my surprise when instead, I learn of my son's death and his widow's ascension to the throne."

"We were fortunate events concluded as they did."

"Just so, just so," the general nodded, studying her with those stony eyes "Though, perhaps you could clarify some details for me? During my brief time in the capital, I must have heard at least five different versions."

*And just how long* have *you been in the capital?* Jenna thought to herself, narrowing her eyes.

She sensed the trap in his words but was unsure how to escape it. There was the official story—that an Elysian had infiltrated the Daughters and seduced the crown prince, then tried to assassinate the royal family—successfully slaying the king and Matron and mortally wounding Theron Falkenrath.

Then there was the *truth*.

How many shades of in between could Jenna feed the general without him spotting her lies?

"Of course, general," she said at last. "Please, ask your questions."

"Your mother knew the truth about my son's lineage—that much is clear in her letter—yet she allowed your marriage to go ahead. Why?"

"To destroy me," Jenna said, toying with her glass. "As I said, she had grown paranoid at the end. She believed I wished to usurp her throne." As she spoke, her heart hammered in her ears, all but deafening her. "I imagine it was a horror, when the very girl she had mentored to displace me planted that dagger in her throat."

"Ah yes, your brother's betrothed. Truly, our enemy grow bold, to have placed *two* imposters into the heart of the

Magisterium," Leonardo replied. "Though it leaves me with questions. Why would this Kaila Dwyn slay my son, if they were working together?"

"Because she did not," Kaila paused, taking a moment to saviour the general's sudden nervousness, before continuing. "My mother used the Aegis to incapacitate your son and reveal his true nature after the ceremony. Unfortunately, that distraction gave the other Elysian her chance to strike. My mother and father were killed before they knew what was happening. She would have killed me as well, but I was able to take the Aegis from my mother's body and drive her off."

"And my son?"

"I killed him before he could recover from his injuries."

Jenna's heart pounded and she held her breath, waiting to see whether Iron Hands would see through the lie.

"I see." The general regarded her for a long time. "Then it seems I am doubly in your debt, Matron. Long has the knowledge that creature lived pained me."

"It must have been painful indeed," Jenna agreed. "Though, apparently not enough to bring that knowledge to the Magisterium."

The general inclined his head. "Admitting my failure would not have brought the creature to justice."

"Yet it might have prevented a greater tragedy."

Jenna rose to stand before the general. She clenched her fist, feeling the power of the Aegis pulsing against her wrist. *So close*. What would it be like to unleash the device? She had connected with it, but when she tried to use its power, it was like trying to hold water with her hands…

"Had I realised the extent of Theron's depravity, I would have acted differently," the general said softly. "Instead, I can only beg your forgiveness, Matron." His head lifted, eyes lingering on Jenna. "And renew my vow of service to the crown of Fresia."

"I am not sure the Magisterium requires a man who would betray his vows in service to his own reputation."

"Perhaps that is so." The general lifted his head to meet her gaze. "But we now share that shame, do we not? Should the truth about my son ever be revealed, the Magisterium would burn us both for desecrating their holy Sanctum."

Jenna's jaw hardened. "Is that why you came here, General? To destroy us both with the truth?"

Finally, Iron Hand's face showed some emotion as he smiled. "On the contrary, Matron," he said quietly. "I thought perhaps this was an opportunity. We understand the Elysian, you and I; the depravity they are capable of. Together, we could finally eliminate these creatures once and for all."

Her heart palpitating, Jenna frowned. "I'm not sure I understand you, General."

"The Elysian outlaws," Iron Hands murmured. "You fear to send the Wardens to deal with them?"

She pursed her lips. "Their kind caused my father no end of grief. Unleashing them in Tah'raus would mean open warfare in the heart of my kingdom."

"Then perhaps my experience can be of use."

Jenna arched an eyebrow, studying the aging general. "What did you have in mind?"

"I will stop the Elysian threat without placing a single civilian life at risk."

"How?"

Iron Hands grinned. "I have a small contingent of soldiers in my service. All I need is your blessing, Matron, and I will see the foul creatures exterminated."

Jenna stomach twisted. This was her chance to appease the noble and merchant factions howling for the Wardens to be unleashed on the population. But…was this really what she wanted? To oversee the extermination of her own kind?

*You're not one of them, not really.*

"And what would you ask in return, general?" she said. This was not her first day as a politician; amongst the Fresian nobility, you never got anything for free.

The general inclined his head. "You were promised the hand of a Falkenrath as your king."

"By your silver-tongued son, yes."

"I would make good on that promise." Smiling, the general laid a hand on her arm.

"*No!*"

It wasn't the most diplomatic of reactions, but Jenna couldn't help it. Just the man's touch set her skin crawling. It just slipped out. She tried to pull away, but his fingers tightened around her bicep…

*Crack!*

On her wrist, the Aegis flashed and a sensation like needles prickling skin shot down Jenna's arm. It was followed by a hiss from the general as his body suddenly went rigid. The light of the Aegis gathered force and Jenna felt a *popping* in her ears. The heat within her grew fiery as a moan hissed from the man's throat…

With a gasp, Jenna tore herself from Iron Hand's grasp. Abruptly, the light went out. Trembling with the sudden absence of energy, Jenna blinked against the darkness. When her vision cleared, Leonardo Falkenrath stood with one hand still outstretched. His face seemed gaunt, the wrinkles of his brow etched deeper than before, his ice blue eyes ringed with shadow. Slowly, he lowered his hand.

"My apologies—"

"*You. Will. Not. Touch. Me.*" Jenna panted, her breath coming in ragged gasps.

The general bowed his head. "Of course, Matron," he rasped. "I meant no offence."

"I…understand," Jenna replied, her voice still hoarse. "And I…apologise for my reaction. Your proposal was just…unexpected."

"I understand." The general's head lifted an inch, so his eyes found hers. "It was not my intention to cause you discomfort. Rather, I understand the Aegis requires two masters. I only wished to offer my aid before others seek to use this weakness against you."

"I see," Jenna murmured. Blood still pulsed in her ears, but she found herself nodding. "In that case, General Iron Hands, I will…consider your proposal."

A smile creased the general's wrinkles as he finally straightened. "That is all I ask."

"Of course."

"I shall wait upon my Matron's verdict," the general continued, seeming to read his dismissal in her tone. "In the meantime, I will speak with my people." His eyes found hers as he laid a hand on the doorhandle to leave. "Let us see if we can't resolve the matter of these troublesome creatures."

The door whispered as it opened—then he was gone.

Jenna waited until the door had closed behind him before sinking to her knees. For some reason, she felt as though a great pressure had left the room. In its absence, her entire body began to tremble.

The general was not what she had expected at all. He hadn't threatened or tried to intimidate her. Yet, for a moment there, Jenna had felt powerless. Like all the work she'd done to become Matron was worth nothing. Here was a man that knew her secret—or half of it at least—who could destroy them both with the flourish of a pen.

Instead, he had offered to help.

It didn't make any sense. Everything Theron had told her about Iron Hands suggested their meeting should have gone differently. That he would attempt to manipulate and blackmail her. And *what the hell had that been with the Aegis?*

Her gaze was drawn to the device. The gold and crystal bands had returned to its usual dim glow. It had never done anything like that before.

Exhaling her anxieties, Jenna pushed her concerns about the Aegis to the side for now. The general's presence changed everything. Whether he was here to help as he claimed, or pursuing his own secret agenda, there was one man who might help her get to the truth.

Unfortunately, he was dead.

Rising from the floor, Jenna straightened her dress. It was past time she paid her dear departed husband another visit.

# 5

Crouched on her bed, knees drawn up to her chest, Kaila cried silently in the darkness. Gone were the days of penthouse apartments and galas beneath the dome of the Sanctum. She didn't even get a room to herself now. She shared this bolthole with half-a-dozen others from Ambrose's organisation—some Elysian like herself, others just humans who'd gotten on the wrong side of the Magisterium.

*I can't even begin to understand how that could have happened…*

She squeezed her eyes closed, unwilling to believe what she'd heard in the tailor's voice. Fear. The most powerful Elysian in the city, a man who's power even *Theron* had respected, was afraid of her. Of what she was capable of.

*You melted their brains, Kaila!*

She shuddered. A part of Kaila feared even herself, knowing what she'd done…

*Knock-knock.*

Her head jerked up at the sound. A light appeared as an oil lantern was unshuttered, revealing curly blonde locks and hazel eyes that were almost as familiar to Kaila as her own face. After all, it was what she'd seen in the mirror every day she'd been inside the Sanctum.

*Eliza.*

"Am I…interrupting?" the girl from Elgoss asked softly. She looked hesitant, standing there in the doorway with a satchel looped over one arm and the lantern in the other.

Kaila's stomach twisted. The pair of them had barely exchanged two words since she'd returned from the Sanctum, where Kaila had successfully ruined Eliza's entire life in the space of a single night. There hadn't been a chance—at first, Kaila had been recovering from her injuries, and later she'd spent most of her time in the city, helping Garrick with raids and otherwise being a general nuisance for the new Matron…

Embarrassed to be caught crying, Kaila carefully wiped her eyes. Forcing her voice to be even, she said: "No, it's okay. Can I help you with something, Eliza?"

The girl didn't immediately reply; instead, she squeezed between the two narrow bunks that Kaila had turned into her little nest and sat on the opposite bed. They stayed like that for a while, Kaila with her back to the wall, knees still pulled up to her chest; Eliza perched on the lip of the mattress, hands clenched tight in her lap. The lanternlight flickered, and Kaila struggled not to stare as it illuminated the pale flesh that ringed Eliza's throat. As if by a will of its own, Kaila's hand drifted to the scar around her own neck, before she stopped herself.

Eliza noticed the gesture anyway. "Does it still hurt?"

Fingers trembling, Kaila lowered them back to the covers. "No more than I deserve."

A frown creased Eliza's brow. "You don't deserve what happened to you, Kaila."

She shrugged. What point was there in arguing? Kaila was done fighting people. She just wanted to curl up here in the darkness and disappear. If she left, no one would miss her. She had betrayed both of the men who had ever truly cared about her, ruined Eliza's life—and now her very existence threatened to destroy everything Ambrose had built.

"What do you want, Eliza?" she said at last, when the other girl didn't move. She couldn't keep the bitterness from her voice.

She might have ruined Eliza's life, but as always, the most beautiful girl in Elgoss had landed on her feet. Despite being a former Daughter of the Magisterium, Eliza had found herself a place in the tailor's organisation. Unbelievably, Ambrose had grown to trust her during Kaila's absence—and so his followers also trusted her.

It was almost like their childhood all over again.

"I want to help you keep fighting."

Kaila's head jerked up at the words. They were about the last thing she'd expected from her former classmate. At first, she thought Eliza must be taunting her, but the girl's face was still, her jaw set tight. Kaila felt a fluttering in her chest that was almost like hope.

She quickly crushed it down. "I can't," she said shortly. "Ambrose banned me from using my Gift."

"There are ways of fighting without using magic," Eliza argued.

Ah, now she understood. Kaila's lips twisted into a scowl. "I tried the other ways," she said bitterly. "They all ended in disaster."

Doubt flickered in Eliza's eyes. She seemed to hesitate, teetering on the edge of the bed, before steeling herself.

"So, what?" she said shortly. "You're just going to give up?"

Kaila didn't respond to the provocation; just stared at Eliza for a moment longer—then deliberately lay down and turned her back to the former Daughter. Hopefully if she ignored the girl, Eliza would just go away and leave her in peace.

There was silence for a long time, followed finally by the creak of the other bed.

Kaila stifled a sigh. *Finally, peace—*

"I never thought I'd see the day Kaila Dwyn turned coward."

"*What?*"

Kaila couldn't help it—she rolled back to face Eliza, lips twisting in rage. Instinctively, she reached for the pocket she normally kept her agimet, before remembering Ambrose had confiscated it. She settled for glaring at the other girl instead. Eliza didn't flinch.

"The daughter of Gideon Dwyn would have never given up this easily."

It was like she'd shoved a block of coal into the furnace of Kaila's rage. The heat started in her midriff, just a tingling at first, but quickly turning to an inferno that consumed all before its path. It was fortunate Ambrose *had* taken her crystals, because in that moment Kaila might not have been able to control what happened next. As it was, she *almost* felt the nexus, its unlimited wealth of energies swirling just out of reach...

"Don't you *dare* speak his name," the words left Kaila in a rush as she rose from the bed.

"Or what?" Eliza snapped back. Her eyes flashed in the lanternlight as she stood eye to eye with Kaila. "You'll destroy my entire life?"

It was like a blow to her solar plexus. The words knocked all the heat from Kaila, leaving her empty, ashamed at her rage.

"I didn't mean…" she stammered, "you know I wouldn't have…"

She suddenly found herself unable to meet the girl's eyes. The others had told her Eliza didn't hold a grudge against her, but Kaila had known it was a lie. No one was that forgiving.

"You took everything from me," the former Daughter whispered, stepping closer, close enough for Kaila to feel the warmth of breath on her cheek. "The least you can do now is not sit here wallowing in self-pity."

Kaila shuddered. It was a struggle, but she lifted her chin to meet the girl's eyes, to face the judgment of the one person whose life she had ruined more than her own.

But to her surprise, she didn't find judgement in Eliza's hazel gaze, but concern.

She blinked.

Eliza Wrenn was *worried* about her?

"Please, Kaila," Eliza murmured, the heat leaving her voice. "We're the only ones left. Please don't leave me alone."

Kaila swallowed. She knew that fear in Eliza's eyes now, recognised it in her own heart. The terror of being the last one left. "You're right," she said at last, slumping back to the bed. "I'm sorry, Eliza." Drawing in a breath, she steadied herself. "What did you have in mind?"

It was like the former Daughter had been waiting for those words. A smile lit up her face as she snatched the satchel from where she'd hung it on the bedframe and sat alongside Kaila.

"Oh, nothing too demanding!" she announced. Drawing out a massive stack of papers, she dumped them on Kaila's bed.

"Ah, what's this?" Kaila asked, dumbfounded.

Eliza wore a grin as wide as the Iron Pinnacles. "Well, it turns out Ambrose has spies *everywhere*. You'd be surprised what they've ferreted out. The only problem is the *quantity* of information passing over his desk. I *know* there are important things we're missing, but there's just so much of it."

Kaila looked from Eliza to the stack of papers. "And so…" she trailed off, a sinking feeling forming in her gut.

"Well, I've been trying to get a handle on it myself, but the papers keep stacking up faster than I can review them."

Kaila groaned. "You want me to *read* all this?"

"Well, you were always Sister Eurador's favourite," Eliza retorted. Dividing the stack of sheets in two, she offered half to Kaila. "It's time you put those skills toward a good cause, don't you think?"

Kaila looked from the papers to Eliza. "This is because I ruined your life, isn't it?"

Eliza beamed. "You really think I'd be that petty?"

Rolling her eyes, Kaila accepted the stack, though not without muttering a few choice words. "At least it's not *that* large."

"Oh, that's just today's briefs. I'm two weeks behind. The rest is upstairs."

This time Kaila's groan could be heard from the ports.

# 6

J enna had always hated the corridors beneath the Sanctum. The upper storeys were different, where light and the noises of the city carried through great windows in the dome.

But down here in the dark, all was silent. That other world, where children played and people laughed, was a distant, forgotten thing.

These corridors were for the doomed, where the Sisters brought their traitors and the Wardens their prisoners. It was a place from which souls never returned, a world that knew only pain and torment and suffering. Though, not death. This was not a place where people crossed to the other side. That was a mercy reserved for those above. The souls in this place were held on the brink, suffering in a perpetual purgatory until their spirits were so withered, there was nothing left when they exhaled their final breath.

This was the threat her mother had held over Jenna and the other Daughters. More than a few insolent Daughters had disappeared over the years, never to be seen again. Jenna wondered if some of them were still here, kept alive by some loyal Sister, even now fulfilling the commands of their dear departed Matron.

But Theron was not in any of these countless dungeons. He was someplace deeper still, in corridors known only to the Matrons. Like her mother before her, Jenna couldn't trust the Sisters with her secrets. They were too dangerous, too blasphemous. Elysian were filth, and all who touched them were corrupted by their magic. If their order ever learned that Jenna Frye had bedded one, Jenna would find herself locked in one of these chambers herself.

*And if they found out she was one of them…*

Jenna clenched her fists, her leather gloves creaking faintly in the silence. Her boots scraped against the concrete floors as she descended, passing finally through a secret doorway and entering passageways known only to the Matrons.

Or so she assumed. When she'd first taken the Aegis from her mother's corpse and placed it on her wrist, a feeling had stirred in the pit of her stomach, a niggling, tugging sensation that had drawn her to these hidden corridors.

The walls changed as she left behind the well-tread corridors, turning from modern concrete to jet-black obsidian and engraved with strange sigils Jenna couldn't read…though they called to her. The air was thick, unnaturally warm, so by the time Jenna reached the last door, sweat beaded her brow.

This door was also built from polished obsidian, though here the runes formed a pattern—spiralling outward from a point in the centre. There was no knob or bolt or any other visible method to open it. Instead, Jenna lifted the arm that wore the Aegis and pressed it to an indentation in the centre of the sigils.

The door slid silently aside, unleashing a burst of light from within. Jenna shielded her eyes against the brilliance, waiting for them to adjust before she entered. Inside was a strange, circular chamber. Like the corridors outside, the walls were obsidian and covered with runes—but here they were different. Those outside had been chiselled by a master craftsman, every line etched with purpose into the harsh glass.

In the chamber, however, the lines were jagged and faltering, as if carved by a novice. They filled every inch of space—not even the floor or ceiling had been spared.

In the centre of the room, resting on a stone pedestal, sat the largest piece of agimet Jenna had ever seen. A forged mesh of blackened wire encased the crystal, anchoring it to the platform. It was the crystal that had drawn Jenna here that first time, she was sure. Even from the doorway, she could sense the hum of its power—the way it called to the Aegis.

Today, the crystal wasn't the reason for her visit, but Jenna obeyed the call anyway. The device had done *something* with Iron Hands—maybe all she needed was patience to unlock the rest of its powers. Her skin tingled as she touched the wire and braced herself.

Thankfully, today there were no visions. The first time she'd been drawn here and touched the Aegis to the wire, Jenna had found herself in darkness. A spirit had come to her there, T'iana, the First Matron. The spirit had spoken to Jenna, but the words had been broken, disjointed, and she could make no sense of it.

When she removed her hand, the Aegis blazed with renewed energy. It faded slowly, the device returning to its usual dim glow. Jenna had no idea where that energy went. Did it somehow transfer to the king's half of the device? Or was that now dead, its crystals drained as it sat in the vault of the Wardens? Was that why she struggled to wield her own piece of the Aegis?

*You were promised the hand of a Falkenrath as your king.*

A lump caught in Jenna's throat as she remembered the general's words. He seemed so genuine, nothing like the cold killer that Theron had warned her about. That was why she'd come here—to learn the truth from the man who'd been willing to sacrifice everything to destroy the general.

As she stepped away from the podium, Jenna's gaze caught on a band of gold lying on the ground. *Her collar.* The first time she'd placed her hand against the crystal and seen the vision, the hated thing had made a little *click* and opened. Just like that, she'd been free.

Her stomach tightened. She had worn that thing her entire adult life. The pride she'd felt the day her mother had given it to her, to be the youngest Daughter in a hundred years…

…but now Jenna knew it had never been about pride or honour, but to suppress Jenna's Elysian power and conceal her mother's shame from the rest of the Magisterium. Jenna's proudest moment had been nothing more than another betrayal by the woman she had looked up to her entire life.

And yet a piece of Jenna still missed the damned woman. It was difficult to admit, the pain she felt in her chest, the sorrow of knowing her mother was really gone. Dead and laid to rest alongside her doting father. She couldn't even hate the woman, knowing at least a piece of her had been trying to protect Jenna, to prevent her secret from escaping into the world.

But she hadn't come to this place to linger on the past—or at least, not *that* part of her past. Wiping an unspilt tear from her eye, Jenna strode across the chamber and into the adjoining corridor at the rear. This place was larger than it seemed, with several smaller room branching off inside. These looked to have been part of a household, with each room created for a different purpose.

There was what she thought might have been the kitchen, with an old-fashioned coal stove, and a washroom with an iron tub and drain—and unbelievably, running water that made her wonder whether her father's inventions were new, or simply rediscovered technology.

The sleeping chamber held only a stone platform where a bed had likely been. Whoever had built this place clearly hadn't cared much for comfort.

She found Theron in the sleeping chamber and paused in the entrance to study him. He lay on the hard stone, eyes closed, chest rising and falling gently beneath the twisted mess of blankets. When she'd first brought him to this place, he had been a mess. Prince Rohan had made a mess of his left hand, leaving only a bloody stump, and his skin had been a terrible grey—the aftermath of his agimet *atar* addiction—but he had regained much of his colour now. A shackle around his ankle chained him to a pillar in the corner. He had enough chain to reach the adjoining washroom, but the rest of the facility was off-limits.

"Ah, my darling wife, is that you?" Groaning, Theron sat up and stretched his arms in a yawn. "Have you returned at last to our marital bed?"

"Please," Jenna snorted as she stepped into the room. "If I wanted to be perpetually disappointed, I'd have become a Sister."

"My dear, you wound me," Theron gasped, clutching his chest.

Jenna rolled her eyes as she approached the bed. Unfortunately, the return of his colour had also revived his awful sense of humour. Ignoring his mocking tone, she set the paper bag she'd brought from the kitchens beside the bed and stepped away, lingering in the doorway.

Taking the bag, Theron peeked in the top, before seeming

to notice her continued presence. He arched an eyebrow in her direction. "What's this? Has my dear wife deigned to grace me with her presence tonight? Or…" He paused, stoking his beard in thought. "Perhaps she has a need of my services?"

Her jaw hardened. As usual, Theron was far too perceptive for his own good. "Not the kind you're alluding to."

Theron, however, ignored her as he set about rummaging in the bag. The kitchen had packaged it all with care, thinking it was for their Matron, so there were several layers of paper to unwrap

"Wait," he murmured, a frown gathering on his lips as the paper fell away, revealing a meat pie and bread rolls. "Is this… it's still *warm*."

Jenna shrugged, lowering herself into the extra chair she'd carried down a few weeks ago for her occasional interrogations of the Elysian. Theron glanced in her direction, then back to the food. This, apparently, was the best way to shut him up. If only she'd figured that out sooner. Half the pie disappeared in a single bite.

"So, what's the special occasion?" he said, mumbling through the mouthful. "Don't tell me it's our anniversary already!"

"If it was, do you really think eating the food I brought you would be the best idea, *darling?*"

Theron paused at the words. They stared at each other for a long moment, before slowly, deliberately, Theron placed the other piece of pie in his mouth. Whole.

"Arg," Jenna muttered. "I can't believe I ever thought you were actually a *noble*."

"Technically," Theron made a popping sound with his mouth as he licked his fingers one by one. "I *am* of noble birth. If you'd ever met my father…well, the resemblance is remarkable."

Jenna's heart gave a little pulse. "I *have* met your father," she said quietly. "He's upstairs right now, actually."

This time, the emotion she glimpsed in Theron's eyes was very real. His pupils dilated and his jaw hardened, fingers tightening around the bread roll he'd just raised to his lips. It was only there for a second, but the emotion was unmistakable: fear.

*Interesting,* Jenna thought to herself.

A heartbeat later, Theron was himself again, shoving the entire bread roll into his mouth and puffing out his cheeks, so his response came out unintelligible. "Whatdidhecometocongratulateus?"

Jenna wasn't buying the act. "You're afraid."

He paused, studying her. Then swallowing in a deliberate manner, he pursed his lips. "You can't get much past a Wraith, I see."

*Wraith* was Theron's nickname for an Elysian with her kind of Gift. He was a Mover—able to shift reality with a thought—while for Jenna…

*The world stood still. Her heart beating hard. A bird frozen mid-flight. Raindrops suspended. A candle burning bright, yet motionless. That feeling of power. Of burning strength in her soul…*

"You know I don't use my magics," Jenna said harshly, thrusting away the memory.

"And *you* know it doesn't matter whether you use it or not," Theron replied, watching her with a strange look. "It's what you *are*."

Jenna scowled, but refused to be drawn down that road again. "Well?" she pressed instead. "Your father? Don't you have anything to say?"

"That depends," Theron mused. "Is he here because of me?"

"Yes," Jenna replied, then hesitated, "and because of my mother. She sent for him, apparently, before her little stunt atop the Sanctum."

"Ah, then he knows about your heritage?"

She shook her head. "She wasn't foolish enough to put anything so damning in a letter."

"That's something, I guess," Theron grunted. "But that's not all, is it? Otherwise you wouldn't look like that."

"Like what?"

"Like you just stood in cow manure."

"*Argh*," Jenna muttered, wrinkling her nose. "Thanks for that image."

Theron chuckled, drawing another scowl from Jenna. Blasted man! What had she ever seen in him? She'd been so desperate for someone, *anyone*, to rule at her side, to finally show her mother she was ready…

…exhaling through her teeth, she returned her gaze to the Elysian. "He made a proposal," she said softly. "He wants my hand in marriage, to make up for his wretched son."

There was a moment of silence. Then Theron did about the last thing she might have expected.

He burst into laughter.

"What's so First-Matron-cursed funny!" she demanded, leaping to her feet and looming over him, the Aegis burning on her wrist.

The laughter died. Theron made a show of wiping the tears from his eyes.

"Don't you think it's just a *little* humorous?" he asked. "After spending all this time calling my mother a cheating whore, now *he's* trying to marry *you*—an Elysian of his own!"

he snorted. "The Trickster does find interesting ways to mock us, doesn't he?"

Jenna's scowl deepened. "I don't see the funny side of it," she snapped. "Even if your father doesn't know about my real mother, he knows I married an Elysian. He could ruin me."

"Oh yes, and don't let the nice guy routine fool you, he's as cold hearted as they come."

"I gathered as much." Jenna glared at him. "Well, what are we going to do about this?"

"*We?*" Theron asked. Raising an eyebrow, he shook his foot, making the chain rattle. "There's no '*we*', my dear."

"No?" she asked. "And what do you plan on doing for food if I'm gone?" She stepped towards the bed, the Aegis glinting menacingly on her wrist. "Do you have any idea, my dear husband, how painful it is to starve to death?" She leaned in close. "I've seen it, you know, in the dungeons above your head. Most of them beg for death before the end. How long do you think you'd survive? A few weeks? You're a tough man—it could be *months* down here, screaming for someone that will never come—"

"Alright, alright, I get it!" Theron cried, raising his hand in defeat.

Jenna glared at him until she was certain he wouldn't continue his mocking. He lowered his hand with a sigh.

"What about the Aegis?" he asked. "You told me it can control people with its power."

"Only those wearing the old artefacts, I think," she murmured. "Daughters and Sisters and Wardens—"

"Wardens?" Theron sat up at that.

She waved a hand to dismiss the thought. Trying to use the Aegis against a Warden would start a war she couldn't hope to win under current conditions. Especially given her doubts about the device.

"It doesn't work, does it?"

Her head jerked up at the words. "*What?*" she snapped. "Why would you say that?"

"I didn't hear a denial in there," Theron replied. "Come on, if you can't talk to your husband, who *can* you talk to?"

She fixed him with a glare that said exactly what she thought about *that*.

He just rolled his eyes. "Jenna, who am I going to tell?" He rattled his chain again. "You know, with the whole *imprisoned-against-my-will* thing."

She maintained her glare, but…the Elysian were meant to be the original owners of the Aegis, weren't they? Maybe he *could* help her with its power.

"Fine," she muttered, "you're right. It doesn't work, except…" she paused, recalling how it had acted when the General touched her. It had repelled him—or at least, she *thought* that's what it had been doing. "Except when I'm threatened," she finished.

Theron sat back, studying her, that familiar, infuriating look of nonchalance on his face.

"Nothing happens?" he asked at last.

"Obviously not," she snapped.

"Ah." To her surprise, Theron actually looked thoughtful. "That is…disappointing."

"Why disappointing?"

"Because you're *Elysian*," he replied. "There are certain legends about the things that would happen if an Elysian ever claimed the Aegis again."

Jenna raised an eyebrow. "My mother said the same thing. Something about a dark god and the end of the world."

"Maybe both king and Matron have to be Elysian?" Theron replied cheerfully. "If you could bring me the king's half—"

"Sure, and maybe I'll just crawl under that blanket with you too while I'm at it, shall I?"

Theron grinned. "I had a dream last night that went something like that."

Jenna rolled her eyes. "It's not the partner thing, alright?" she muttered. "My mother used it just fine, even after she murdered my father."

"True," Theron muttered. "A shame you went and murdered her; *she* probably could have told you what was wrong with it."

"Oh yes, if only I'd stopped to think about that *when she was trying to kill me…*"

"Oh, would you relax." Theron raised his hands. "Come on, if anyone understands patricide, it's me. Speaking of which, wouldn't that solve your whole General Iron Hands problem? If you're suddenly feeling squeamish, I could…" He made a throat slitting gesture.

Jenna gave him a look. "I'm beginning to suspect the murderous one in your family isn't your father."

Theron snorted. "It probably wouldn't help anyway. Knowing my father, he'll have some form of guarantee against you taking action against him." He paused, looking thoughtful. "Look, let's not panic here. Don't forget, if my father implicates you, he implicates himself as well. He'll only expose your secret as a last resort. So, delay him. Give us time to come up with another plan."

Shaking her head, Jenna began to pace. "I can't believe this is *happening,*" she muttered, allowing her rage to bubble over. "Just once, *once,* couldn't things go my way? I thought finally, *finally,* I might have a chance to prove myself. To show the sisters and Fresia and moth—"

She bit off that last word. Fists clenched, she came to a halt, glaring at the rune-etched-floor. Even after everything that had happened, after she'd poisoned the old woman's tonic and pressed the pillow into her face until she no longer breathed, *still* Jenna craved her mother's praise.

Maybe that was why the Aegis wouldn't obey. She was too pathetic to command its respect. Trembling, she turned to stalk from the room.

"Are you okay, Jenna?"

She froze at the question. For once, there had been no hint of mockery in the Elysian's voice.

"What do you care?" she whispered, not daring to look at Theron for fear he would see the pain in her eyes.

"Well, as you pointed out, you're the only one who knows I'm down here," he said softly. "Plus, you know, it wasn't terrible, the time we spent together."

She snorted. "You lied about who you were for weeks so you could steal the most powerful relic in the kingdom," she muttered, finally trusting herself to face him. "And, you know, destroy my life."

"Technically, I didn't *actually* lie."

She glared at him, but he smiled back until she relented. "I suppose it wasn't the *worst* month of my life," she admitted, pinching the bridge of her nose. "Though to think, if I'd just cut your throat on that first night…"

"And miss out on all this *fun?*"

"You think this is *fun?*"

"Why not?" he grinned. "Jenna, you're a *Wraith.* Why are you worrying about the Aegis? *You can control time itself.* If you're not going to enjoy it, *what's the point?*"

"Enjoy it?" Jenna frowned.

Wasn't *that* a foreign concept? Her entire life had been dedicated to a woman for which she would never be good enough. What was *fun* and *joy* to someone like her? And yet…she found her hand creeping towards her pocket, where she kept the piece of agimet she had taken from Theron.

She hadn't touched it. Not since that first night when she'd held it in her hands and felt the *atar* flowing through her veins. The night she'd finally known the truth—that Eliana Frye had never been her mother, but her abductor, the woman that had stolen Jenna from her true mother as a negotiating ploy.

*She was Elysian.*

That was the truth. She was one of the monsters whispered about in children's bedtime stories. And yet, she didn't *feel* like one of them. Theron had shown her how to use her power, but…

"It still doesn't feel like a part of me," she said quietly.

"You've been closed off from your Gift for your entire life," Theron said gently, then hesitated, before adding: "Would you like me to help you practice?"

She swallowed. *Practice?*

The Gift was something evil—that was what the Magisterium taught. A monstrous power to be feared. Not *practiced,* as if it was no different from learning to fight with a knife or studying dinner etiquette.

"I'm not giving you a crystal," she said, glaring at the Elysian.

It had been weeks since he'd last asked—and even longer since he'd launched himself at her like a mad dog at the end of its chain. But still…

"I wasn't suggesting it," Theron said quietly, and she saw him shudder, "but maybe I can help it feel more…natural."

Pursing her lips, Jenna considered the offer and then nodded. Carefully, breath held in apprehension, she reached for the crystal.

The moment her fingers brushed its gleaming facets, a tingling spread across her skin. The light in the room changed, shadows recoiling as the glow in her eyes flared. Clutching the crystal tight, she drew it out, holding it before her like something dangerous.

"What does it feel like when you use your power?" Theron asked. There was no missing the hunger in his eyes as he watched the agimet, but he didn't move from the bed. "How does the *atar* feel to you?"

"Like it's something foreign," she replied after a heartbeat, "like its invading my body."

"And when you *use* your power?"

She swallowed, remembering that first time. Always, her life felt like it was rushing away from her, like she was a wagon barrelling out control towards some terrible collision.

Except in those brief moments when she had stolen time and the entire world had stood still.

It should have been abhorrent. To think, someone could hold that power. It was everything the Magisterium had warned against, this unnatural inversion of the world, a corruption of the natural way of things. And yet to Jenna it had been…

"*Exhilarating,*" she whispered. "To just stand there and know…"

Theron grinned. "Good," he said, "and what about when you move?"

Warmth crept into Jenna's cheeks. "I haven't gotten that far yet," she muttered. "When I tried…it was like I couldn't *hold it.* My concentration broke and everything started moving again."

She didn't mention what had happened *after* she'd lost her concentration.

"That's only natural." The dancing in Theron's eyes suggested he knew anyway. "You're trying to run before you've even learnt to crawl. There's a lot you need to know about the

Gift and how it works before you become a master assassin like your mother."

Jenna's heart pulsed at the mention of the woman most had known only as the Reaper. "What was she like?" she asked, seating herself carefully alongside Theron. They had talked about this before, briefly, but Theron had been half out of his mind with withdrawal at the time. "Why didn't she ever come back for me?"

"I only knew her a few days," Theron's voice was uncharacteristically sad as he replied, "but she wasn't well. *Atar* addiction had trapped her in Iselador. It has the only nexus for miles around, you see." He hesitated. "I think she wanted to leave, but speaking from experience, detoxing isn't exactly easy."

Recalling what he'd been like in those first weeks of his imprisonment, Jenna couldn't help but agree.

"I wish I had known..." she started, before clenching her lips shut. Letting out a sigh, she stood. "I need to return to my duties."

"What will you do about my father?"

"Stall him, like you suggested," Jenna replied. "At least until I can think of another way to appease him."

"You could switch sides," Theron offered, his face growing serious. "Bring me the other half of the Aegis and we can escape together—"

"The Wardens have it under lock and key," she said quietly. For some reason she found herself unable to meet his gaze.

"It doesn't matter," Theron said, his voice growing eager as he sensed the opportunity. "My friends are still out there. You're one of us, Jenna, they'll help—"

"*No,*" the word tore from her with more force than she'd intended. "No, I am *not* one of you," she hissed, glaring at him. "I don't care what you say, I will never be Elysian. I didn't sacrifice half my life to get where I am, just to throw it all away because someone thinks they can bully me." She met Theron's eyes. "Tell me you wouldn't do the same, if you were in my shoes."

Theron opened his mouth as if to say something, then seemed to reconsider. His gaze dropped. "You're right, Jenna," he murmured. "I've never been where you are. But I know a man who *has* been there. And I know what *he* would choose."

"Then it's a shame he isn't the one in my cell."

Theron nodded. Letting out a sigh, Jenna turned and stalked away. As she reached the door, however, she paused, one hand on the frame. Lowering her head, she felt that trembling within, the sense of uncertainty, like her entire world was turned on its head. Drawing in a breath, she glanced back at Theron.

"You can really help me? With my power, I mean. Even though you're not a Wraith?"

His head lifted and she read the surprise in his eyes. "I can do my best."

Clenching her jaw, Jenna nodded. "I'll be back tomorrow." She hesitated, glancing at the crumbs that were all that remained of the pie. "I'll see what I can do about the food."

Then she turned and stalked back out the way she'd come. The visit had disappointed her. She should have known Theron wouldn't be able to help her against the general. Though strangely, she did feel a *little* better as she closed the door to the hidden chamber behind her and started the climb back towards the other world above.

# 7

On Kaila's first night in the Sanctum, the old Matron had locked her in a dark room and forced her to stand for hours in the dark. Under the control of the Aegis, the torture had left every muscle in Kaila's body screaming in agony. It had taken days for her to recover enough to just stand up straight.

But after two weeks spent poring over the endless pages of intelligence reports from Ambrose's agents, she was fairly certain Eliza would have made a better persecutor than even the best in the Magisterium's employ. Her eyes burned and the letters on the page kept jumping around as if possessed by *atar.* She had to squint just to make them stay still.

She couldn't even escape when she rested, as everything she'd read that day returned to haunt her nightmares. Grain sacks rolled off wagons to crush her and wandering roosters clawed at her eyes.

Truly, Eliza Wrenn could not have found a more effective method of torture, even if she really *was* trying to torment her archnemesis from Elgoss.

Which, to be fair, Kaila couldn't be entirely sure that was not the case.

She might have been convinced otherwise, in fact, if the blasted girl hadn't spent the entire time at Kaila's side, reading and taking notes from her own dense stack of papers. Ever the suspicious one, Kaila had checked that there were really words on Eliza's pages—and even insisted they swap on occasion, in case the former Daughter was deliberately giving her the dull edition.

None of it made any difference. Eliza Wrenn simply whistled a cheerful tune to herself and continued her work, flipping through report after report on cattle movements and temporal droughts, and…

Kaila muttered a curse, realising she hadn't absorbed a single word on the page in front of her. It was a dry account from the duke of her old province, the Iron Pinnacles, and a successful rice delivery from the town of Elgoss…

*Huh?*

She frowned, staring at the page. Elgoss?

*Elgoss?*

A pulsing began at Kaila's temples. That…that was impossible! Everyone in their hometown had been butchered after she and Theron escaped. That was what the Magisterium said…

Her blood ran cold as the throbbing spread through her entire body.

"Liars," she whispered.

"What's that?" Eliza was sitting cross-legged on the bench across from Kaila. She had the tip of her pencil between her lips, gnawing on it like she had back in Sister Eurador's classes. She also only had a few reems of paper left in her to-do-pile.

"They lied," Kaila croaked. Her voice rose to a scream. *"Eliza! They lied!"*

That finally got a reaction. "About what?" Eliza gasped, her head jerking up, eyes darting from Kaila to the page on the bar. "About the Aegis?"

"No." Her mouth suddenly parched, Kaila slid the report to the girl. "Look at the date," she added as Eliza scanned the page

"Five days ago," she whispered, eyes widening. "That's… that's not possible…"

"Unless…" Kaila cursed beneath her breath. "How could we have been so stupid? They must have spread the story to keep us away."

"My parents…" Eliza's hands began to shake. "They… they could still be alive."

Kaila swallowed. She hadn't even thought of that. But if her theory was correct…Eliza was right, if anyone would have been spared, surely it would be the Earl and his family. But…

"There's something else," she added hesitantly.

Eliza's jaw tightened. "The rice?"

*The rice.* Kaila nodded. The town was high in the mountains and was more often than not in drought. What little they *did* produce from the barren soils had been to supplement the sporadic shipments of food from the capital. *Rice?* Elgoss didn't produce *rice.*

It did, however, produce Agimet.

"They've reopened the mine," Kaila whispered, her heart suddenly pounding.

Eliza was still staring at the paper, but with those words, she seemed to shake herself. "We have to bring this to Ambrose." She was halfway to her feet before she seemed to realise something. The excitement faded from her eyes. "I can't…"

Kaila's stomach tied itself in a knot as she realised what Eliza was saying. Ambrose was somewhere in the city—and Eliza Wrenn was a wanted woman. Ambrose had given her one of his weavings—tied to a timepiece Eliza wore on her wrist—but she was meant to save that for emergencies, since the tiny agimet crystal inside would only last a few hours.

"You'll have to go without me," Eliza continued, sinking back into her seat.

"No." The words were out of Kaila's lips before she had a chance to consider them. "Searching these records was your idea. You should be there when we tell him."

"Kaila, this can't wait."

"Then don't make him wait." She offered her hand. "Come on, let's see what your new face looks like."

Eliza's lips twisted downwards as she studied the offered hand, and Kaila thought she might still refuse. There was something more in her eyes than just worry though, almost… almost like Eliza was afraid of what waited outside.

*Of course.*

It had been months since Eliza had walked freely through the streets of Tah'raus. Kaila should have realised it sooner.

"Relax," she said gently, "you'll be with me. If the crystal runs low, I can top it up."

The other girl swallowed. Kaila could see the fear now, shimmering behind her hazel eyes. But after a long moment, Eliza gave a curt nod and grasped her hand. Hauling her up, Kaila grinned and gestured to the timepiece.

Grimacing, Eliza touched a finger to the timepiece. The device was one of the modern varieties. Ambrose had been experimenting with the information they'd gleaned from her time in the Sanctum, like what materials they needed to transport agimet around for the Trials. The boxes used a composite of lead and gold string, which when combined, Elysian magic couldn't penetrate.

Replicating that on a smaller scale had been difficult, and so far Ambrose only had a few working devices. The one Eliza wore contained two crystals—a cut decoy that powered the timepiece itself, and a second uncut gem hidden within a lead and gold sphere. Ambrose had attached his weaving to this crystal, but it remained contained until someone twisted the face of the timepiece, which would open the…

The breath caught in Kaila's throat as magic rolled over Eliza like mist, distorting her features for a heartbeat. When they returned, her hair had changed to a vivid scarlet, falling in loose waves that brushed her shoulders. Her cheeks sharpened and her skin warmed to a sun-kissed bronze. Only her hazel eyes remained the same—watchful, intelligent, wary.

"Wow," Kaila murmured.

"What?" Eliza's head whipped left and right as though looking for her reflection, but there was no mirror in the bar.

Kaila smiled. "Nothing." She walked in a circle around Eliza, checking there were no flaws in the weaving. It was flawless, of course. The tailor himself had made it. "Ambrose did a beautiful job."

The hint of a smile touched Eliza's lips, before she glanced at her wrist. "What about the crystal? Is it…"

Kaila held out her hand. Eliza made to place her wrist in her palm, before hesitating.

"Ambrose said you weren't meant to touch any agimet…"

"There's barely a speck in there," Kaila muttered, rolling her eyes. "I couldn't even break down a door with that much *atar.* Come on, hand it over."

Still looking doubtful, Eliza did as she was bid and placed her wrist in Kaila's hands. A hiss escaped Kaila's throat as *atar* passed from the crystal into her flesh. She reached for the nexus and drew a wisp into the crystal, instantly replenishing it's stores. Now it would last at least another hour.

Content, Kaila hesitated to release her friend. The feeling of *atar* in her veins was satisfying after weeks of going without. Strange, to think there had been a time in her life she hadn't even known this sensation. She didn't want to let it go now she had it back…

Abruptly, Kaila released Eliza. She recognised those emotions. Her heart was suddenly hammering. She wasn't addicted to the *atar*. She had never used a broken crystal, like Theron. She didn't need it.

Did she?

"Everything okay?" The illusion Eliza wore was frowning.

"Everything's fine," Kaila said quickly. "Your illusion will last at least an hour now. If we're out longer, we can find someplace quiet and I'll charge it again."

This time the smile that lit Eliza's false face was genuine. "Thank you, Kaila."

Kaila forced a smile to her lips. "Come on then," she continued, "let's go tell Ambrose how your bookwork is going to change the course of the war."

***

It took them an hour, but they finally tracked down Ambrose through Garrick. The tailor might wear a different face each day, but when he was about the city, he was rarely seen without his hulking bodyguard.

They found them in Soul Square. The illusion he wore today was of a beggar—one of many scattered across the notorious plaza. Times were lean in the city, with spare ration chips almost as rare as actual gold. Judging from their numbers, the guards would be showing up any day now to move them on—or worse, conscript them. Fresh bodies were always needed *somewhere*—to hold a pick or a shovel or a sword.

Kaila felt a pang in her stomach. Their efforts to disrupt the Magisterium were only adding to the suffering of these people. But what else could they do? Lay down and let the Wardens stomp them into the dirt?

So along with Eliza, she marched across the plaza to where a rather diminutive looking beggar sat alongside a hulking figure that could only be Garrick. The pair saw their approach and rose, wandering into a squat concrete building that overlooked the plaza. It was one of many colonnades in the city—facilities built by the Magisterium to oversee the populace—but given the unsavoury nature of its location, the local sister was rarely seen on the premises.

Even so, the hairs on the back of Kaila's neck stood on end as they entered through the enormous double doors. She hadn't been back on enemy territory since the night she'd battled her way out of the Sanctum. And she hadn't been in a colonnade since Theron had helped her flee Elgoss all those months ago.

Ambrose led them across the antechamber and the grand nave, where a few souls from outside had given up begging the living for their pity and turned to more spiritual aid in the form of the First Matron. No one in the Magisterium had ever claimed that T'iana had been divine, but it was a practice they made no effort to discourage.

The tailor ignored the worshippers, however, leading them instead to the rear of the colonnade. As they passed out of sight of the public, his visage changed, shifting to become a woman in a garnet-red habit with a silver collar around her throat.

"Come, children, let us speak in here," the tailor said, gesturing towards a private room.

Just the image of a Sister of the Magisterium sent a shiver of dread through Kaila's spine, but she pressed the fear aside and did as the tailor said. Inside, they found a room sparsely furnished with a few wooden chairs and a desk.

"Well, what have you found?" Ambrose was suddenly himself again as the door closed behind them.

A lump formed in Kaila's throat as she looked into the man's obsidian gaze. Suddenly, it wasn't Elgoss she wanted to discuss, but her Gift and whether the man had been able to find out what was wrong with it. It had been *weeks*, surely he must have found something…

"It's Elgoss," Eliza chimed in before Kaila could recover her wits.

That got the tailor's attention. He turned, sharp eyes catching Eliza. "What about it?"

"We think it's still there," she said breathlessly, striding across the room to stand before the tailor. "They didn't destroy it…" she trailed off, as if thinking of something, "or maybe they found new workers…"

A frown creased the tailor's forehead as the girl's voice cracked.

"They're hiding something up there," Kaila said, coming to Eliza's rescue. "One of the reports mentions a shipment of rice from Elgoss."

"I imagine that's meant to mean something to me?"

"Elgoss never grew rice!" Kaila exclaimed. "It's perched on the side of a volcanic mount, for Trickster's sake. There's only one thing that shipment could have been."

Finally, Ambrose seemed to understand what they were saying. "Agimet."

"They've reopened the mine," Kaila agreed, before

glancing at Eliza. "Either they never destroyed it in the first place, or they've found new workers, like Eliza said."

Silence fell over the room. The tailor wore a pensive frown as he ran his thumb along the edge of his cufflink, as if the crystal embedded in the gold might help him think. Eliza looked nervous, almost bouncing from one foot to the other while she waited for Ambrose to speak. In the end though, it was Garrick who finally broke the taboo.

"Trickster's balls," the Bruiser muttered. "Didn't Theron say he saw an entire *cart* of uncut agimet leaving that place?"

"Two hundred twenty pounds a week," Kaila replied. Her cheeks grew warm as all eyes in the room shifted to her. "That was what my father averaged."

"Well, boss?" Garrick asked, turning to the tailor. "What do you think?"

Ambrose was nodding slowly. "We'll want to do it right this time," he said at last. "Theron never told me the details of his plan—but after his first attempt, it's obviously going to be well guarded." His eyes travelled around the room. "This is need to know only, got it? Garrick, how many Elysian do we have at *The Rusted Gull?*"

The Bruiser pursed his lips. "Five," he hesitated. "Six, counting Kaila."

"It'll have to be enough. I don't want word of this getting around. We have to assume the Magisterium has at least a few ears to the ground."

"*Yes!*" Kaila hissed, punching her fist into the palm of her hand. "When do we leave?"

This was it, the job Theron had dreamed of pulling off, the one that would change the balance in the war forever. Without that agimet supply, the Magisterium wouldn't be able to power its devices—which were growing more common by the day. And the Elysian would no longer be limited to a handful of crystals. With that much agimet, even the Wardens would have to be cautious.

Such was Kaila's excitement, it took her a moment to notice the silence that followed. She looked around at the others, noting how their eyes seemed to be looking anywhere but her. All of them but Ambrose. A lump lodged in her throat as she caught his gaze.

"Kaila," he said gently, "I still don't have any leads on your…anomaly." He drew in a breath, and she knew what he was going to say before the words left his mouth. "If this is really the chance we think it is, I can't risk having you with us. I'm sorry."

# 8

"I'm sorry, General, but the Matron was quite precise with her orders—she is not to be disturbed in her meditations. No exceptions."

Leonardo Falkenrath glowered down at the diminutive sister, but she stood her ground and eventually he was forced to relent. Grunting, he turned on his heel without another word and retreated down the corridor. The rattle of armoured boots against hard concrete followed as his soldiers fell in behind him.

Since his arrival, he had been glad to find his allies in the capital remained intact, despite the previous monarch's best efforts to undermine his power. His associates had been playing their roll well, stirring up resentment toward the last regime.

Leonardo grimaced as he made his way through the twisting corridors of the Sanctum. He had warned Alaric not to go down this path, creating machines from the crystals of their foulest enemy. But the man had been possessed, convinced the machines were a gift from the Aegis.

*Fool of a man.* The Aegis was a tool of the enemy. It had once served humanity well, but over the centuries foolish kings and wicked Matrons had been corrupted by its burden. Now a Matron dared threaten its power against the Wardens, preventing them from completing their sacred duty. If not for her cowardice, the black-armoured soldiers would even now be hunting down the wicked in this city, instead of babysitting the sisters and Daughters inside these walls.

*She must be controlled.*

Unfortunately, ever since their first meeting, Matron Jenna had evaded his every attempt to speak with her again. What game did the girl think she was playing? He could ruin her with a word! Did she not care, or had she simply decided avoiding him was the best course of action?

Leonardo's fingers tightened into fists. For just a moment, he let the anger wash through him. How dare she ignore him! Were all Daughters of the Magisterium taught such insolence? His first wife had certainly thought herself an intelligent woman. It had taken more than a few beatings to set the insolent creature straight.

A smile stretched Leonardo's lips as he imagined the young Jenna Frye on her knees, begging for his lenience. He would give it, of course. Eventually. Once he was sure she had learned her lesson.

He sucked in a breath, restoring the easy smile to his lips. He should have known the girl wouldn't accept his proposal— if Jenna was anything like her mother, she would be a master of guile. He would have to be patient, play the kindly father figure, the trusted advisor she could turn to when the rest of the world threatened to swallow her whole. The Sisters were already pressing for a suitor to be chosen to sit alongside her, and the Wardens would not suffer on the sidelines for long. Not with the Elysian growing ever more bold.

And then there was her brother…

His smile grew as a thought occurred to him. He could be patient, but every day that passed increased the likelihood of another stealing this opportunity. If he wanted to be sure, he needed to add urgency to her decision. A certain web was already being spun. It would entangle the Elysian causing strife within his kingdom—but perhaps the Matron could be ensnared as well.

All he needed was the right bait…

Diverting his path, he soon arrived at an ornate door of polished silver. Casting a glance at his guards, he nodded for them to remain outside, before stepping up to the door and knocking. The *thump* of his fist against metal echoed dully through the corridor.

He was forced to wait several frustrating minutes—in war, a general was *never* made to wait—before the rattle of the doorknob announced the presence of someone inside. Finally, the door swung open, revealing Prince Rohan. Surprise showed on the boy's face.

"General Iron Hands?" he stuttered.

Leonardo smiled. Good, at least introductions would not be needed.

"Prince Rohan," he said, careful to keep his voice respectful. "I thought we might talk."

He stepped through the doorway before the prince had a chance to refuse his entrance.

"T…talk?" Rohan repeated, his eyes tracking Leonardo as he came to a stop in the middle of the apartment.

"Yes." The general clasped his arms behind his back. "About certain sensitive matters regarding your former bride —and my son."

"Your son…" Rohan's eyes bulged. The blood drained

slowly from his face, before he seemed to find his wits again. "Of…of course, sir."

"Perhaps you should close the door."

Rohan's knuckles bled white as he gripped the door and pressed it shut.

Leonardo smiled. "That's better."

He allowed his eyes to roam. It was a gloomy place, as were all the quarters within the Sanctum. The thick outer walls allowed for only small, slit-like windows in anywhere but the upper stories. Sunlight barely made it inside during summer—let alone at this time of year with winter approaching. Even so, the apartment was dingier than most, with only a single oil lantern set on the desk for light.

"*Whatareyoudoinghere?*"

The words tumbled from the prince in a rush. Leonardo supressed a sigh. The *correct* convention for a meeting with someone of his rank was to offer a drink and at least five minutes of polite conversation. But he knew the princes story well—he had spurned his parents and the Magisterium at a young age, only returning to the shelter of the Sanctum after the unfortunate incident with his fiancé. Given that knowledge, Leonardo supposed he could not expect proper manners from the boy.

"I'm here to talk," he replied. "As I said."

Stepping around the boy, he moved to the desk where the lantern burned. By its light, he studied the papers haphazardly spread across its surface. Several were wanted paintings of the Elysian that had disguised itself as the prince's fiancé. He studied them, committing the raven-black hair and burning eyes to memory.

*Kaila Dwyn.*

Strangely, he knew the name. A report mentioning the same girl had been delivered to his desk in Bermish months ago, sent from a Warden that had gone to investigate an attack in Elgoss. His smile grew. Would this girl take his bait? She was obviously dangerous. That Warden had never returned from Elgoss, though after some standard cleansing, the town had of course been restored to full functionality. It was too important to sit idle.

He flicked through the rest of the papers, taking in the various reports about sightings—even a few that seemed to have been procured from private citizens. Yes, he could see the potential here. The boy was driven. It wouldn't take more than a nudge to send him down the path Leonardo desired.

Heavy footsteps warned him of the prince's approach. "If you're here to talk, then *talk*."

Smiling, Leonardo turned to look down at the boy. "I came to see what kind of man would lie with the monster that slew his parents."

"*What?*" the word hissed through Rohan's teeth like an arrow from a bow.

"That's what happened, isn't it?" Leonardo pressed. "You invited that creature into your bedchambers." He advanced on the prince. "Then you brought her to the Sanctum." The boy tried to retreat, but Leonardo was surprisingly quick for his age. His hand snapped out, catching him by the wrist. "Into the *heart* of our Magisterium—and stood by while it slew your parents—"

"*No!*"

With a snarl, Rohan tore himself loose of Leonardo's grasp, then staggered back, teeth bared, fists raised.

"Well?" Leonardo offered when the prince didn't move.

Spreading his hands, he invited the boy to strike him. He stood a foot and a half above the prince, and while the years had certainly stolen some of his strength, he hadn't earned the name Iron Hands for nothing. After a moment, the boy lowered his hands.

Anger stirred in Leonardo's stomach. "So it's true," he spat. "The son of Alaric is a coward."

That brought Rohan's retreat to a halt. He still didn't move, just stood trembling as Leonardo advanced.

"What?" he snarled. "Does the Prince of Fresia need his big sister to protect him?"

"No," the reply came out as a whimper.

"I think he does," Leonardo snapped. "Otherwise, he would defend his honour!" He leaned in close. "I can see why they chose you now, why the Daughter Eliza was taken. Don't you see, *boy?* They took her because you were *weak!*"

"*No!*"

Finally, the boy cracked. Screaming, Rohan launched himself at the general. Leonardo could have dodged—the blow was wild and poorly aimed—but avoiding pain was not the point of this venture, so he allowed it to fall. The *thud* of bare knuckles against his cheek barely nudged him on his feet. In fact, it seemed to do more harm to the prince, who cursed and clutched his hand.

Leonardo made a show of wiping his lip—as though the pipsqueak could have drawn blood from *him*. Then he returned his eyes to the young man. Fear shone from the prince's face.

"Good," he spoke softly, almost gently, "there is some fight in you after all. Maybe you can yet redeem yourself."

Rohan wore uncertainty on his face like a mask. "Redeem?"

"You were corrupted by the enemy, boy," Leonardo said quietly, allowing the smile to fade from his lips, "because of your failure, our king and Matron lie dead. A Warden and a dozen soldiers gave their lives fighting that monster."

To his surprise, the prince did not deny the accusation. "I would give anything to take back what happened that night," he said quietly, his eyes darting away, "to save Eliza from that creature." He sucked in a breath and placed a hand on his chest. "I can still feel it. What that *thing* did to me."

"And yet," Leonardo said, lifting one of the sketches from the desk and waving it in the prince's face, "Eliza's killer still walks our streets."

"Eliza is *not dead*," Rohan hissed. His hand snatched the paper from Leonardo's hand.

Leonardo chuckled. "It is good to have hope," he said, "but even should she live, by now she is beyond redemption. What good can a whore of the Elysian—"

This time, the blow actually took Leonardo by surprise. Red flashed across his vision and he rocked back on his heels. If the prince had chosen to follow up his attack in that moment, he might have even fallen.

Instead, settling back on his feet, Leonardo rubbed his jaw and for the first time considered the prince seriously. The young man stood *glaring* at him, rage seething in his eyes.

"Eliza Wrenn is my wife," he hissed. "Not some piece of garbage to be tossed aside. Understood?"

Lowering his hand, Leonardo offered a nod. The boy had pride. He could respect that. "Very well," he said quietly. "Should the Daughter live when this is all over, she will be yours to deal with as you please."

Rohan frowned. "What do you mean, when this is all over?"

Leonardo returned the paper to the desk. "I am here because you are not the only one in need of redemption, Prince Rohan."

"Why…" Rohan trailed off as realisation struck him. "Theron."

Clenching his jaw at the creature's name, Leonardo nodded. "I have offered your sister my services to exterminate the Elysian infesting this city." He studied the boy, considering. "Tell me, Rohan, why is it that Kaila Dwyn still lives?"

Rohan frowned. "She escaped that night before the Wardens could corner her."

"But Jenna Frye was able to use the Aegis to stop my son."

Rohan opened his mouth, then closed it, suddenly uncertain. Leonardo did not miss the hesitation.

"Kaila Dwyn slaughtered your parents and a dozen guards," Leonardo continued. "Even a Warden of the Nameless. But she left you and your sister alive." He advanced slowly, until he loomed over Rohan. "Why?"

The prince held his gaze for only a heartbeat before it fell. "Because Kaila saved my life."

For the first time that night, Leonardo was truly surprised. "Why?"

"I don't know," Rohan trembled as he spoke, "but I don't care." His fists tightened as he lifted his eyes to meet Leonardo's gaze anew. "All I know is that if I ever see that monster again, *I will not hesitate.*"

That brought a smile to Leonardo's lips. "Good," he rasped, "then I will make sure you have that chance."

A frown creased the boy's forehead. He still didn't understand. "How?"

"Come with me, Prince Rohan," Leonardo replied with a laugh. "And I will serve that creature to you on a silver platter."

# 9

S eated on the rooftop of a warehouse, Kaila stared at the tower rising against the Tah'raus night. Seven stories tall, its apartments glowed with agimet lights—except at the top. The great penthouse, crowning the wealthiest building in the city, remained shrouded in darkness.

*He's really gone.*

Kaila swallowed. She had wanted to come back here for so long, just to check, to see whether it was true. If he had really gone back to them. Rohan. Sweet, innocent, wonderful Rohan. The man she had loved.

The man she had betrayed.

Tonight, she had finally found the courage. Afterall, what else did she have to lose?

*Everything.*

The penthouse was empty. Rohan had returned to the Sanctum. Back to the protection of the Magisterium, where she couldn't see him, where she couldn't *talk* to him, explain *why*.

Though even three months later, Kaila still wasn't sure what she would say.

Her eyes slid closed as the tears fell freely. She had wandered blindly through the city after the meeting with Ambrose. It might not have been the smartest of choices—given her lack of agimet—but she had her knives. She might be rusty after relying on magic for so long, but she was far from helpless.

Eventually, she had come here.

*If this is really the chance we think it is, I can't risk having you with us. I'm sorry.*

Ambrose's words still rung in her ears, mocking her. It wasn't fair! She had done everything he had asked; stayed out of the fighting, away from trouble. She had helped Eliza find this lead! She had done *everything*—but it wasn't enough. It would never be enough.

*You're broken…*

The fear rose in her stomach, returning again and again to occupy her mind, to whisper those terrible words. It was the only explanation that made sense. Her powers had worked fine before. Sure, there were still things no one could explain—like why the first time she'd touched agimet, her powers hadn't woken.

It hadn't been long after that that she'd encountered Theron in the mine. Only when she'd wrestled the crystal from him had she seen the building blocks of creation.

From that day on, the universe had danced to her tune—until the night she'd sworn her vow to Rohan. *Something* had happened when they'd spoken the words of unity before the Aegis. The device had done *something* to her soul, hadn't it? Cold as any blade, it had cut away a little piece of her.

A moment later, she'd been restored.

But maybe the damage was deeper than she'd thought.

Maybe the device had a safeguard against Elysian. T'iana had stolen it from them, after all. The First Matron had left a message for her predecessors in the Aegis after all—could she also have left a trap inside the device, to ensure no Elysian could ever reclaim it?

Or was something *else* happening to her, something to do with her power as a Warden, like Ambrose suggested?

Kaila closed her eyes, wishing she still had Theron to discuss all this with. Behind that teasing smile was a cunning mind. He would have figured it out by now, she was sure.

Instead, their last words had been filled with hate and distrust.

*Do whatever you want with that red-haired whore, just do not marry her!*

Her eyes burned, but she had no more tears left. She needed to be strong. To push down this weakness. Theron was gone. So was Rohan. Nothing Kaila could do would change that.

Rising, she made her way down through the abandoned storehouse, taking care not to step on any of the sleeping bodies. Most of the disenfranchised who had taken up residence here had already retreated beneath their thin blankets to escape the autumn's growing cold. The few cookfires that had burned earlier had long since reduced to embers.

"Your fortunes have changed since you came here last, girl."

Kaila jumped as a voice spoke and spun, catching a hint of silver amidst the shadows. For a heartbeat, she thought it was agimet—but as the gloom in the storehouse resolved, her eyes found a woman looking back at her. Unlike the others, she was awake, seated on a crumbling stairwell that had probably serviced a second storey before it burned away. The woman looked almost as old as the stones, her skin wrinkled and folded, her hair bleached white. Her robes were worn to the point of threadbare. Only her eyes told a different story. Their emerald gaze was unwavering as Kaila crossed the factory floor.

Kaila frowned, considering the old woman's words. The first time she'd come here, it was disguised as a beggar. No one would have looked twice at her back then—let alone made the connection with the plain-clothed outfit she wore today. The woman was probably mad, muttering words that might or might not make sense, depending on how receptive the audience. Deciding to ignore the disturbance, Kaila started again for the exit.

"Does my appearance so frighten you, child, that you flee from this old mother?"

The words brought a grimace to Kaila's lips. While she had thrown off the yolk wrapped about her by the likes of Sister Eurador, the lessons of an entire childhood could not be so easily ignored. The elders of Fresia were to be respected.

"Forgive me, elder," she said over her shoulder, "but the hour is late."

"Has the prince forgiven you then, that you rush back to his side at this late hour?"

A chill spread through Kaila's veins. Suddenly, there was a pulsing in her soul, a tingling at the back of her neck that screamed *danger*. She glanced at the sleeping bodies, suddenly aware of her peril. Were these really the unfortunate, or were they sleeping soldiers, waiting for the command to pounce.

Her eyes shifted to the old woman seated on the stairs. She was a Sister, surely. Had they realised Kaila had used this building to survey the prince all those months ago, and set a trap in case she returned? Carefully, she slipped a hand into her bodice, closing her fingers around the hidden blade. Unfortunately, without agimet she was going to be outmatched if it came to a straight fight, considering the number of bodies nearby.

"I'm warning you…"

A rasping laughter echoed through the ruin. "Easy, girl—before you cut yourself." The woman patted the stone beside her. "Come, I only wish to talk."

Kaila wasn't buying it. "Who are you?" she growled. Steel flashed as she slid the dagger from its hidden sheath.

The old woman did not reply, but her eyes began to glow.

"You're Elysian," Kaila hissed with a sharp intake of breath. "Who are you?"

The woman inclined her head. "I was told you require assistance with your Gift."

Kaila's heart pulsed. "Ambrose sent you?"

Before the woman could respond, a snort came from Kaila's feet. Her head whipped to the sleeping men nearby. If they woke…

"Peace, child," the woman said quietly. She leaned forward, elbows resting on her knees. "I have arranged so that we can speak uninterrupted."

Hesitantly, Kaila nudged the sleeping figure with her foot. They didn't stir. Alarmed, she swung back to the old woman. "What have you done to them?"

"The mind is a complex thing," the woman replied, "far more so than the average human would believe."

"You're Psionic?"

The woman smiled but said nothing, only tapped the stone again. "Come, girl. Let us speak."

Kaila narrowed her eyes. "You haven't even told me your name."

"You may call me Cassandra."

Swallowing, Kaila nodded. She cast a last glance at the sleepers, distinctly aware she was defenceless against an

Elysian's power, then wove her way across the storehouse until she stood before the broken stairs. She didn't sit, however. Instead, she crossed her arms and fixed her face in a glare. If Ambrose thought he could appease Kaila by sending a Psionic to help with her magic, the tailor didn't understand people half as well as he thought.

"How did you know I would be here?" she snapped. "Does Ambrose have people following me?"

The old woman said nothing, just studied Kaila with those emerald eyes. The *atar* had faded to a mere shimmer, just enough to cast back the shadows of the warehouse.

"You are the rightful Matron of Fresia."

Kaila blinked. Of all the things she might have expected to come out of the woman's mouth, those words hadn't even been *close* to making the list. How could the woman know anything about *that?*

"I'm not…" she started, before trailing off and drawing a breath. She glanced in the direction of the tower, as if she could see through the thick stone walls. "He rejected me. I'm nobody."

"A vow before the Aegis is not so easily broken."

"What would you know about the Aegis?" Kaila snapped, angered despite herself.

"Perhaps I am a student of history," the old woman replied. "Or perhaps I simply know more about the Elysian than you, child."

Kaila ground her teeth to keep the angry words from sneaking out. "So you're here to help with my broken Gift?" she said once she had control of herself.

The woman smiled. Rather than deepening the wrinkles on her face, they seemed to grow lighter, giving her a younger look. "You are as bright as I had hoped," she replied. "As for your Gift, why do you think it is broken?"

"Because it doesn't work the way I want it to."

"Whoever said a Gift must work the way *we* want?"

Rising, the old woman made a flourish with her hand. A piece of agimet appeared between her fingers as though from nowhere, shining with *atar*. Kaila frowned. That had looked like a Weaving.

"I thought you were a Psionic?"

"I never said that," the woman replied. "Now come, show me this broken Gift of yours."

She tossed the crystal. Kaila gasped, reacting instinctively to snatch it from the air before it shattered on the ground and became unusable.

Instantly, she felt the burning of *atar* flood her veins. Light spilled from her eyes, casting a silver halo around her person. Exhaling, she closed them, feeling the power, savouring its return. Her fingers tightened around the stone. When she opened her eyes again, she did so with her *atarsight*. The old woman's *soullight* hummed with the energies contained within, but it gave Kaila no more hint as to her identity.

"Ambrose banned me from using my Gift."

The woman looked around sharply, eyes widening. "Why, I hadn't realised the tailor was amongst us," she mocked. "Please, mighty Elysian of the silks, forgive my insolence."

Despite herself, Kaila snorted. "How *exactly* do you know Ambrose?"

The smile left the woman's lips. "Enough questions, child. Show me your Gift or hand back the agimet. The night grows long."

Kaila gritted her teeth, but after so long without the power she was reluctant to give it up. So instead, she drew a whisp of power from her *soullight* and directed it towards a piece of fallen mortar. The connection came easily through her Gift.

The command was but a formality. Stones rattled as the chunk lifted into the air.

"Good," the woman said. "Now, what happened the last time it went wrong?"

Kaila grimaced. "I don't know," she said softly. Absently, she turned the stone in the air. "One minute, it was working, then I was distracted and…" she trailed off with a shrug.

"Is that so?"

Abruptly, the world shifted. Kaila was no longer in the storehouse, but in a dark, empty room. The walls shimmered, jet-black glass, smooth, untouched by human hand, without a single nick or blemish of imperfection. Crying out, Kaila reached for the nexus, only to find it gone. The world was an empty, black place and she was alone in inky darkness, abandoned, empty…

…a piece of Kaila fought against her new reality. This was a Weaving, an illusion created to torment her. She struggled for a way to fight back, but there were no *soullights* here, no reality to shift with her powers, nothing.

Except…a pulse remained inside of her, almost smothered, but it lingered in her senses, a candle against the storm. *Atar.* What she had taken from the crystal. She grasped for it, that tiny speck and threw it against the walls of the Weaving. She didn't understand what she was doing. This was something she couldn't Move, but she needed it to move anyway.

The world flickered.

For a second, it was like she stood in two worlds. One was the darkness. The other was the abandoned warehouse. The old woman had an arm stretched in Kaila's direction. Threads of silver power bound their *soullights*.

Somehow, Cassandra was doing this to her.

Fury flushed through Kaila.

*Enough!*

She'd had enough of others thinking they could intimidate her. That they could push her around, like she was still the green girl from a backwater town. She was Kaila Dwyn. Daughter of Gideon Dwyn. Soldier, warrior, *Elysian*.

And she was done taking orders.

"*No!*"

In her vision of the twin worlds, the silver threads that bound her to Cassandra tore loose. They snapped back to the stone she had lifted. A high-pitched humming filled the stone as power surged through the connection. In a rage, she unleashed it at the old Elysian woman.

*Crack!*

Abruptly, there was just one world again. Kaila was standing in the abandoned storehouse. The sudden shift left her dizzy and she stumbled before righting herself. Blinking, she looked from the dark walls to the suddenly empty crystal in her fist. She had drained it dry. Then, belatedly, she realised what she'd done…

She spun, the woman's name on her lips. "Cassan—"

The old woman stood behind her, arms crossed, lips twisted in a thoughtful expression. "Interesting."

"You…" Frowning, Kaila looked around for the rock she had sent rocketing at the woman.

She found it embedded in the wall a few feet off to her left. Her expression deepened. Hadn't the woman been standing there just a moment ago…

"I could have sworn…" She shook her head, eyes narrowing. "What did you do to me?"

"I'm sure I don't know what you're talking about, child." The woman smiled as she advanced. "However, your Gift seems to be working just fine."

"That rock should have cut you in two," Kaila whispered.

"A good thing your aim was off."

Kaila eyed the woman. She was quite sure there had been nothing wrong with her aim. Maybe Cassandra was just a Weaving? But no, Kaila had seen the woman's *soullight* when she'd broken the illusion.

There'd been a moment before the rock struck, a flicker in the material realm, as if something had changed in a way Kaila hadn't seen before.

*What are you?*

She kept the thought to herself, though. Instead, she turned the conversation back to her own power. "That proves nothing," she said. "It's only happened once."

"And maybe it will never happen again," the woman replied. She began to circle Kaila, stepping around the sleeping bodies that still littered the floor.

Kaila swallowed. If only she could believe that. "Is that all you have for me?" she asked quietly. "Cheap tricks and hope for the best?"

"I have found questions to be more useful in this world than a wrong answer offered helpfully."

"What the hell is that supposed to mean?" Kaila snapped, her anger finally getting the best of her.

The woman came to a halt before her. "It means you're different, girl," the woman replied. "Haven't you worked that out yet? You can do things other Elysian cannot."

Kaila's scalp tingled. "How do you know that?" Her Warden's blood was a secret Ambrose would have never revealed—not without telling her.

Cassandra just smiled. "Perhaps it was a guess."

Something was wrong about this entire encounter. Who was this Cassandra? Why had Ambrose not mentioned her in their meeting earlier? Hesitantly, Kaila opened herself to the nexus. With only empty agimet, she couldn't see the threads spun by other Elysian, but as a Warden she *could* sense distortions in the nexus where Elysian were using their powers.

The nexus was all around them, centred deep beneath Tah'raus, but spreading across the city. At times its swirling loops invaded even her dreams. Tonight, it was acting strangely, its swirls not languid but spinning quickly, forming whirlpools like those in the harbour where the tides met the currents of the ocean.

Heart suddenly racing, Kaila glanced again at the old woman. She saw no agimet on her person, but the disturbance in the nexus was clearly centred around her. She must have a veritable *fortune* of agimet on her person to distort the nexus like this.

She opened her mouth to demand answers, then thought better of it. Cassandra had already demonstrated to Kaila that she was in no position to make demands. Instead, she glanced at the sleeping people again.

"I have a friend who's Psionic," she said softly. She hadn't seen Quintin in months, not since he'd caught Theron in his web of lies and quit their team. "Funny—he never said his power could make people sleep."

"It takes a great deal of skill," Cassandra replied. Raising a hand, her eyes flashed silver. The empty crystal in Kaila's hand jolted from her grasp and flew across the room, landing in the old woman's palm. "However, I never said I was a Psionic."

Kaila's skin crawled. "You're a Mover?" How many Elysian were watching her right now, concealed by the Weaver? She had counted at least three powers. Were there others?

Cassandra smiled. "Good night, child."

Swallowing, Kaila nodded and turned away. However, as she reached the doorway, Cassandra's voice chased after her.

"You will rise again, child."

The words brought Kaila to a halt. She felt again the ache in her chest, the shattered shards of love that she had once hoped would change the world. Tears threatened, but she batted them away and swung on the woman.

"Who are you to…" she trailed off as her words echoed through the storehouse. Several bodies stirred and lifted their heads, blinking sleep from their eyes. There was no sign of the old woman.

Kaila departed before her presence raised questions. As she weaved her way through the dark streets, her heart was racing. The encounter had left her strangely disturbed. She'd met many different Elysian by now, but Cassandra seemed… different. Stronger.

Or maybe it was just her eyes.

Kaila had seen no fear in them, no hint of the terror that haunted every other Elysian in this world.

She swallowed, recalling the way the nexus had trembled. With that sort of power, maybe a woman like Cassandra had nothing to fear? The Wardens might be able to draw on the nexus, but with enough agimet, perhaps that wouldn't matter. Wasn't that why they wanted the crystals from Elgoss? So they could fight back for real?

The flicker of hope died in Kaila's chest. Whatever the woman claimed about Kaila's Gift being different, Ambrose had already made his decision; until she learned how to control the anomaly, she would remain on the sidelines.

Kaila continued on her way, passing through the markets to avoid some of the more dangerous parts of town. They no longer thrived like they had a year ago when she'd first arrived in the capital, but they were still safer than the backstreets at this hour. The detour cost her time, however, and she didn't reach the safehouse until well past midnight.

She wasn't surprised to find it empty. An agimet mine was too much of an opportunity for Ambrose and his organisation to sit still on. As he'd said, they would need everyone to capture the town.

She had been left alone.

Despair settled on Kaila's soul as she wandered into her quarters and sank onto her bunk.

To her surprise, it shifted beneath her—followed by a *yelp*. Kaila leapt so high in surprise she hit her head on the bar of the bed above. Cursing, she staggered in the darkness, while behind her a bedraggled Eliza sat up, blinking sleep from her eyes.

"Oh, hey, Kaila," she murmured through a yawn. "You're back late."

"Eliza!" Kaila gasped, her heart still racing. "What the hell are you still doing here? And what are you doing on my bed?"

"Oh…" Blinking, she looked around and seemed to realise where she was. "I came in here to wait for you after the others left. I guess I dozed off…"

"You…you're not going with them?" Kaila asked with a frown. For some reason, she'd assumed Ambrose would bring the former-Daughter with them.

Eliza shrugged. "I don't have magic and I can't wield a sword to save my life, Kaila," she said with a smile.

"But what about your parents?"

"What about them?"

Kaila swallowed, remembering some of the things Eliza had told her about her mother and father, the way they had coldly dictated their daughter's fate, sent her off to be used and abused by the Magisterium so they could raise their status in the kingdom.

"Besides," Eliza continued after a pause. Rummaging around on the bed where she had fallen asleep, she lifted a stack of papers. "If I was off chasing ghosts, who would help you get through the daily reports!"

For once, Kaila didn't groan at the sight of the familiar papers. Instead, despite everything that had passed between them—the anger and the jealously and the pain—Kaila Dwyn threw her arms around her old friend and hugged her tight.

"Thank you," she whispered when they finally broke apart.

"For what?" Eliza asked, a confused look on her face.

"For being a right pain in my ass," Kaila replied with a grin. Turning to the papers, she picked up the top leaf. "Now come on, these aren't going to read themselves, are they?"

And for the first time in their weeks of working together, it was Eliza's turn to groan.

# 10

J enna breathed, steadying herself, focusing on the *atar* simmering in her soul. It still felt strange, that sensation of energy inside her, at once foreign and yet so *natural*, like it filled a hole she had never known was there. It was more than just power. It *connected* her to the outside world. It was like she had been moving through the world without ever really being a part of it—until the day she'd removed her collar and touched agimet for the first time.

The way Theron described his Gift, it was deliberate, targeted. He could create threads of *atar* and attach them to individual *soullights,* which then moved on his command. It wasn't like that for Jenna. When she held the forbidden crystal, she felt *everything*. Like all of Tah'raus, of Fresia, *the planet,* was a part of her.

All of them, connected by that singular force that touched everything—*time*.

It flowed around them, *through them*, carrying the world along in its unrelenting currents. Connecting them. Connecting *her*.

*Atar* flowed through Jenna's soul as she set it to work. It was instinctual, and yet a piece of her rebelled at wielding this power. It created resistance. Hesitance. But slowly, the connection formed.

And the world stood still.

Jenna opened her eyes. Across from her, Theron was half risen from his chair, lips parted as though to speak. He didn't move, however, as Jenna counted the seconds. Didn't so much as blink.

A shiver ran through her soul.

Could she accept this part of herself? Her Gift went against everything the Sisters of the Magisterium preached. Power over others, imparted by birth, immutable. Power like this was meant only for those bound to higher ideals—like the Wardens with their vows to guard Fresia and humanity itself from the darkness.

Except, was that *really* the way the world worked? Whatever her mother might have preached, she had certainly bent those ideals to serve her own ends. The woman had exploited the powers of an Elysian to eliminate her rivals— and then used her authority as Matron to cover up what she had done amongst the Sisters.

Even the Wardens seemed to have their own designs. Far from using their powers to serve humanity, they had tried to thwart her father's machines at every step—devices which gifted the power of agimet to the masses.

She could feel the *atar* burning in her soul, like a soft fizzling that grew with each thump of her heart. The magic was almost gone and she still had not completed the task Theron had assigned her. Drawing in a breath, she steadied herself. It would work this time. How hard could it be?

She took a step—

*Crack!*

The moment she moved her foot, Jenna's grasp on the world slipped. Instantly, she was restored to the flow of time. Theron still didn't have an exact explanation for what happened next—only that losing control of your Gift in the middle of using it tended to have unpredictable consequences.

For Jenna, that meant her footstep mistimed, and rather than one small step, she slammed shin-first into the stone bench that served as Theron's bed.

*"Gah!"*

Hoping on one leg and clutching at her shin, Jenna let out a stream of curses she'd picked up from the Sanctum guards over the years. Theron's laughter accompanied her cries.

"You know, I think you're actually getting worse."

Jenna scowled as she finally got a hold of herself. They'd been holding lessons on her power for a week now, but so far, progress had been frustratingly slow. Just *moving* while using her powers still seemed as far off as the western wastelands. And each time she *tried,* the unpredictable effects would most often result in her flying several feet through the air in which-ever direction the fates decided appropriate.

It was disconcerting to say the least. The way Theron described it, her real mother had been able to keep the power going for an entire battle between Mover and Wraith.

"What am I doing wrong?" she muttered, still rubbing her latest bruise.

When a reply wasn't forthcoming, she looked around to find Theron staring at the covers on his bed—or rather, the shining agimet she had dropped there.

Her heart lurched in her chest. Breath held, her gaze darted from the crystal to Theron, wondering whether she could grab it before he could. What if she threatened him with the Aegis? She had already told him she couldn't control it, but it still might make him hesitate…

"No," he spoke the word as if it cost him a great deal. He seemed to be speaking more to himself than her. Then, to her disbelief, he rose and retreated until his back was to the wall.

Trembling, unsure what had just happened, Jenna carefully recovered the crystal. Holding it tight, as though to reassure herself she really had it, she turned to Theron.

"Why didn't you take it?"

He shook his head, not bothering to hide his fear. "I'd rather not talk about it," he murmured. Silence fell between them, before he seemed to shake himself. He waved a hand at her. "What happened that time?"

Jenna pursed her lips. She still wasn't sure what had just happened. But she knew Theron well enough by now to know you couldn't force these things with the man.

"The same thing—I couldn't hold it." She cursed softly, tightening her fist around the crystal until her veins glowed red. "Why can't I do this?"

"Don't think like that," Theron replied quietly. "You'll get it. But it's not like you just developed this power. It's been there all along, just blocked. The Gift grows stronger with age —but normally you get to practice with it as it grows. You don't have any of that experience yet. It makes this…harder."

"No kidding," she muttered.

She watched him as the silence returned. The question was still eating her up inside. Was it because the crystal was almost drained? That didn't make sense. He still could have freed himself with what remained.

"I'm afraid of what it will do to me," Theron spoke suddenly, surprising her.

Jenna's head jerked up and she opened her mouth to question further, before deciding better of it.

"The last time I touched a crystal, I almost died," Theron continued, his head bowed, eyes averted. "I have control of the withdrawal now. I almost feel normal." He shook his head. "But if I use *atar* again, even from regular agimet, I'm afraid I won't come back."

Remembering his joy earlier when he'd spoken about the Gift, Jenna wondered what it must be like, to have lived with this power for so long. To feel the very world shift at your command—and now have all that taken away.

"I'm sorry," she whispered.

"Don't be," Theron said with a shrug. He gestured to his plate, which he'd barely touched tonight. "Care to share a meal? Using the Gift can build up an appetite."

Jenna's stomach rumbled by way of agreement. She was tempted, but in the end she shook her head. "I can't. I have to go back, before someone comes looking for me."

He arched an eyebrow. "Aren't *you* meant to be the Matron? *They're* meant to scamper at *your* shadow, not the other way around."

"Probably," she said, "but my hold over them is tenuous at best, Theron." She hesitated. "Tomorrow?"

He smiled. "Same place?"

Despite her best efforts, a smile touched Jenna's lips. She bid him good night and headed out past the great agimet on its plinth, then out into the bowels of the Sanctum, where her mother's office waited for her.

Strange, how even all these months later, she still couldn't think of it as her own. Unfortunate, since the veritable mountain of paperwork waiting on her desk was all addressed to her. She dropped into the worn leather chair, her eyes feeling strained just looking at the sheer volume of it. How had her mother ever kept up with all of this? At least with the late hour, she should be spared any unexpected visits from the general. True to Theron's warnings, he had only grown more insistent as the weeks progressed. The time was approaching when she would need to deal with him.

For now though, she had reports to sort.

She flipped through them one by one, scribbling notes for Sister Margery—her administrator during daylight hours. Another attack in the south docks. A minor dispute between minor Houses over inheritance rights. Requests for increased grain shipments to the southern provinces, again. And complaints, somewhat strangely, about a pair of Daughters —Max and Jasmine from house...

Orpheus? She didn't know that name. And Daughters? They must be recent recruits from the Dominions, the last of her mother's intake. Pursing her lips, she scanned the list of grievances. Broken curfews, missing silks, prolonged absences, *fighting*…her eyebrows rose at that last one—and the list continued. How long exactly had these two been a part of the Magisterium?"

Rising from the desk, she returned to the outer office where Sister Margery kept the Matron's files from the last year. Thankfully, the woman was a great deal more organised than either Jenna or her mother, and it didn't take long to hunt down the records of the pair.

Her frown deepened as she scanned the page. Both had sworn their vows as Daughters on the same day…in a *private ceremony with her mother*. Jenna's eyebrows lifted. While the Matron was always present with the Aegis for Daughter's to take their vows, usually those ceremonies took place with upwards of twenty girls.

What's more, these two weren't from the Dominions at all. According to the file, they were from Tah'raus—and both were younger than Jenna had been when she'd first worn the golden collar. And they had been admitted to the order just a week before the Summer Gala.

Her skin prickled. Who *were* these two—

A tap came from the doorway. Irritated by the interruption, she was ready to give some poor servant a tongue lashing when she saw the shadow darkening the entrance to her office. An inexplicable sense of dread spread through Jenna—even before the shadow stepped into the lanternlight and revealed Theron's father.

"General Falkenrath," she said, caught off guard. "What are you doing wandering the Sanctum at this hour?"

"I might ask the same of you, Matron," he murmured. "Mind if I join you?"

He closed the door behind him without waiting for a response. Her heart began to palpitate in her chest and her fingers twitched towards the agimet in her pocket—before she remembered she'd drained it almost dry. It would be hours yet before the nexus naturally restored its charge.

The general advanced into the room until he stood over her desk. Jenna tried her best not to quail in her seat. Despite his age, Leonardo Falkenrath still carried the air of a soldier about himself. He stood with his hands clasped behind his back, those stony eyes watching her with a coldness that set her spine to tingling.

"You look tired."

This time, Jenna managed to keep her voice steady. "There are many matters the Matron must address."

He nodded, the action slow, measured. "It has been some…time," he murmured. "You have considered my offer?"

Jenna swallowed. This was it, and they still didn't have a plan. Rising, she stared across the desk at the man. Even on her feet, he towered a full foot over her. Looking into his aged face, she tried to convince herself he was the kindly man he pretended to be. That it would all be okay.

"I have," she said, lifting her chin. "I'm sorry, General Falkenrath, but I must respectfully decline your offer."

"I see."

The silence stretched out as the two stared at each other across the heavy oaken desk. Jenna was the first to break the contest, her eyes darting to her cup of ink.

"Yes, well, if that was all…"

Reaching for her quill, she sat and gave her best impression of returning to work. Bending her head to the next report, she began scratching words in her notepad.

The general did not move.

After a few heartbeats, Jenna gave up on the act. Letting out a frustrated sigh, she leaned back and looked up at the man.

"Was there something else, General?"

"I understand I am perhaps too old for a young woman of your vigour," he replied, and in place of warmth, she heard disdain in his voice. "However, this Magisterium will not allow your rule to continue without a king at your side."

"General Falkenrath, I *am* the Magisterium," Jenna growled, matching the man's gaze as she regained her feet. Rage spread through her veins, and she felt the Aegis pulsing on her arm, as if responding to the emotion. "And I am warning you, I have heard the end of this matter."

"I could destroy you."

It was like he'd dunked her into a barrel of ice water. There it was—the threat she'd feared. Still, she wasn't without an arrow in her own quiver.

"As you said before, revealing the truth about your son now would only ensure your own mutual destruction."

"I am an old man, Jenna," the general replied. "It would be a fitting end of my life, to see a traitor removed from our throne."

That was it. Her one shot. But if the threat did not hold…

She watched him, wondering. *Could* she do it? Marry this man, make him king. He was right—sooner or later, the Magisterium would force her to marry or give up the position anyway.

As soon as she actually considered it, she knew it wouldn't work. This was not a man that wished to share the throne. Once Leonardo had what he wanted, he would ensure her own power was removed in short order.

"I will never marry you," she said the words simply, without anger or fear. As if that would matter to a man like this.

"Very well," the general, despite her expectations, maintained his calm. It sent a chill right to the tips of her toes. "Considering your storied history, I had hoped you might see reason and accept I am the best you will get, but I cannot say I am surprised."

Hands clasped behind his back, still the blasted man did not budge.

"I think I've heard quite enough of your *reason*," Jenna snarled, clenching her fist and making a show of the Aegis's blazing light. "Now, I suggest you leave, or I will be forced to give you a demonstration of the power of this office."

To her surprise, the general only smirked. "But then who will help your brother, Matron?"

That caught her off-guard. "My brother?"

"Yes," he replied. "You see, I had hoped to spare his involvement, but after learning of his…affliction…" He shrugged.

The Aegis actually flashed this time as Jenna advanced around the desk, until they stood barely inches apart.

"You will leave Rohan out of this," she said, the words hissing like boiling steam from her lips.

She wanted to smash the man, to call on her guards and order them to cut him to pieces, but she doubted the Wardens would obey that command. So instead, she snarled and spun from him, racing from the room.

She didn't notice whether he followed, nor the Wardens stationed outside—all she knew was the pounding in her chest and the red that pressed at her vision. She raced through the dimly lit corridors, barely noticing the occasional servants she brushed from her path, until finally she came to her brother's quarters.

The door was unlocked.

Inside, she found an empty, unmade bed.

She stood there, fists clenched, knees trembling. Each breath came as a desperate gasp, as if the air had turned to liquid. For as long as she could remember, it had been her and Rohan against the world. Even when he had left the Magisterium, they had still shared a connection through their shared loathing of their mother. But now, now…

*Rohan, what have you done?*

Footsteps were approaching outside, but Jenna didn't want to turn, didn't want to confront the man that had played her like a fiddle.

"What have you done with him?" she whispered when she sensed his presence enter the room.

"I only gave him what he so desperately wanted."

"You sent him after Kaila Dwyn?" she cried, spinning finally to face him.

The man actually had the nerve to smirk. "That creature corrupted him, destroyed the prince in the eyes of our people. He has no future in this kingdom, not while that monster still walks this land. I gave him the chance to restore his reputation. That is all."

"Restore his reputation?" she cried. "The Elysian will *slaughter him…*"

She choked on those final words. Would they kill him? She had spared Kaila, hadn't she? And from what Theron had told her, their relationship hadn't been entirely fabricated…

But Rohan didn't know any of that. She cursed herself for a fool. Why hadn't she told him the truth about Eliza and Kaila, about everything? She had tried, that night on the roof, but he'd been raw, hurting. He had never believed her, not really.

And now he was out there somewhere, ready to kill the woman he loved to save a phantom that had never really existed.

She bowed her head, feeling the tears shimmering in her eyes. She had thought she could resist this man, that she had known where the knife would strike, but she hadn't even been close.

"Don't cry, little one," his voice was pitiless as he approached. "There is no shame in losing to one's betters. You will understand that, in time."

A rough finger brushed her chin, lifting her head to look into those glacial blue eyes. She flinched, stumbling backwards from him, but he advanced, not allowing her the time to escape. Fear fluttered in her chest as she tripped and fell over a coffee table. His smile spread.

"What do you want?" she whispered.

"You will announce our engagement to the Magisterium."

"I won't do anything until you bring back my brother—"

"*You*," the general bellowed, "will do whatever I say, *girl*." His hand snatched out, catching her by the arm and dragging her back to her feet. She tried to look away from the burning in his eyes, but rough fingers grasped her by the chin. "*Tonight.*"

Jenna clutched her fist, feeling the pulsing energy of the Aegis there, but even had it chosen that moment to obey, she could not have used it. Rohan was somewhere out there, alone with men loyal to the general. If anything happened to Leonardo Falkenrath, she was under no illusions about what their orders would be.

Grudgingly, desperate, she managed a nod.

"Excellent." Abruptly, the general released her. His voice became light as he continued. "There will be no backing out of our agreement then, understood?"

*What kind of monster are you?* Jenna thought as she staggered back from him, rubbing at her jaw. For his age, he had a surprising strength.

"Understood," was all she could manage.

"Very good, in that case, I will send word that no harm is to befall the boy."

With that, he snapped his fingers. A moment later, one of her Wardens stepped through the doorway. The sight was the final twist of the knife in Jenna's chest.

"Warden Ross, you are a Caller, are you not?"

"Yes, sir."

"Would you please reach out to your comrade, Warden Laura, and report that for the next twenty four hours, she is to protect the crown prince at all costs?"

"And after that, sir?"

The general smirked at Jenna. "Why, that depends on our young Matron here, doesn't it?"

Jenna's blood boiled as her own guard's armour lit up with the glow of *atar*. *Her own guards* were working for the man. She clutched her hand around the Aegis, *yearning* for its power, to break that barrier that kept her from unleashing it on this man.

"Of course, sir," the Warden replied in that metallic voice they all shared. "It is done."

The general turned to Jenna and smiled. "You see? That wasn't so hard, was it?" His smile faded. "Now, how about we assemble the Sisters before our good Matron gets cold feet."

---

"Here you are, sir."

Leonardo nodded his thanks as he accepted the handkerchief from his servant. Wiping the stench of the wretch girl from his fingers, he tossed it aside and continued down the corridor. Free of the cloying perfumes of the woman who styled herself as Matron, he allowed a smile to reach his lips.

The announcement before the Council of Sisters had gone over well. The hags had already been jostling for the girl to select a king, and her choice of experience over youth had been to their liking.

All in all, it had been a prosperous day. Even the fear in the girl's eyes told him she was no longer any kind of threat to him. Obviously, her control over the Aegis was tenuous at best. Better and better. When he claimed the other half as king, he would become the true power in Tah'raus.

His heart pulsed. All this time, and finally his plans were nearing fruition. His excitement was pulpable—he was of half a mind to march back to the council and demand their vows be taken on the spot. Unfortunately, that would raise questions. He would have to wait just a little longer, but Leonardo was accustomed to patience by now. There had already been more than a few setbacks in his path to the throne—the business with his children had certainly been an unwanted diversion.

But the Nameless had his own plans, it seemed, and even

that unfortunate business had eventually lead him back to the true path.

Now there was just one loose end to clean up.

"Warden Ross?"

The Wardens that had guarded the Matron had left her alone after their meeting. Their order had never served weakness.

"Yes, sir?"

"I need you to contact Warden Laura again."

"Sir?"

He pursed his lips. "Tell her to disregard my previous order. The Warden is to continue with our previous plan, understood?"

"Of course, General. I'll send the message now."

# 11

ooden boards creaked beneath Kaila's bare feet. She stumbled as rough hands shoved her from behind, forcing her up the rickety steps.

Above, swinging lazily in the breeze, the noose waited.

All around the platform, the mob howled. Their faces were smeared with ash and blood, twisted in hatred. Their mouths gaped wide, their shouts swallowed up by the roar. Kaila didn't need to hear their words to understand, though.

She flinched as a cabbage sailed through the air to strike the twisted boards, splattering her with rotten pulp. The rattle of stones against wood followed, before a ring of darkness pressed against the crowd, forcing them back. Not to protect the prisoner; but to ensure the king's justice was served.

Kaila tried to speak as the shove from behind came again, only to find her mouth was gagged. Rough hands grasped her and dragged her forward, towards where a masked man waited. Long fingers drew the noose wide as Kaila approached.

Screaming, she tried to run—but her strength was gone and instead *her knees buckled. The air was thick, cloying, the sky above an ugly, churning grey. The crowd pressed closer and the black wall bulged inwards. The screams rose as somewhere in the distance a familiar bell tolled…*

*And then Kaila woke.*

YAWNING, KAILA LEANED BACK IN HER CHAIR AND RUBBED HER eyes. Nightmares—or rather the same nightmare over and over again—had plagued her all night and now the words on the page were blurring again. This was impossible. Contrary to her suggestion the night before, they had retired without touching the mountain of papers collected by the tailor's network of spies.

First light, however, had seen Eliza alert and dragging Kaila from her bunk. *To catch up*, she claimed. Apparently, yesterday they had been slacking, going off to find Ambrose to report their discovery.

Unfortunately, Kaila was distracted to say the least. Her mind kept darting off in other directions. It had been so long since she'd thought about Elgoss and its people. Tomas and Sister Eurador and Sareen and so many others kept drifting through her mind. The faces of her childhood. A piece of her still longed to see them again, though they had betrayed her long before she'd thought them dead.

And then there was that strange Elysian, Cassandra. Who was she? *What* was she? A Mover? Or had everything Kaila witnessed all been an elaborate illusion? If so, she was a better Weaver than even Ambrose. His master, perhaps? Was that why he had sent her to Kaila?

There were no answers. The tailor was gone and with him

Garrick and most of the other Elysian who had operated out of *The Rusty Gull.* The poor barkeep had arrived in the early hours only to find he had no one to cook for—Eliza had prepared them a pot of oatmeal, while Kaila shook off the last dregs of sleep. It wasn't even burnt—somewhat of an achievement for a young woman who until recently had never worked a day in her life. It was a little lumpy though.

None of that, however, helped with the papers.

They'd started by going back through some of the older stacks, searching for references to their home. There was no mention of its name in the older piles, but now they knew what they were searching for, the pair began to pick out other discrepancies that might have pointed them towards Elgoss. A mention of food supplies to a recovery team in the Iron Pinnacles; defective iron ore strangely diverted to the capital for inspection; prisoners of a riot commissioned to work in a mine, the name of which had strangely been left off the documents.

The hints had been there—they just hadn't spotted them.

It was understandable. In the Sanctum, there would be hundreds of sisters working on documents like these. Ordering, filing, auditing them to ensure none of their noble families got too greedy with their thieving. They didn't care about the little folk, of course. Those who tended to the fields or dug the ore from the earth were little better than pack-horses—animals to be used and tossed aside when a better alternative came along.

Though after everything she had been through, Kaila wasn't sure she cared about them either. Every time she thought about the commonfolk of Fresia, she saw again the hatred in their eyes when they spoke of her kind. Part of her longed to condemn them all with the same brush, to watch them suffer along with the Magisterium when the Elysian finally had their victory. It would be easier, after all.

But Ambrose still cared. Despite his snobby way of looking down on others, the tailor still wanted to help the people of this city. Not even Theron had wanted that. He might not have *hated* them, and had at times gone out of his way *not* to harm them, but he hadn't ever tried to *help* those retched souls.

But Theron was gone. It still hurt to think about that. How she had left him that night, broken, bloodied, in the hands of their enemies.

So, she didn't.

Instead, Kaila set aside the pile she'd been working on and reached for a fresh stack of sheets. She found it helped at times to switch between piles. Pretend one was more interesting than another.

On this occasion, it happened to be correct.

A tingling sensation crept across her scalp as she glimpsed a familiar name on the top page.

*Rohan.*

Instantly, her heart was racing. Rohan. She hadn't heard a word about him in months. Hadn't *wanted* to know.

*Get away from me!*

His final words to her rung loudly in Kaila's ears as she stared at the name on the page. She could still see his face that night, the confusion, the *loathing* in his eyes. It hadn't mattered that she'd saved him—the moment he saw the glow of *atar* in her eyes, everything had changed. That light meant it didn't matter who she was or what they'd shared. He had already decided what she was. A monster. Nothing could ever change that.

She didn't even notice the tears building in her eyes until they fell to the page. Only then did Kaila find the will to tear herself from her grief. She had been a fool to dream of a world where Elysian and human could live side by side. Too much hatred had passed between their species for that to ever be possible.

Angrily, she rubbed away her tears and returned her attention to the page. A piece of her didn't want to know anything about Rohan's life. It was easier to pretend he had just vanished that night. But Kaila had to face that truth sooner or later. Rohan was still the crown prince and his movements might be important. So with trembling hands, she lifted the page from the stack of papers and began to read.

*A squad of fifty soldiers has been sent north to the Cascades, where a storm recently wrought havoc on vital orchard plantations. The force is led by Prince Rohan, who will coordinate relief efforts and restore trade output from the Dominance. He is accompanied by Warden Laura and a force of fifty soldiers. The Magisterium awaits further assessment by the prince, to be sent by carrier pigeon upon his arrival…*

That was it. After that, the writer turned to other comings and goings from the capital. Apparently, this was from an agent on the north gates, who Ambrose had collecting information on travellers who came and went from the city.

Kaila swallowed as she found her mouth suddenly parched. Blood pulsed in her ears and there were stars dancing in her eyes before she realised she hadn't blinked in quite some time. Setting the paper back on the stack with a reverence usually reserved for sisters at prayer, she stared at it, trying to process what she'd learned.

Rohan was gone. He had left the city. Off to help a Dominion in strife, apparently. A sharp pain came from her thigh. Belatedly, she realised she was gripping her leg so tightly her fingernails had cut through the fabric of her pants into her flesh. It took an effort of will to make them relax.

Drawing in a long breath, she tried to do the same for her

racing heart. This news didn't matter. Rohan was gone, but he was irrelevant. If anything, this helped. The report suggested supplies would not be arriving from the north anytime soon—it would accelerate the Magisterium's desperation.

Unfortunately, however much Kaila told herself Rohan Frye didn't matter, somehow, he did. It was like their separation had torn a chunk out of her—and now the hole that had been left was a putrefying, festering mess. Yet holding that page, she could almost image they were still connected, that even through time and distance, some force bound them as one.

It was a lie, of course. A comfort she told herself instead of confronting her grief.

"Everything okay, Kaila?"

She looked up at the question. It took her a moment to focus on Eliza. The other girl sat across the table, her own stacks of papers already dwindling. Just now, however, her eyes weren't on the papers, but Kaila.

Her first instinct was to lie. Rohan wasn't something Eliza needed to be concerned with. And as for Kaila's own sense of hurt and pain…well, that was her own damn fault, wasn't it? Except, that concern in her friends eyes wasn't just going to go away.

"It's…Rohan," she whispered, surprising herself. "He's left the capital."

Eliza's eyebrows lifted into her blonde fringe. "Let me see," she said, extending her hand for the paper.

Kaila handed it over without a word, then watched her friend scanned the page. She thought perhaps Eliza read the note several times, before finally lowering the paper and meeting Kaila's gaze.

"It sounds like he could be gone for some time."

Clenching her jaw, Kaila offered a single, curt nod.

"How do you feel about that?"

"I…" Kaila wasn't sure if she trusted herself to speak, but Eliza had asked. "Not…not great," she admittedly, doing her very best not to choke up.

The other girl saw through her act anyway. She was on her feet and around the table and wrapping Kaila in a hug before her warrior's instincts had a chance to kick in. And then it didn't matter, because instead of pushing her away, Kaila found herself hugging the other girl back. Softly at first, and then as the tears gathered, with a desperate loneliness she hadn't realised had been building inside.

"I'm glad you stayed," she gasped between sobs. *Please don't leave me!*

Eliza's hands tightened around her. "I'm glad *you* stayed," she rasped, leaning back and wiping tears of her own from her eyes. "There's nothing for me out there anyway."

"What do you mean?" Kaila hiccupped. "What about your parents?"

Her nose was dripping and her vision blurred. Trickster above, she was a mess. Rising, she moved to the bar and collected a couple of handkerchiefs—or rather, the grotty rags that pretended at handkerchiefs. She ignored the barkeeps pointed look. They were meant to be keeping a low profile outback, but it wasn't even midday yet and the few customers that tended to frequent *The Rusty Gull* wouldn't be making an appearance until the evening.

"They never cared about me. I was just another means of improving their fortunes." Her lips pressed into a thin line. "You and Ambrose are the only people who've ever actually cared about *me*."

Kaila swallowed. She couldn't imagine two parents being so cold towards their own flesh and blood, but she didn't try to refute the words. Theron's father had been a noble, after all, and he had hung his own daughter. Family evidently meant something different to their kind.

Eliza had set the paper back down on the table. Kaila lifted it carefully, looking one last time at the name on the page. In those words were her last connection to Rohan, to the man she thought she had loved. But whatever she felt inside, whatever they had shared on those quiet nights together, that part of her life was over. It was time she let it go. Carefully, she set the paper aside.

After that, they tried to get back to their task. Despite her resolution, however, Kaila's mind kept returning to Rohan, wondering how his journey north was going, what it would be like in the Cascades. The road there continued on to the Iron Pinnacles and eventually her home, though they hadn't come that way when she and Theron had journeyed to the capital…

Her eyes returned to the paper she was meant to be reading. She hadn't taken in a word. With a sudden burst of frustration, she tore it from the stack, scrunched it up into a ball and tossed it across the tavern.

"*Gah!*" she cried. "This is *literal* torture!"

"It's really not," Eliza muttered, though Kaila noticed the girl had been staring off into space as well.

She pursed her lips, considering the young woman—then abruptly, she made up her mind and rose.

"Come on."

"Huh?" Eliza muttered, looking around in confusion.

"I think we've earned ourselves a break, don't you?" Kaila said, placing her hands on her hips. "So, let's go for a walk."

Eliza raised her eyebrows. "Kaila, do you really think that's a good idea?"

"Why not? You've got the weaving."

"I'm only meant to use it in emergencies, remember? In case I drain the crystal."

Kaila rolled her eyes. Catching Eliza by the wrist, it took all of a second to connect the crystal inside her timepiece to the nexus again.

"One hour," she insisted, fixing the girl with a look. "Come on, let me show you the city. It's the least I can do, after, you know…"

She didn't have to finish that particular train of thought. Thankfully, Eliza must have been just as distracted, because she offered no further objection as Kaila dragged her to her feet. Together, they headed out the front door—Eliza activating her Weaving as they did so—and into the narrow alleys of the port.

They made their way towards the coast in silence, where they eventually emerged onto a bustling street around the docks. Here, great ships loomed above like buildings and fishermen hustled back and forth with mechanised vehicles stacked high with goods. With their recent issues getting supplies from the Dominances, the Magisterium had been sending out its fishing fleets more frequently.

Of course, this only served the tailor's plan. While the Magisterium had neglected this part of the city for years, the tailor had invested a sizeable sum of his business empire into these ships. It was said he already owned the port's heart and soul. Thus, for some strange reason, the holds of the fleet recently had been coming back half empty. At least, officially.

"Kaila." As they wove through the traffic, Eliza stopped abruptly and turned to face her. "There's something I've been meaning to tell you."

Taken aback, Kaila almost crashed into her friend. "Ah, is this really the place, Eliza?" she asked, glancing at the people pushing by.

The crowd didn't appear to take any notice of them, but you could never be too careful in Tah'raus. The new Matron might not have as many ears in her purchase as the old one, but the Magisterium still had power.

Eliza glanced around, seeming to second guess herself, before recovering her resolve. "What you did, Kaila, you don't have to feel guilty about it anymore," she said. "I didn't lose anything I miss." Her hand drifted to her throat. The scars were hidden by the weaving, but they were still there. "Or pay a price I wasn't willing to pay."

Kaila opened her mouth to object, but instead found herself speechless. She wasn't sure what she would have said anyway. What was one *meant* to say to something like that? So instead, she managed a quick nod. That was apparently enough, as Eliza responded to her awkward silence with a smile.

Then they were on their way again. Even at midday, the docks weren't the sort of place two young women should hang around alone, especially with Kaila without her powers. Though as they moved into the city proper, Kaila noted the differences were less than they had been in the past. The starving were no longer confined to the Soul Square. You could hardly go a block without passing a beggar with their bowl extended in search of ration chips. Not that those would sate their hunger—where once a single chip had meant a day's food—three were needed now for a single meal at the kitchens. There simply wasn't enough to go around.

Kaila felt a pang somewhere in the vicinity of her stomach. She had to remind herself that these people would tear her apart if they knew what she really was. Besides, this was war—one the Elysian had been losing for a long time. It was only right the humans took their turn suffering.

Wasn't it?

Eventually, they made their way into the merchant quarters, where the streets finally grew clean and the last dredges of the lower class made way for the true wealth of Fresia. Though even here there were differences, if you knew what to look for. The shops no longer displayed their wares in the open, where they might fall victim to an opportunistic thief. Now that ration chips were as good as worthless, people were looking for alternative currency.

There were also more guards. *A lot* more guards. Stationed outside storefronts, on streetcorners, even patrolling the dwindling crowds. Thankfully, there was no sign of the black armour of the Wardens. Ambrose's weaving wouldn't last long beneath their piercing gaze.

They wandered through the clothing section first on Eliza's insistence—you could take the girl out of the Daughter, but apparently you couldn't take the Daughter out of the girl. She was fascinated to see what fresh styles had taken root in the capital in the tailor's absence.

They did not disappoint. Despite the approaching winter, more than a few of their fellow shoppers sported a risqué style that could only have been inspired by the designer Marriats. Kaila's cheeks warmed at the reminder of her own disastrous experiment with one of his dresses.

The smile slid from her lips, her good mood fleeing with the reminder of Rohan. Nodding to Eliza, she left the girl to her exploration and wandered from the store. Outside, she spied a fruit store nearby.

"Apple slices, ma'am?" the older woman at the store asked, offering a tray.

Smiling, Kaila accepted a piece. She was surprised at the crispness as she bit into the tangy fruit.

"This is great," she murmured. "How is it so fresh?"

The woman offered a warm smile. "Agimet chiller," she replied. "Allows our suppliers to deliver fresh from the Cascades." She gestured to the table, which was laden with all varieties of fruit—apples and cherries and several varieties of citrus. "The driver had to change the crystal a few times, but it keeps the fruit much fresher than ice."

Kaila nodded absently, even as something in the words tugged at her. Times like these, she wondered at the marvels humanity and the Elysian could have achieved had they just worked together, instead of in opposition. Agimet devices had the power to change the world—if the Magisterium didn't so jealously guard the secrets of agimet, concealing its value from the very people who dug it from the earth.

She passed a silver piece that were the favoured currency among merchants to the vendor and indicated several apples and a pomegranate. While these were placed in a basket, Kaila glanced at the dress store. Eliza was just visible through the open door, engaging in a rather animated discussion with the owner. Kaila couldn't work her out. Eliza Wrenn should *hate* Kaila for what she'd done, destroying her life, robbing her of the privileges of the Magisterium.

Instead, the young woman from Elgoss seemed *happy*. Kaila hadn't seen Eliza happy since…well, when they'd been children, before the nightmares of war and duty had stolen away their innocence. They had both been through so much since then, lost so much, and yet there Eliza was, reborn with a new face, happy and seemingly carefree, despite everything she'd lost.

*I didn't lose anything I wasn't willing to lose.*

Shaking her head, Kaila finished off her apple slice and went to rejoin Eliza with her basket in hand. Seeing Kaila's approach, Eliza bid her goodbyes to the owner and they wandered away. They had missed lunch, so most of the stores with hot food were already closed for the afternoon, but venturing into the branching alleyways that surrounded the market brought them to more affordable offerings. This was where staff who cleaned and maintained the shops would generally find their meals—these days, if the merchants wanted honest staff they had to provide some form of payment instead of ration chips.

Between the hot pasties, stuffed dumplings, and simple sandwiches, they eventually settled on sausages on skewers. Kaila couldn't keep the smile from her lips as she watched Eliza devour the meal. She'd already gotten a splotch of sauce on her chin. Even without the new face, Kaila could hardly reconcile this woman with the pretentious girl who once tormented her at school.

It made her reconsider Eliza's earlier words. She'd just assumed the girl was trying to make her feel better after guilting Kaila into helping earlier. But what if it was true? She could have lived a life filled with banquets and galas and gowns tailormade for her by the best designers wealth could afford. That was the image the Magisterium sold its people— that anyone could be chosen for this life of privilege, if only you were studious enough, and dedicated enough, and loyal enough.

But that hadn't been the life Kaila experienced, when she'd replaced Eliza. Instead, she'd found herself alone. The other Daughters barely talked to Eliza, and the Matron had only been interested in what *Eliza* could provide her. In the end, the Daughters were just like everyone else in this cruel kingdom—servants to the needs of the Magisterium

And they hadn't even been fed well.

Watching Eliza finish her sausage and wave for a fresh kebab from the storeowner, Kaila's own stomach rumbled. Smiling to herself, she handed over a coin for a kebab this time. The meat still steamed from the agimet cooker set up in the back of the cart. Unlike the sausage, there was a bite to its flavour, the sort that set her eyes to watering.

She exchanged a glance with Eliza, who's eyes were already shimmering. "You know," she said to distract herself from the burning. "I can hardly believe you're the same person from Elgoss sometimes."

Eliza shot her a sidewards glance. "What, you think someone's gone and replaced me?"

Kaila spluttered, her cheeks warming as the other woman laughed.

Kaila scowled. "I just could never imagine Eliza Wrenn from Elgoss walking through the streets with sauce running down her chin."

"*What?*"

It was Kaila's turn to grin as Eliza frantically tried to clean her face with a rag that probably added more dirt than it removed.

Kaila couldn't help but chuckle at the sight. "Okay, now I see her."

Eliza flashed her a glare. "Is it gone?"

It wasn't. Kaila nodded anyway and Eliza sighed in relief. Setting aside the rag, she sat on the stool outside the stall and stared at her kebab for a full minute.

"Maybe it's because *I* don't know who I am," she said at last.

"I'm sorry," Kaila murmured.

To her surprise, the other girl laughed. "Don't be," she said. When she lifted her head and turned to Kaila, there was a smile on her lips. "Don't you get it? It's *exciting*, not knowing! All my life, I have been what my parents wanted me to be. And then, what the Magisterium wanted. But now…" She shrugged, still grinning. "I get to decide."

"So, what you said earlier…that was the truth?"

Eliza nodded.

It should have been a relief to Kaila. Knowing she didn't

have to feel guilty about at least *one* of the terrible things she had done. And yet, there was no ignoring that empty feeling in her chest. The piece of her that trembled and shook when she thought about her friend's words.

*I get to decide.*

Despite everything that had happened to her, Eliza had discovered something she'd never known she wanted—a choice.

It just also happened to be the one thing that Kaila would never have.

She forced herself to smile anyway, and after finishing the kebabs, they wandered back in the direction of the marketplace. Eliza wanted to collect the vendors details in case she had time another day to pass by his shop. They were coming to the end of her crystals charge and the former Daughter preferred not to take any chances.

As she waited outside, however, Kaila felt again that strange sensation of disquiet. Turning suspicious eyes on the dress store, she tried to pinpoint the source. Maybe it was seeing those dresses again, the reminder they provided of the day's *she* had been disguised as a Daughter, how it had felt with all those eyes on her. Yes, she'd hated it. Yet standing there in her plain cotton dress, indistinguishable from anyone else in the crowd, Kaila thought maybe she missed being a Daughter more than Eliza did. Even the night she'd worn that scandalous slip of Marriats; she'd been mortified, yes. But it had also been *exhilarating.* And the look in Rohan's eyes, the *hunger* of the kiss they'd shared…

He wouldn't even look twice at her now.

Swallowing the sudden lump that had formed in her throat, Kaila forced herself to look away from the store. That had to be it, the source of her unease. Remembering everything she had lost.

Yet as she moved away from the store, the feeling seemed to grow. Frowning, she looked up and down the street. Was the fruit vendor watching her strangely? Did she recognise Kaila? Her image hadn't been as widely circulated as Eliza's, but it had begun to appear on occasion after her involvement with the attacks throughout the city.

She watched the store for a few minutes before discarding the possibility. The woman was too busy plying her wares to a fresh set of customers. If she really thought she'd spotted one of the infamous Elysian terrorists…

Kaila's heart began to pound as realisation struck. She had already taken a step towards the stall before she caught herself. It wasn't the store she had to check. It was the records. Or failing that, someone else that had read those same records.

"Eliza!" It was careless to use her friend's real name, but if she was right, there was no time to consider an alias. "Eliza, quickly, where was the storm?"

Eliza wore a frown as she turned from the vendor. "Kaila, what are you talking about?"

"The storm that—" At the last second, Kaila bit back the name Rohan. Sucking a breath through her teeth, she continued. "The storm our…friend went to help clean up, where was it again?"

The frown on her friend's brow deepened. "The Cascades. Why?"

That was it. Confirmation. Blood pulsed in Kaila's ears as she snatched up Eliza's hand. "We need to go, *now!*"

---

"Kaila, what's going on? Kaila, stop—"

Ignoring the voice behind her, Kaila stormed through the

common room of *The Rusty Gull*, past the bar and kitchens, into the dormitory. Eliza chased after her, panting from the struggle to keep up through the winding streets of Tah'raus. The documents were exactly where they'd left them, tucked away in a cupboard beside the bunks. She tore through the pages until she found it.

"Kaila," Eliza gasped. "*Please*, tell me what's going on."

*A squad of fifty soldiers has been sent north to the Cascades, where a storm recently wrought havoc on vital orchard plantations…*

There it was, clear as day. The lie they'd missed, one so far away and unimportant, no one but a fruit merchant would have seen it. Her knees suddenly weak, Kaila sank onto her unmade bed. Silently, she passed the page to Eliza. The other girl took it with a frown, her eyes darting across the page as she reread the words, before returning to Kaila.

"So I was right about it being the Cascades?"

Kaila nodded wordlessly, offering the basket she'd brought from the marketplace. The fruit was no doubt banged about from the race back to the inn, but she'd lost her appetite anyway.

"If a storm destroyed the orchards," she rasped, "how is there a merchant in Tah'raus selling *fresh apples from the Cascades?*"

For the longest moment, Eliza stood staring at the page in her one hand, the basket in the other. Slowly, though, the colour drained from her face. She dropped to the bed, looking faint.

"But why…"

"It's a trap," Kaila whispered. "Rohan has fifty soldiers and a Warden. They're not for a cleanup—they're for *me*."

"But why would he think…"

Kaila gestured to the stack of papers. "Don't you think it's strange that after all this time we *suddenly* started finding hints about Elgoss?"

Abruptly, she stood and began to pace. It was all so, so *obvious!* She should have seen this immediately. The Magisterium was never careless. Its Sisters were meticulous, concealing the location of Elgoss, keeping the secrets of the Wardens—even hiding the existence of agimet machinery *from the people that mined the crystal from the earth.*

And then suddenly, they'd let the town's existence slip in a random report about a non-existent rice harvest?

Yes, they should have seen through it instantly.

Instead, she and Ambrose and everyone else had been blinded by the opportunity of a lifetime. The chance to steal agimet right out from under the nose of the Magisterium before it could be rendered useless. The clues had all been there—right up to the increasingly frequent mention of the town, as though someone wanted to be *extra* sure the message had gotten through.

This couldn't have been Rohan though, could it? She had seen the hatred in his eyes that night on the rooftop, but surely he wouldn't go this far…

Would he?

"Kaila, if you're right…"

"Ambrose," she rasped. Swallowing, she continued, "Garrick, the others…they're going to walk straight into it." She clenched her fists and turned to Eliza. "We have to get a message out to the other Elysian. Eliza?" She frowned when the other girl didn't move. "Eliza, did you hear me? We need to find the other Elysian!"

As her voice rose to a shout, Eliza finally jerked out of whatever trance her mind had taken her into. Blinking, she looked at Kaila with a frown.

"The other Elysian?"

"The ones in Ambrose's organisation," Kaila replied. "You must know how to contact them, right?"

Slowly, Eliza shook her head. "Only Ambrose—and maybe Garrick—know how to reach everyone."

For a moment, they both just sat there. Kaila could taste the familiar tang of despair. It rose in her throat, making it hard to breathe, threatening to choke her. Spots danced at the corner of her vision and she swayed where she sat, panic well and truly setting in.

"No," Eliza said suddenly, her voice firm. "I won't let this happen." Her hazel eyes found Kaila's. "We have to go after them."

"*What?*" Kaila couldn't believe what she was hearing. "Eliza, they left yesterday on *horseback*—we'll never catch them in time!"

"I can find us horses," Eliza said. "If we push hard, maybe we can catch them before they reach Elgoss."

"And if we can't?" Kaila whispered.

"Then we fight."

There was a strange resolve in Eliza's eyes as she stood. Moving to the cupboard where she kept her things, she rummaged inside. A light appeared as she withdrew and offered her hand to Kaila. A piece of agimet rested in her palm.

*Kaila's agimet.*

"Where…"

"Ambrose gave it to me before he left." Eliza shrugged. "Just in case you needed it."

Her mouth suddenly dry, Kaila licked her lips. "Are you sure?" she asked. "We still don't know what happened last time. It could be dangerous to be around me…"

"Kaila, if they take Ambrose prisoner, *all* of our lives are forfeit," the former Daughter replied. "We need you."

Kaila swallowed, suddenly finding herself at a loss. She hadn't realised how much it meant to hear those words. Wordlessly, she took the crystal from Eliza's hand.

Immediately, *atar* surged through her, restoring her connection to the world. It was a relief, feeling that power, knowing that *someone* at least trusted her with it. Unfortunately, its return also brought with it a realisation.

"There's no nexus in Elgoss," she whispered. "I won't be able to recharge crystals."

While in Tah'raus, the power of the nexus had meant she could recharge agimet almost instantly. But in a place like Elgoss, miles and miles from the nearest nexus, there would be almost no ambient *atar* to draw on to restore the crystals.

Eliza pursed her lips, but her resolve didn't waver. "Nor can the Warden though, right?"

It was true. Not even a Warden could create energy from nothing. Except, most Wardens carried at least five crystals embedded in their black armour. Being able to recharge her crystals from the nexus had evened the odds for the Kaila in the past, but she didn't like her chances of outlasting someone with *five crystals* to her one.

Especially with her Gift was malfunctioning at the best of times.

But Eliza was right about one thing—if they lost Ambrose, it was over. The resistance, any hope for a better life, all of it. The tailor was the linchpin that everything rested on; if he was compromised, the rest would either crumble or simply fade away.

She looked at Eliza, her fingers tightening around the agimet. The girl had so recently rediscovered her love of life. Now she was willing to risk it all for a cause that wasn't even her own. It wasn't right.

"You should stay behind."

"*What?*" Eliza's head jerked up at that, her eyes widening.

"I mean it, Eliza," Kaila whispered. "You're not Elysian. You can barely lift a sword. You should stay in Tah'raus, *live*. Let me go after them. I don't have anything left to lose anyway."

Standing across from her, Eliza looked at Kaila with a strange look, as if she wasn't quite sure how to respond.

"No, Kaila," she said at last, "I'm tired of being left behind. Tired of being the helpless girl sitting in the dark, waiting for someone else to come along and decide whether I live or die. So I'm coming with you—and that's the end of it."

Looking into Eliza's eyes, Kaila swallowed. She recognized the emotion there—that hollow helplessness, as if her choices, her life, no longer belonged to her. Whatever fleeting joy Eliza had found in the marketplace had already been swept away by the weight of reality.

Still, she couldn't just let her friend throw her life away. "Ambrose would want you to stay."

"Ambrose would want *you* to stay," Eliza shot back. Drawing in a breath, she met Kaila's eyes. "Enough, Kaila. There's no more time to argue. Ambrose and the others already have a head start—we have to leave, *now*. I'm coming with you and that's the end of it."

Kaila sighed—she knew when she was beaten. "Okay," she murmured, rising and extending her hand towards Eliza. "I give up. You can come."

Eliza actually grinned. "Who knows, maybe I can help you with your power. How hard can it be?"

Despite the levity in Eliza's voice, Kaila found herself grasping the crystal tight in her palm. In her mind's eye, she felt again that blinding pain in her skull, heard the screaming and the scarlet darkness. If she lost control against a Warden, if her Gift backfired and she lost consciousness…

"You're…sure you don't know any other Elysian who might be able to help us?" she rasped.

Eliza looked ready to shake her head—then paused. Lips parted, she stared at Kaila for the longest time, as if considering whether she dared speak her thought aloud, until finally…

"Actually, there might be someone."

# 12

The light had found its way through the drapes again. Groaning, Quintin tried to roll over on the broken sofa to escape the awful glow, but it barely made a difference. Raising a hand to shield his face, he searched for the source of the light. The wind had tugged open the drapes, allowing the morning's sunlight through. It caught on the empty bottles scattered across the coffee table, setting the room alight.

Moaning, Quintin pulled a pillow over his face and tried to ignore the pounding in his skull. It didn't work, however, as a short time later the great clock tower began to toll—the tower in which Quintin was currently present.

*Dong, dong, dong!*

The sound was like a knife stabbing through his eyeball and scraping against the back of his skull.

*Dong, dong, dong!*

Each chime drove the blade a little deeper, until six had passed. Silence returned. In full wakefulness now, Quintin shuddered at the emptiness. His world was now a silent place, devoid of emotion. He no longer held the blessed crystals. He had betrayed everything about what he was, who he wanted to be. He didn't deserve the blessing the Trickster had Gifted him.

He did deserve this. To be alone. It was better this way. Better that the curse ended with him. He thought of his daughters; finally safe, free to live without fear. They would break the circle, escape the cycle of hatred that had consumed their parents.

They weren't free. But no one in Fresia would ever be *free*. What was the point in dreaming of an impossibility?

Another tremor. Groaning, Quintin pulled himself to his feet and stumbled to the drapes. He yanked them closed. Yes, it was better this way. Max and Jasmine might be denied their birthright, but they were *safe*. The day would never come when he had to bury his own children.

His skull aflame, Quintin returned to the couch. He had just slouched onto the worn cushions, when the banging started at the door.

Groaning, he covered his ears with the pillow and prayed whoever it was would go away. But this wasn't like the clock-tower, a familiar agony he could persevere. Whoever was outside was not going away. At least, not without encouragement.

"Leave me alone, whoever you are!" he bellowed, lurching upright on the couch. "Before I tear the soul from your body and feed it to the demons of the night!"

The banging stopped abruptly. Letting out a sigh, Quintin had just laid back down, when he heard what he thought was the whisper of door hinges. Frowning, he squinted in the darkness, but his vision was still watery from the earlier sunlight, and he saw nothing—until the drapes were suddenly torn open.

"Arghhh!" he cried, throwing up his hands as though to protect himself from fire.

"Oh, don't be so dramatic," a young woman's voice spoke from the burning light.

His heart lurched. In Quintin's befuddled, desperate state, he thought it must be one of his daughters, returned to him somehow. Despite everything he'd sacrificed to send them away, he found an aching hope swell in his heart. It had been so hard, giving them up forever.

Unfortunately, as his vision cleared, Quintin found himself looking at a familiar young woman, yes, but she was most definitely *not* his daughter.

"Kaila," he muttered, slumping back on the couch. "What are you doing here? No, never mind. Get out, you're not welcome. Close the curtains on the way out."

He squeezed his eyes closed and prayed the girl would take a hint for once in her life. Silence was his answer, and for a few minutes, he thought he might have actually won—though the awful girl hadn't closed the curtains. He was just contemplating whether it was better to suffer the brief agony required to get up and close them again, or just to lie there and suffer until night fell, when the squeak of a floorboard warned him of the girl's return.

Unfortunately, he was too slow to react.

"Gahhhhh!" he cried as a pail of *freezing* water was poured over his head.

Lurching bolt upright, spluttering and coughing he swung his hands about himself to fend off further attack.

"First Matron be damned, you're a sorry sight," Kaila said instead.

Muttering expletives that would have made a sailor blush, Quintin thrust aside his pillow. He found Kaila standing over him with hands on her hips.

"Huh, I actually didn't know a few of those curses," she commented.

"I thought I told you to go away," he muttered, rubbing his temples.

"And I did," she replied. "But then I thought about how you were probably thirsty, and how you don't have running water in this flat." She shrugged. "So, I fetched you a pail from the well."

Quintin fixed her with a glare. She replied with a sheepish smile. A growl hissed his lips as he pushed himself to his feet —muttering several curses he was sure Kaila *did* know. Brushing past her, he stomped across to the pile of crates that he'd left discarded in the corner of the apartment. There, he rumbled around amongst the empty bottles, searching for one he might have missed.

"Quintin…" Kaila followed him, but he ignored her. If Kaila was here, this was *not* a conversation he wanted to have sober.

Finally coming up with a bottle that still had a few sips of ale inside, Quintin raised it to his lips and downed it in one gulp. It was flat and warm and tasted something awful, so he cast around for another. Unfortunately, the rest were empty. He thought there might be another crate up in the loft though, one he hadn't touched.

He glanced at Kaila. She stood with her arms folded across her chest, watching him with judging eyes.

"Quintin, please, would you just listen to what I have to say?"

Grimly, he turned to the ladder and dragged himself up the rungs while Kaila muttered something indiscernible behind his back. Above, Quintin hesitated. He hadn't visited the loft in months. Not since the day he'd given his daughters to the Matron.

The old woman hadn't known they were Elysian, of course. She thought he was just another servant, hoping to give his children a life he never could have hoped for himself. She had made them Daughters of the Magisterium. They would live in luxury for the rest of their lives, their Gifts concealed by the golden collars they now wore. They would never know the fear of life as an Elysian—and all it had cost Quintin was the life of his oldest friend.

Staring at the empty, unmade beds, the trembling began in his hands. To his relief, he spotted the crate, tucked in the corner. He strode over, yanked out a bottle, and exhaled—his memory hadn't failed him. It was full. Shaking in earnest now, he twisted off the cap and raised it to his lips. The ale was still warm but didn't have the sour spoilt taste. He drank long and deep, listening to the sound of Kaila climbing the ladder.

He was onto a second bottle by the time she appeared. She seemed hesitant—most unlike the girl he'd known as Theron's apprentice. His fingers tightened around the bottle at the thought of his former friend.

*He got what he deserved…*

But guilt was stronger than any spirits. It would not be dismissed so easily.

"Well, spill it," he snapped, turning his anger on the girl.

Kaila stood at the top of the ladder, watching him with those sad eyes. For a long time, it seemed like she would say nothing…

"Ambrose is in trouble."

Quintin's head jerked up. The words were so softly spoken, he'd almost missed them. He stared at the girl, wondering if he'd heard her right.

"What do you mean?"

Her eyes met his. "He's walking into a trap…"

The way she trailed off, left the end hanging, Quintin

knew there was more. Eyes narrowed, he took a step towards her. "What aren't you saying, girl?"

She swallowed, fists clenched, shoulders straightening. His heart dropped into his stomach as she told the story—about their discovery and Ambrose's plan to rob the mine, then how they'd worked out the trap. The soldiers the prince had taken with him, the Warden. And finally…

"It's my fault," she said quietly. "Rohan wants *me*. But Ambrose took the bait, so…" she exhaled. "It doesn't matter. We're going after them, right now."

"We?"

"Eliza is coming with me."

Quintin blinked. "The Daughter?" He wanted to laugh. "You're going to go rescue the tailor from the Magisterium, just the two of you—a Mover who's barely had her powers a year, *and a human without any magic whatsoever?*"

Kaila swallowed. "I thought you might help us."

This time Quintin did laugh. It was a cruel thing to do, but the girl needed to learn. This was Fresia and they were Elysian. Ambrose might like to pretend otherwise, but their kind only ever worked together for one thing—profit. And there was no profit in a suicide mission against the Magisterium.

Kaila wilted, though she did not retreat, and when his laughter finally died away, she was still watching him with those eyes.

"If they take the tailor," she said quietly, "sooner or later, he'll break. And they'll know everything. There won't be any safe place left for the Elysian to hide."

Quintin's stomach churned. The girl was right, of course. Ambrose was the closest thing to a leader the Elysian had. But that didn't change the facts.

"I'm sorry, Kaila," he said, softly this time, "but Ambrose

knew the risks of this business. Thank you for warning me, but you needn't have bothered." Even if Ambrose told them about the clocktower, it mattered little now. What did he have left to live for anyway?

"What happened to you, Quintin?" Anger crept into Kaila's voice. She advanced a step, eyes shimmering in the sunlight from below. "I know Theron lied to you. I don't blame you for walking away, or…or for what happened next." Her voice cracked, before she drew in a breath. "But afterwards…we needed you. *I needed you!*"

Even through the liquor and the haze he had drowned himself in these past months, Ambrose felt the hurt in her voice. He cringed, retreating from her, as though distance might help him forget the past, the thing he had done. But there was no escaping that guilt, the knowledge that he had been responsible for his friend's death.

At first, Quintin hadn't believed the rumours. Theron had faked his death before. It never seemed to stick. Not even the Warden he'd encountered in the Iron Pinnacles had been able to put the man in the ground.

But the rumours persisted, and the silence from Theron remained.

Then had come the knock on his door. Ambrose. Quintin should have known he couldn't keep the truth from the tailor.

*I never want to see you again, traitor.*

And that was it. Ambrose hadn't told anyone else, as far as Quintin knew, but it didn't matter. He had been banished from the world of the Elysian, from his own life, really. It was what he deserved.

Now, standing before Kaila, he saw the price others had paid for what he'd done. It hadn't just been Theron who'd suffered because of his betrayal, but Kaila as well. The guilt filled his chest, the weight of what he'd done suffocating him. The truth almost spilled from him there. Almost.

"I'm sorry," he said instead, "after what happened to Theron, I couldn't…"

"No one blamed you, Quintin. He lied to all of us about his addiction. You had every right to walk away."

He winced at those words. They were like a dagger to his chest. His mouth suddenly parched, he walked to the great glass windows above the clock and looked across the city. Dusk was falling over Tah'raus, and a dark, unsettling red lit the horizon. Tomorrow would be a fine day.

"What happened to your daughters?"

He let his eyes flicker closed. "Gone," he said, not daring to meet her eyes. "Someplace they will be safe."

"You and I both know none of us will ever be safe so long as the Magisterium rules."

Opening his eyes, Quintin allowed his gaze to be drawn to the terrible dome looming over the city. That concrete monstrosity had shadowed his entire life, staining everything he'd ever experienced. It wasn't just a threat—it was a prom-ise. It didn't matter where you went or what you did, how you behaved. If the blood of the Elysian flowed in your veins, they would find you, and they would kill you.

"What do you want, Kaila?" he whispered at last. "Why are you here?"

"I'm going to save Ambrose."

Quintin turned to look at Kaila. *Really* look at her this time. She was different to the naïve girl he'd delivered into the bowels of the Sanctum all those months ago. Life had churned her up, breaking off the soft, vulnerable parts and leaving a young woman in her wake.

But it didn't change the facts.

"Kaila, they have a Warden," he said quietly.

"I've beaten their kind before."

"When you had a nexus to draw from," he retorted, "and when they were alone. This one has an army." Maybe he should have left it alone, but he still felt the guilt inside, the acrid burning that whispered this was his fault, that he had driven her to this fate. So, he advanced on her until he was looking down into those hard emerald eyes. "I know you're strong, Kaila. But this is a battle you cannot win."

To his surprise, she did not look away. "Maybe it is," she said, "but what other choice do I have, Quintin?"

"You could *stop*. Forget about the tailor and the Magisterium and *live*, Kaila."

"Live?" she asked. She gestured to his loft. "Is this what you call living, rotting away in this cesspool?"

He snorted. "If the Magisterium captures you, the hole they throw you in will make this *cesspool* look like a vacation house on the Vermillion Coast."

"I spent weeks inside those walls, Quintin," Kaila murmured. "Don't you think I know what will happen if things go wrong?" There was a tremor in her voice, before she pressed on. "But I don't care. I have to do this. I can't just let them win again. I can't let it all be for nothing. I'd rather risk everything than just give up."

"Then don't," Quintin snapped, his voice growing harsh. "Just don't include me in your death wish."

He turned from her and strode back to the crate. It was too late for her. She was too far down the path of hatred to turn back. He could see that now. Another soul, lost to the *cause*.

*Bang.*

Glass rattled as he tripped and struck the crate with his boot. Cursing, Quintin clutched the wall to steady himself, his vision swimming. The alcohol was finally beginning to take effect, numbing the memories, the faces that haunted him each night…

"Please, Quintin. I can't do this without you."

He froze at the desperation in Kaila's voice, one hand outstretched for the next bottle. The faces swam before his eyes; his daughters the day he'd handed them into the arms of the Magisterium. Trickster above, that had hurt, knowing what he was doing, what it would cost them. But if it meant they were safe, that they wouldn't have to fear discovery, or be hunted…

"Why me?" he rasped. He didn't dare look at her.

"Because there's no one else. You're all I have left."

His eyes slid closed. He couldn't do this. He *couldn't*. He was done fighting. He'd given up. Sacrificed everything—his hopes, his belief, his life, all so his daughters could have a chance to live a regular life.

*Men like my father, they won't go quietly, Quintin. And so long as they rule, there will never be hope for anything better. There will only be…this.*

The memory of his old friend's words cut like an arrow to Quintin's heart. What would have happened if he'd just trusted the man? If just one last time he had put his faith in Theron Falkenrath. Could they have actually succeeded? Reclaimed the Aegis and shattered the illusion of the Magisterium?

He would never know now.

*What do you have left to lose?*

"How exactly do you plan to save the tailor?"

# 13

*The crowd surged, faces snarling, voices jeering. Spittle flew from screaming mouths as they pressed toward the scaffold.*

*Black-armoured sentinels barred their path, unmoving, expressionless. They would not save her. They were there to see justice done.*

*Kaila climbed, each step laboured. Her limbs were heavy, her soul torn, her spirit a pale flicker of what it had once been.*

*At the top, the noose waited…*

Gasping, Kaila tore herself from the nightmare. Clutching her chest, she tried to calm her racing heart. For five long, gruelling days she had ridden with Eliza and Quintin towards the north. And with every night came the vision, that promise of death.

Eliza's horses had turned out to be two aged mares that even in their heyday had probably only ever been used as packhorses. Their uneven gait left an ache in Kaila's spine that had her wondering if she'd even have the strength to draw her sword when they finally caught up with Ambrose.

The sleep—or rather, her lack of it—didn't help either. She hadn't told the others about the dream. The fact her powers might not work the way they were supposed to was terrifying enough. Prophetic dreams about the hangman's noose was a worry she didn't need to share. Even if it woke her in a cold sweat each morning.

Kaila released a breath she hadn't realised she'd been holding. Darkness still clung to the world, but a glow had begun on the horizon, silhouetting the familiar peaks. As the light grew, the sky turned a deep, dark scarlet.

They were in the Iron Pinnacles now; yesterday they had bypassed the ruins of Iselador and camped in the pass that would lead them down into the valley of Elgoss. They'd pushed themselves hard, hoping to catch Ambrose and the others before they reached the town, but now they were out of time. If they rode hard, tonight they would arrive in Elgoss.

*Home.*

A shiver ran through Kaila. The last time she had been in Elgoss, people she had known her entire life had turned against her. Was that why the nightmare plagued her? A reminder of what she was, really, when all was said and done? Just another monster to be put down.

Rising, she moved to the mouth of the pass and looked out across the valley. The winter snows hadn't yet arrived, but unlike the verdant land around Iselador, the basin before them was barren, all scarlet dirt and broken rock. Little grew on this harsh land, little except the tiny town that could just be made out in the distance, perched on the side of the volcanic mount.

Elgoss.

Was Rohan there already, waiting for her to spring his trap?

She glanced over her shoulder, to where Quintin and Eliza still slept. The Psionic had said little on the journey. She still wasn't sure what had changed his mind. He was a shadow of his former self, but at least he had agimet and his Gift.

Her eyes shifted to Eliza. Her once enemy. In a way, all of this was happening because of that hatred they'd shared. Now they were friends, but they couldn't undo the damage they had done. Rohan was setting this trap because of Kaila, because he thought he could avenge the real Eliza.

It hurt to think about that.

Pushing aside the thought, she wandered over to wake them. They were running low on supplies by now, so they skipped breakfast and packed up their sleeping bags. They were on the road before the sun had cleared the horizon. The path down from the pass was as steep as Kaila remembered, so they went on foot leading the horses between them. Sweat soon drenched their skin and their clothes clung to them like wet rags.

But they pushed on, chasing the dwindling hope they could catch Ambrose before Elgoss, that this entire journey hadn't been an exercise in futility.

As the day crept on and the sun passed its zenith, even that hope faded. They reached the valley floor and rejoined the road. Kaila rode with Eliza—the former Daughter had more practice with the beasts than the miner's daughter— while Quintin mounted the second of the mares.

Another hour crept passed with still no sign of Ambrose. If the other Elysian had already reached the town, it meant they were likely already dead or taken captive, and their task went from a simple warning to a nigh impossible rescue.

Then, as the valley turned a corner and the great volcanic peak of Elgoss appeared, they finally saw movement. Below, the land dropped away steeply through a gorge, before the climb to Elgoss. The road wound down the scarlet slope, zigzagged its way through twisted terrain, before regaining its altitude to reach Elgoss.

Far below, at least an hour ahead, a nondescript carriage and half a dozen riders had just reached the bottom of the hill and started into the gorge.

Eliza sat bolt upright in the saddle. "Is that…"

Kaila's heart pulsed. She squinted against the dust rising from the trail. "I…I don't know."

They shared a glance, then turned to Quintin in question.

The Psionic shrugged, though he worked his jaw before he responded. "It could be anyone."

"What do you think, Kaila?"

She said nothing. Her eyes were fixed on that distant carriage and its riders. Any moment now, they would disappear amongst the crags of the canyon. There was a pulsing in her ears as she reached for her agimet and drew in a drop of *atar*. They had passed beyond reach of Iselador's nexus now. There would be no more replenishing the *atar* in their crystals —even with her Warden's Gift, the ambient *atar* was all but non-existent.

Her vision shimmered, the *soullights* of those far below flickering before her eyes. Even with her *atarsight*, she could barely make them out, but just before they vanished around the bend, Kaila caught a glint from the man seated in the front of the carriage. Just the briefest of glimpses, but enough to know the driver carried several pieces of agimet.

"It's them," she whispered, turning to the others.

They didn't need to speak for Kaila to read their expressions. Eliza's eyes shone with renewed hope, while Quintin's face remained grim, as though he couldn't quite bring himself to believe—or perhaps he simply didn't care.

"Come on," she said softly. "We can catch them in the canyon if we push the horses."

Eliza's eyes shone as she nodded and nudged their mount towards the trail. Kaila gritted her teeth as they set off at a trot, the vibrations running all the way up her spine. The rattle of stones from behind announced Quintin was following.

Unfortunately, the road was little better than a goat path in the way it clung to the mountainside. Dust swirled around them as they picked their way down, the switchbacks coming fast and tight, forcing them to slow.

More than once Kaila felt the mare falter, its hooves sliding on the broken stone. Each time it did, her stomach lurched into her chest cavity as she found herself staring over the ledge. Thankfully, Eliza was able to drag back on the reigns, righting their course.

Kaila clung to her friend, counting down the minutes, knowing each one narrowed the gap with their quarry—even as the sun crept towards the horizon and the shadow of Mount Elgoss stretched towards them.

They didn't pause at the bottom of the slope. By then, the carriage and its riders could only be ten minutes ahead. Walls of scarlet rock loomed as they pressed on into the gorge. The temperature plunged as the shadows swallowed them up, and with the sweat soaking her clothes, Kaila soon began to shiver. She steeled herself against the discomfort, resisting the urge to draw from her crystal.

*Faster.*

They were so close now, yet the knowledge did nothing to calm her panic. They *had* to warn the tailor before he reached Elgoss. She could sense the volcanic mount above, felt its presence like a malevolent shadow on her soul. It was a reminder of what she had been before Theron, and what this place would make her again, if she let it.

*Nothing.*

A rattle echoed through the gorge. Kaila and Eliza leaned forward on their horse, seeking a glimpse of their quarry. *So close*. Any moment now, Ambrose and Garrick and the others would come into view and they could wave for them to stop. Then they could explain everything, why they had to turn back. It would all be okay.

*Clang!*

A sound, sharp and metallic, echoed from the scarlet walls. Not the rumble of wheels, but the clashing of steel. Abruptly, Eliza dragged back on the reins. The mare snorted, stumbling to a halt. Quintin followed suit, and suddenly they were motionless. Kaila held her breath, straining her senses as the mare trembled beneath them.

*Clang!*

The sound rang out again, unmistakable. Somewhere ahead, weapons clashed.

They were too late.

The ambush had begun.

# 14

The world stood still.

It was finally working. Jenna breathed it in as she strode up and down the chamber, listening to the impossible silence. The energy didn't slip through her fingers now. Time was hers to command, and she moved through it without hesitation.

*So, this is what it was like for my mother.*

And all it had taken to master was the existential dread of a noose closing around her throat. Days had passed since the general's threat, and still there was no word on whether Rohan was really alive. The general insisted his soldiers would keep the prince safe, but the man could be trusted about as much as a lone wolf amongst sheep.

It gave Jenna the briefest of chances. She had told the sisters the marriage wouldn't move forward until her brother returned to the capital for the ceremony. Falkenrath didn't like that, but it was her only leverage.

Silence echoed through the chamber as she reached the

wall and leaned her head against the cold obsidian. Her skin tingled at the contact, the *atar* flickering inside her. She closed her eyes, listening to the impossible silence. Not even her footsteps made a noise here. Sound required time, apparently.

Too bad this mastery had come too late.

Falkenrath was ruthless. He'd swiped Rohan right out from under her nose. If she so much as flinched the wrong way, he wouldn't hesitate to have him killed. She was backed into a corner.

Exhaling, she released her grip on time.

"He's going to kill me, isn't he?" she whispered.

On the other side of the obsidian chamber, Theron stirred in his chair and looked around. A few minutes had passed for her, but to Theron it would have only been a heartbeat. She'd circled the room so many times she wasn't even sure where she'd started, so to his perspective she would appear to have teleported.

He pursed his lips. "Most likely. My father is not the type to share power. He'll want a nice, compliant wife—not one who talks back." He offered a faint smile. "Not exactly your specialty, my dear."

Jenna huffed, resuming her pacing—this time without her Gift. "I can't let him hurt Rohan," she murmured. "This is my mess. He should have never gotten caught up in this."

"You know once the General has what he wants, your brother will be—at best—an inconvenience. At worst, the prince will be a threat to his position."

"Don't you think I know that?" Jenna snarled, swinging on him. "I'm *trying*, but he has the Wardens. They don't even pretend to obey me anymore."

"You could go to my friends," Theron said quietly.

Jenna let out a long breath. Crossing to the stone slab that served as Theron's bed, she sunk onto the blanket. "And say what?" she whispered.

He hesitated, then crossed the room and sat beside her. "That you're one of us." He pressed his lips into a thin line, before he went on. "I know you'd rather keep living this lie; but this is something all Elysian have to face eventually."

He gestured around the room. "You can pretend all you like, but the Magisterium will never forget. They'll never let you rest. And one day, they *will* uncover the truth. Then it won't matter how wealthy you are or how many friends you have in high places, even your rank as Matron—they'll take it all."

Jenna swallowed. She clenched her fist, feeling the inert power of the Aegis pulsing on her wrist in response. A faint tingle spread across her skin, but nothing more. She muttered a curse under her breath. The power was inside—she just couldn't use it.

"It still won't work for you, will it?" Theron asked.

She shook her head. What more could she say? She'd tried everything she could think of—but the only time it had done anything was to protect her against a direct threat to her person.

"T'iana must have done something to prevent an Elysian from using it," she muttered. "A safeguard if we ever stole it back."

"I doubt that," Theron replied. "It would have prevented *her* from using it."

"What do you mean?"

"Because T'iana was Elysian," Theron replied absently.

Jenna stared at him, speechless. A pounding began at her temples as she struggled to find the words she needed. As the silence stretched out, eventually Theron looked up, before his eyes widened in realisation.

"You didn't know?"

"*Know?*" Jenna finally managed to squeeze some words from her throat. "How could I *know?* That…it would be…blasphemy!"

"I guess your mother never got the chance to tell you," Theron said sheepishly. "The Elysian call her the Great Betrayer."

Jenna swallowed. "That's…"

She couldn't find the words again. T'iana, the First Matron of Fresia, who had formed the Magisterium and lead the war against the Elysian a thousand years ago, had been one of the enemy herself.

Just like Jenna.

Jenna stared at the floor between her feet, her body trembling, her mind racing through the implications.

"Why would they cover something like that up?"

Theron shrugged. "Because it doesn't fit their narrative," he said. "We're meant to be monsters, dark creatures corrupted by the taint of our dark magic. Unless you've recently developed a taste for the blood of unborn children, you might have noticed that's not exactly true either."

"So, what? They lie about the First Matron, make the Elysian out to be monsters. Why? What's the point?"

"Power, my dear wife," Theron whispered, leaning towards her. "That's all men like my father or your mother ever cared about. The Elysian have power the Magisterium can't control—so they hunt us, turn the people against us."

"That…that can't be all of it," Jenna whispered.

"I suppose we also make an easy enemy to lay the misfortunes of the kingdom upon. A drought in the north? The Elysian cursed the crops. A plague in the capital? Dark Elysian magic…" he trailed off, his lips curling down.

Jenna shivered. Could it really be so simple? It felt like

there needed to be more. But as the silence stretched out, Jenna thought about her mother. Eliana Frye hadn't ever really cared about Jenna's blood—just that she wouldn't become Matron and reveal her secret to the rest of the Magisterium.

Her heart hurt to think of the agony the Magisterium had inflicted upon the Elysian, all so they could maintain their rule.

"How do you do it?" she asked at last.

"Do what?"

She looked at him. "Keep going. Persevere, even when the whole world is against you."

His lips twitched. "Bad humour, mostly." Then he sighed, growing serious. "You shouldn't follow my example, Jenna. You saw what I was willing to do to destroy my father. There was no line I wasn't willing to cross, no deed too foul to achieve my goal."

To her surprise, Jenna found herself smiling. "Oh yes," she said, stretching her arms and falling back on the covers with an exaggerated yawn, "you poor thing, you had it *so hard*, seducing a princess for your devious plan."

Theron chuckled, but the mirth in his voice quickly faded. "I can't say I regret the company," he said, looking down at her, "but for what it's worth now…I'm sorry I lied to you, Jenna. Quintin was right. I was so obsessed with my father, I lost sight of what was *right*."

Jenna sat up suddenly, her heart thudding. *Quintin? That name…*

Her eyes widened as she remembered where she'd heard it. The Daughters her mother had invited into the Sanctum, their father had been *Quintin Orpheus*…

And she understood. Finally, she knew how her mother

had figured out Theron's plan before herself or his father. Because she *hadn't.*

Someone had told her.

"Jenna, what is it?" Theron was watching her closely, a frown on his face.

"I know how my mother found out you were Elysian, Theron," she said softly.

"What?"

"A few weeks ago, there were complaints about some new Daughters. They were the last ones my mother ever initiated into the order—just a few days before the Summer Gala, in fact. And they were young; even younger than I was when I swore my vows."

As she spoke, Jenna saw the understanding dawn in Theron's eyes. Her heart twisted at the sight of it.

"These Daughters, what were their names?"

"Jasmine and Max."

Theron bowed his head, his eyes flickering closed. "Quintin…betrayed me."

Jenna reached for him instinctively. "Theron, I'm so sorry."

"Don't be," Theron rasped, offering that poor, broken smile again. "Thank you for telling me."

Silence fell between them. Jenna watched him, the hurt etched into the lines of his face. Yes, he persevered, but it wasn't with the easy, impervious smile he presented to the world. That was a lie. Inside, this man was as vulnerable as any of them, each blow a knife to his soul. A tremor shook her and finally she looked away.

"I should go," she murmured, starting to rise.

"Don't." A hand rested against her shoulder.

She paused. Looked around. Saw him watching her, his

eyes wide—pleading. Her heart gave a quiet little thump. After a moment, she nodded and sat down again.

"Okay, Theron. I'll stay."

Silently, she reached for his hand. Warmth spread through her fingers as they held his. Neither moved. Eventually, Jenna shifted so she could lay her head on one of the pillows. Hands still entwined, Theron did the same. They stayed like that for a long time, until sleep took them both.

# 15

Crouched on the mountainside, Rohan listened for the rumble of wheels on stone. For over a week, their hunting party had camped in the ruins of Elgoss, waiting for sign of their quarry. The town was a dead place, its streets silent, the buildings empty. The only sounds came in the dead of night, when strange *cracking* noises came from below, as if the earth itself spurned the evil that had been committed on its holy soils.

*Kaila Dwyn.*

Rohan's heart pulsed hard in his chest. She was close—he could *sense* it. Like a moth to the flame, she had been drawn back to this place by Iron Hand's ploy, to the place where her darkness had first stained this land.

And the light that would finally purge her evil from this world.

This morning, the scouts had reported her approach. After weeks of agony—first the long journey through the mountains, then the hours of waiting—finally, the time had come. No more would he be haunted by the memories of that night, the moment on the rooftop when the creature had revealed itself, with his rage for his helplessness that day.

Finally, he would have his chance for vengeance.

His sister had urged him to move on these past months. To forget Eliza and the monster that had taken her from him. And he had tried, for a time.

But the truth was, Rohan didn't *want* to forget. That monster had taken everything from him—now he would not rest until he did the same to her. His hatred had become the blood in his veins; his rage, the air in his lungs. They fuelled him, consuming everything else, until all that remained was this one, burning purpose.

And now, thanks to the general, all he had to do was wait a little longer.

His knees ached from crouching on stone. The other soldiers were spread out across the slope, hidden by the shadow of the hill. Rohan could sense their tension. Their quarry were not ordinary men, but Elysian sorcerers, with vile magics that could warp reality, changing faces and send men flying with a thought.

But Rohan Frye did not fear the enemy. He had surrendered his fears that night atop the Sanctum, when Kaila Dwyn had stolen the one thing he cared about more than life itself.

Besides, the Nameless had not left his followers defenceless against his enemies in this war.

Rohan's eyes were drawn to the black armoured woman that stood on the slope with them. The Warden Laura did not hide like the rest of the Fresian soldiers, but stood on the slopes like a silent guardian of the Pinnacles. Her chest blazed with the fire of five agimet crystals. She would stand with them today and turn back the dark powers of the enemy.

"Prince Rohan," as if sensing his attention, the Warden

spoke his name with the rasping, metallic voice of her order. "Join me."

"Warden?" he said, surprised. The woman had hardly spoken the entire journey.

The black helmet turned and despite his faith, Rohan couldn't help but shudder under the weight of her gaze. Rising, he carefully picked his way across the rocky slope. More than a few of the soldiers exchanged nervous glances he passed them

"The enemy are close," the Warden said as Rohan joined her. "Are you prepared?"

His skin prickled. "It is all I have dreamed of since the night my wife was taken."

A piece of him had broken that night, like Kaila had stolen a little piece of his soul, leaving him hollow. Her betrayal had taken so much from him. Rohan just hoped that today, at last, he might reclaim the missing pieces of himself.

*Crack!*

From somewhere below came the clatter of wheels bouncing off stone. Watching the road, Rohan held his breath, waiting for the first signs of movement.

"Anger is good," the Warden rasped when nothing appeared. "The Nameless calls for passion from his soldiers."

Rohan swallowed. "I pray for his blessings this day."

"And you shall have it."

Holding out her hand, the Warden formed a fist. Black liquid shimmered between her fingers, extending from her gauntlets into a blade of black steel. Reversing the weapon, she offered the hilt to Rohan.

Mouth agape, he stared for several heartbeats longer than was appropriate, before reaching out to take the weapon. Its handle was surprisingly soft in his fingers, more like leather than the hardened metal he had expected. A tingling sensation spread through his arm as he held it, swelling until it filled his entire body. It grew no worse, however, and eventually began to fade.

The Warden had been watching him closely, as though waiting for something, but now she nodded.

"Strike your enemy with the blade and it will draw the magics from her veins," she said with her metallic voice. "Kaila Dwyn will be your task in this battle, prince. I will handle the other Elysian, but the general insists it must be you who strikes down the traitor. Only this can redeem your soul in the eyes of the Nameless."

Rohan bowed his head. "I will not fail, Warden Laura."

As if in answer, a hiss of warning came from the soldiers below—and then they appeared. First one rider, then a second, before the carriage itself emerged from the shadows of the gorge and started along the road below.

Instantly, Rohan was alert, his fingers tightening about the strange blade. It still prickled against his skin, as though its magic sought a way inside his flesh, where it might drink the power of his soul. He steeled himself against its touch, however, and looked to the Warden.

Laura still did not move, though around them the soldiers of the Magisterium rose carefully to their feet, weapons in hand. They were hidden deep in the shadows of the gorge, where their quarry would struggle to make them out against the dark red stone. Poised above the road, they awaited the command to strike.

Rohan's heart pounded hard against his ribs as he watched the group advance. There were half a dozen riders, plus the driver of the carriage. Even with their vile magics, the Elysian were badly outnumbered. It would be a slaughter.

A smile touched his lips as he turned to the Warden. Her armour seemed to blend with the darkness, even the agimet crystals momentarily dimmed. She held no weapon, though this did not seem to concern her in the least. Lithe as any predator of the mountains, she started forward, and her voice rang out through the gorge.

"Soldiers of Fresia, for freedom!"

The men shouted their accord and surged past the Warden. Their voices echoed from the cliffs, building into a roar that carried before them like an avalanche. Below, the men on horseback dragged back on their reigns, even as the beasts panicked and fought against them. For a moment, it seemed chaos would consume them.

Then the driver of the carriage stood and threw out a hand. Silver blazed in his fist, casting back the shadows.

Rohan's heart stood still. *Magic.* He held his breath as the Elysian's magic swirled, the black sword clutched before him like a shield. The world stood frozen, as Elysian and human soldiers weighed the other's resolve.

Then movement came from the carriage. Canvas flaps were thrown back, revealing a dozen men in a hidden compartment. Each carried a blazing crystal, their eyes burning silver as they spilled from the carriage. The Fresian charge faltered as the enemy ranks swelled. Now, almost twenty foul Elysian stood against the brave heroes of Fresia.

Fear swept through Rohan as he saw the general's carefully laid plan about to crumble. This was meant to be an ambush; taking the enemy by surprise, crushed by their superior numbers before the enemy's magics could be brought to bear. Now the enemy had turned the ambush on its head. It would be the soldiers of Fresia who were crushed. Already, Rohan saw some of their men glancing back, searching for a path to flee.

"Courage, men!" Warden Laura's voice rung out through the gully. Her armour glinting with the light of agimet crystals, she strode forward through the ranks of soldiers. "Let not the foul magics of the enemy deceive you! This day is ours!"

Rohan gaped as she cleared the last of their soldiers and advanced towards the enemy alone. Below, twenty blood-thirsty monsters waited, teeth bared, eyes burning with that horrible glow. She would be slaughtered, her armour cracked and broken, her life snuffed out by their dark magics. The day was lost—no human could stand against such power…

…a shiver crept down Rohan's spine. Something…something was happening to him, wasn't it? To all of them. This fear, it wasn't natural. Across the hillside, the brave soldiers who until a few minutes ago would have marched into the flames of hell for their kingdom stood frozen with fear, unmanned by the sight of a few enemy Elysian.

Trembling, Rohan looked at the sword in his hands, then back to the Elysian. He could almost *feel* their power, the promise of death in those malevolent eyes. That night in the Sanctum, he had seen the after aftermath of their power, the bloody corpses Kaila Dwyn had left in her wake. To attack now was suicide.

*I have dreamed of since the night my wife was taken…*

His body made the decision before his mind could rebel. Rising, Rohan took one step, then another towards his quarry below. As he moved, he felt the weight of their eyes fall upon him. The terror redoubled, a screaming that split his skull, demanding he flee.

Gritting his teeth, Rohan fought against his own mind.

It didn't matter how many were waiting for him. He had only one goal, one desire left in this world—to destroy the monster that had killed Eliza Wrenn.

He felt the moment the spell broke. It was like a glass barrier had been placed around his mind and then filled with a terrible pressure. But as he pressed against it, there came a *crack*, followed by a rush of relief. Fear still remained, but now it was a tiny thing, a trembling inside that reminded him of his peril.

There was more to the enemy's deception, however. As he returned his gaze to their quarry below, there numbers seemed diminished—and with a start, he realised there *were no reinforcement.* Just the carriage and its original riders.

In fact, the enemy were using their magic to cover their retreat—as the carriage and its horses turned and fled back the way they had come.

Thankfully, Warden Laura had seen through their deception. With a burst of motion, she cut across the slope and hurled herself at the cowardly creatures. Her gauntleted fist lashed out as she landed amidst them. A horse screamed and crashed to the ground. The riders scattered—some thrown from their saddles, others struggling to rein in their panicked mounts.

Amidst the chaos, the Warden struck.

Heart pounding, Rohan watched with a terrible fascination as she downed another of the horses. She was preventing their escape, he realised, crippling their mounts so none would slip from their fingers.

But she was alone, and eventually the Elysian would regain their composure.

Grimacing, he looked to their soldiers. They stood unmoving, frozen by the terrible fear of the enemy. The Sisters had warned of the tricks Elysian could play on the human mind— how they could twist it, turn it against itself. How could they fight a magic like that?

"Soldiers of Fresia!" he bellowed, marching through their ranks and brandishing the black sword. "Your kingdom calls on your courage!"

A few stirred, blinking in the shadows of the gully, as

though struggling to wake. Taking heart from the sight, Rohan threw out his arm, pointing the black blade at the battle below.

"Look, men!" he cried. "Our Warden calls for your aid! Will you let her fight alone?"

As though to emphasis his words, a roar carried up the valley. Below, a massive hulk of a man charged at Warden Laura. Eyes aglow and a massive hammer in hand, he struck her a terrible blow. She fell, black armour disappearing momentarily amidst the surging bodies. Her cry echoed from the cliffs.

And just like that, the last dredges of the spell broke. Straightening on the slopes, the soldiers lifted their weapons and looked to Rohan.

Grim-faced, he pointed his blade. "For freedom!"

With a roar, the soldiers of Fresia charged.

"What do we do?" Kaila whispered.

They sat on their horses, listening to the clashing of steel and screams of the dying as they reverberated through the gulley. She looked to Quintin, but the Psionic sat trembling on his horse, his face drained of blood.

"We have to help them."

There was no give in Eliza's words. Before Kaila could argue, the mare surged beneath them—urged on by a shout from Eliza. They charged past Quintin, hurdling the scattered rocks that littered the path, onwards across the torn ground. The scarlet cliff-face flashed past on one side, while on the other a precipice yawned, worn down by the endless passage of time and water. The road narrowed, until Kaila felt sure

Eliza's recklessness would see them both dead—and then widened abruptly as the cliffs gave way to a jagged slope.

Ahead, all was chaos.

Of the five horsemen they had seen earlier, three had lost their mounts and were just now staggering to their feet. The remaining two struggled to keep control of their horses as a black-armoured monster lurched towards them.

Before the Warden could down another, however, Garrick slammed into the creature with a *thud* that could be heard from sixty feet away. The Warden, however, was unphased and already beginning to rise when Garrick struck again. His warhammer rose and fell, clattering into her helm and gauntlets with superhuman strength.

As the other riders tried to go to Garrick's aid, the enemy reinforcements arrived—and suddenly they too were fighting for their lives. Crystals appeared and four sets of eyes glowed silver.

The soldiers of Fresia were undaunted.

Blades at the ready, they charged the Elysian.

The two Elysian on foot stepped forward to meet them. The first raised a hand and with a gesture, several of soldiers went hurtling backwards, caught by an invisible force. The eyes of the second glowed bright—and three men screamed and fell to their knees clutching their skulls.

Unfortunately, it wasn't nearly enough. Not against so many. The remaining soldiers swept past their ill-fated comrades, determined to bring down their enemy.

Kaila glanced at Eliza. This was it. No more time for hesitation. Before she could stop herself, she leapt from the saddle.

"Kaila!" Eliza screamed. Confronted with the reality of battle, her face had turned pale. "What are you doing!"

"Find Ambrose!" she called back, pointing to the carriage

that had stopped in the centre of the road. Eliza couldn't do anything in this fight, but maybe she could still save the tailor.

Then she turned to confront the soldiers. The *atar* in her crystal leapt eagerly at her call, like it *wanted* to be used. For once, though, its power seemed desperately inadequate. There had to be at least fifty soldiers in the road—and she had only one crystal to confront them. Quintin had a second, but glancing over her shoulder, she saw no sign of the Psionic.

Her stomach twisted. She was alone again. Maybe that was better though—if her powers went awry, she would hurt only her enemies.

Fingers tightening about the crystal, Kaila opened her *atarsight*. Unlike the other Elysian, she wasn't under immediate threat. It gave her a second to consider her options. The pair were encircled now, though none of the soldiers had gotten close enough to land a blow yet. It wouldn't last. Kaila could sense the *atar* in the pair's crystals. It was already burning low.

Kaila would have to be efficient to have any chance of success. A difficult prospect, considering their numerical disadvantage. Connecting to each individual *soullight* would burn through her *atar* within a few heartbeats. Briefly, she reached out with her Warden's Gift for any ambient *atar* in the canyon, but an entire mountain range separated them from the nexus of Iselador. There wasn't so much as a drop of power in the air to replenish their crystals.

Fortunately, Theron had shown her there were other ways to use her Gift.

Reaching within, Kaila spun out a single line of power. There was plenty of debris in the gorge that she could turn into projectiles, but every thread demanded more power. Instead, she selected a single boulder the size of her skull and wrapped it in her magic. Ponderously, it rose into the air and hung there, awaiting her command.

With a thought, she sent it hurtling at her enemies.

The first she struck died quickly, his lungs obliterated by the crushing force of the boulder. A second perished without ever knowing what had struck him, crumpling to the ground as his spine was shattered.

That finally got the attention of the others.

A smile touched Kaila's lips as she felt their pause. They hadn't flinched at the magic of the others, but another Elysian, appearing seemingly out of nowhere, made them hesitate. She took the opportunity to check the *atar* in her crystal. So far, the single thread had consumed only a fraction of its energy. That would change if she had to face the rest of the soldiers alone. Hopefully, the others had something left.

Garrick and the Warden had vanished somewhere in the chaos. Maybe the Trickster would smile on his children today and Garrick would get in a lucky shot on the black-armoured monster. Taking her out of the fight would change their odds dramatically.

Grimacing, she turned back to the soldiers. Strangely, they still hesitated, watching her from where they had surrounded the others. Kaila clenched her fists.

"Come on then!" she challenged. "Who's next!"

She started towards them. To her surprise, a ripple went through their ranks. For a heartbeat, she thought they would flee. Then several stepped aside, allowing one among their rank to step from the circle to meet her.

It was Rohan.

Kaila froze. She shouldn't have been shocked—she'd known he would be here. It had been his name on the report that had caught her attention in the first place. But knowing was one thing. Standing face to face with that truth was another.

"Hello, Kaila."

His face was hard as he strode towards her, lips pressed into a thin line. He carried a black sword in one hand. *A Warden's sword.* Her heart pulsed, but Kaila didn't move. Couldn't. Her *soullight* trembled, the fragments that had twisted and broken inside threatening to tear her apart. She could feel herself losing control over the boulder, the thread unravelling.

"What, no words for your dear husband?" Rohan's voice was bitter. "Truthfully, it's nice to finally know who I'm speaking to. Kaila Dwyn. The Elysian who destroyed Elgoss." He paused, glancing over his shoulder in the direction of the town. "I'll admit, when General Falkenrath told me his plan, I didn't think you would be stupid enough to take the bait." He shrugged, a cruel smile spreading across his lips. "I should not have expected so much from a creature that would murder its own father."

"No…" It came out as a plea. She shook her head in denial. "Please, Rohan, that's not…" Her voice cracked and her knees began to tremble. She could feel the strength draining from her body, her grasp over the *atar* in her soul fraying.

"Come on, Kaila," Rohan mocked. He was close now, that terrible blade held before him, eyes filled with a dark hatred. *"What are you waiting for?"*

The last words came out as a roar as he surged towards her. The sudden movement finally snapped Kaila from her stupor. She flinched back from him and the black steel lashed through the space where she had stood, slamming into the ground with a *thud*. Snarling, he drew back to swing again.

Heart thundering in her ears, Kaila lashed out at him with her Gift. The thread formed instinctively, shooting from her like an arrow from a bow to pierce his *soullight,* connecting them. She only wanted to stop him, hold him still so they could talk…

…but the moment her power touched Rohan, Kaila knew she'd made a mistake. There was something different about the way her Gift formed this time. Something more—as if she'd woven all the sorrow and pain and anger in her soul into that silver thread.

And as the connection formed between them, she felt a reverberation back from the prince. For one, frozen moment, she heard music—harsh and haunting and beautiful all at once. The loss of love, of a world that had once been vibrant colour, but could now only ever be grey.

Distantly, she was aware of someone screaming.

Of Rohan, his pain, his grief.

Kaila felt it in her soul, in the connection she had formed, and the piece of her that had been broken—and then healed.

Kaila felt it all.

It hurt. It *overwhelmed.*

The world shimmered. She felt the cracks, her soul splintering, slicing her apart, *breaking her.*

Control fled. Threads of *atar* unwound, spinning out of control.

But they did not break.

They spread. Lashing out. *Connecting.* Binding to the *soullights* all around her.

With each fresh connection, Kaila felt another piece of herself break. The shards twisted in her soul, the agony building, one atop of the other.

She was screaming by now, her throat bloody. She felt her soul begin to unravel, crumbling in the flame of connection…

…and the darkness, rising to swallow her whole.

# 16

Steel clashed on steel and screams rent the air. The roar of battle all around, Eliza crouched low in the saddle and urged her horse on through the chaos. The aging mare bulked as men stumbled across her path, but with a firm hand, Eliza held it to the path. Her heart hammered as she scanned the battlefield for a way through to Ambrose's carriage.

*So close.*

She could just make it out—some sixty feet ahead, where it had collied with a boulder and tipped on its side. Blood stained the canvas flaps, but Eliza knew by now not to trust her eyes when it came to a Weaver. She wouldn't believe Ambrose was gone until she felt his cold flesh in her arms—

Eliza yanked the reins as a shadow lunged at her. The mare shrieked, veering hard as a soldier hacked at where her neck had been moments before. Crying out, Eliza kicked and the mare surged forward. The soldier cursed as a hoof caught him in the shoulder, spinning him to the ground.

She had tried to skirt the edge of the battle, but the soldiers had poured down the slope from one side of the trail, forcing her towards the precipice on the other side. Seeing the edge approaching, she tried to slow the racing mare. But the ground was broken and uneven, and before she could regain control, it stumbled, steel shoes catching on a hidden rock.

*Crack!*

A scream tore from her throat as the beast began to fall. She dragged back on the reins, trying to direct it onto steadier ground, but the old mare had finally reached its limits. Screaming, it collapsed to the broken stone, flinging Eliza clear. The world spun and she hit the ground hard. Momentum sent her skidding several feet, sharp shale tearing through clothe and flesh alike.

Dazed, struggling for breath, Eliza lay there a moment and struggled to put the world back up right. Through the ringing in her ears, she heard the heavy tread of approaching boots. They didn't sound friendly. Clenching her teeth, she pushed herself up—even as her arm screamed and her stomach rebelled.

Three soldiers loomed, blades held at the ready, chainmail rattling as they charged.

Gasping, Eliza staggered to her feet, but the sudden movement set her vision swimming. She stumbled, catching a glimpse of the carriage, still just out of reach. Letting out a growl, the first of the soldiers raised his weapon…

The world warped, then blurred. A ripple ran through the battlefield, like a wave through water. As if reality was being stretched and rewritten. For a heartbeat, the soldiers stood frozen…

…then without so much as a whimper, they turned on their heels and fled. One fell, scrambling in the gravel, but the other two didn't so much as pause to help him back up. They didn't look back.

"Eliza Wrenn, would you care to explain exactly what you think you're doing here in the middle of a battle?"

Eliza turned slowly to find the tailor standing alongside her. His coat was immaculate, untouched by blood or dust, and his silver hair was styled like it always was—or at least, that was the image he showed to the world. Today, however, he allowed the silver *atar* to shine in his eyes. A lump lodged in Eliza's throat as she met that gaze.

"It's a trap!" she gasped, the words tumbling from her lips before she could produce a better explanation.

Arching one eyebrow, the tailor turned to regard the battlefield. "You don't say."

Eliza swallowed. "There's a Warden," she continued, "and Prince Rohan is here somewhere. I think he wants to kill Kaila."

The tailor's eyes widened. "Kaila is *here?*"

At that moment, the world *trembled.*

It began as a pulse, like the reverberation of a drum through the battlefield. But with each beat, it grew louder—stronger—until Eliza felt it not just in the stone beneath her feet, but her own flesh and bone.

And as its power grew, the changes began. First was the stone. As reality itself seemed to lose meaning, the cliffs shimmered, then slagged, stone bubbling like wax beneath the hot sun. Metal groaned and the air itself grew heavy. Men screamed as shadows bent in the wrong direction, but found themselves unable to move, their very bodies no longer theirs to command.

Then came the sound—sharp, screeching, *alien.* Music, almost, but wrong. Twisted, tainted, no soul that heard it could fail to feel the grief and the fury of its maker. It wrenched at something deep within Eliza's soul, emotions she'd thought buried—the pain of betrayal, of loss, of all the hurt and pain the world had caused her. Kaila and Ambrose and Theron and Garrick and Quintin. They had destroyed her life, taken everything from her.

The pain swelled until Eliza felt herself screaming, clutching at her ears, anything to make that awful music stop.

And still the drumbeats grew.

Across the battlefield, light warped, swirling about a point of radiance, the wrongness at the heart of the sound.

Kaila.

She stood in the middle of it all, eyes blazing with the familiar silver light, boots planted wide, hands extended as though to fend off an attack. In her hand, she clutched a blazing crystal. All around, the soldiers of the Magisterium and Elysian alike had fallen. They writhed on the ground, their voices crying out in agony.

Only one man remained unaffected.

Rohan loomed over Kaila, draped all in grey, black sword extended. The pair stood frozen in a silent tableau, as though each were waiting for the other to move.

Black sword against blazing agimet.

And then, just as suddenly as it had begun, the music cut off.

The light in Kaila's eyes flickered, then blinked out.

The crystal in her hand went dark.

Silence fell across the canyon, terrible in the aftermath of what they had just witnessed.

It was broken by a soft *thump* as Kaila crumpled to the ground.

As quickly as the stillness had begun, movement returned. The wind came howling down from the peaks, whistling through the narrow stones as stunned soldiers dragged themselves back to their feet.

"What…what the hell just happened?" Eliza gasped, still struggling with what she had seen. What she had *felt*.

"I…I honestly have no idea," Ambrose's voice was uncharacteristically feeble, "but…I know I never want to feel that again."

Eliza swallowed, still unable to tear her eyes from where Kaila had fallen. Strangely, the stones around her friend remained twisted and deformed.

*That wasn't an illusion,* she realised with a chill.

Metal rasped against stone as the soldiers regathered their weapons. Then, almost as one, they started towards where Kaila had fallen.

"We have to help her," she said, finally turning to Ambrose.

The tailor looked wane, his face drained of colour. As she spoke, however, he seemed to shake himself. He took a step. "Maybe…" he faltered, "maybe it would be better…" His hand clenched into a fist. "No, you're right. Come."

He took another step and seemed to regain some of his strength. The colour returned to his face, and then he was all but dragging her across the battlefield. She could just make out the grey of Rohan's cloak through the soldiers. He hadn't moved from where he stood. Eliza thought she saw his lips move, but the words were lost to her.

"You gave her agimet, didn't you?" Ambrose asked, interrupting her thoughts.

"I had to," Eliza rasped. "So we could help you."

His hand tightened around Eliza's wrist, and stumbling to a stop, he swung on her. "Eliza, listen to me very closely," he said, eyes wild, "whatever else happens here today, *do not* let Kaila touch agimet again."

"*What?*" she gasped. "But—"

"She's dangerous, Eliza," he hissed. "I don't know *what*

that was just now, but…there have always been myths amongst our kind. Most are just stories invented by the Magisterium, but that…" His lips drew into a thin line as his eyes shifted to where Kaila had fallen. "Now I'm not so sure."

Eliza forced herself to look again, to see the twisted stone and broken bodies. Many of the soldiers had not regained their feet. Swallowing, she nodded.

"Good, now come on. I don't want any—"

*Thump.*

The pair of them leapt backwards as a body landed at their feet. Eliza gaped as Garrick, bloody and dazed, struggled to push himself to his hands and knees. Before he could straighten, however, a black boot slammed into his back, driving him face first into the dust.

"Well, well, well, look at this collection of rats," a mocking voice spoke from behind the black visor.

Eliza's breath hitched. Even before she'd left the Magisterium, the Wardens had terrified her. There was something unnatural about the way they moved and spoke. Now, as she found herself face to face with one of the black-armoured monsters, her terror was like a physical weight, creeping through her body, stealing away her breath.

"I'll admit, the Bruiser stretched me for a minute," the Warden continued. She nudged Garrick's limp form with her boot. He didn't move. "A good thing he only had one stone." The helmet lifted, regarding Eliza and Ambrose. "Eliza Wrenn, I presume?" Laughter sounded from within the helm. "Looks like I won a bet with the general."

"Go, Eliza," Ambrose hissed, stepping between her and the Warden. "Get to Kaila."

"But—"

"*I said go!*" the tailor did not look back, but she heard the pain in his voice.

The laughter came again, echoing from within the armour, twisted and inhuman. "Yes, run along little Daughter. I believe the prince was looking for you."

Eliza hesitated, frozen in place.

The Warden moved slowly, circling Ambrose like a wolf stalking a stag brought low after a long chase. Her black armour gleamed dully in the shadows, her movements fluid, as if the plates were more liquid than solid steel. Her visor remained fixed on the tailor, unreadable.

Ambrose didn't retreat. He held his ground, silver hair swirling in the breeze, spine stiff against the Warden's threat.

"Go," he repeated, not looking back. "Remember what I told you."

Eliza took a single, trembling step.

The Warden lunged—and the world twisted. With an explosion of colour, the battlefield broke in two. The ground seemed to move beneath them, splitting them apart. In an instant, the tailor and the Warden were a hundred yards away, and she was alone. She watched, heart trembling, as the pair came together with a *crash.*

Then Ambrose was gone. Vanished into the weaving.

No more time to hesitate. Spinning on her heel, Eliza charged in the direction she hoped was still where Kaila had fallen.

She had failed. The entire plan, *everything*—it had all fallen apart.

Eliza ran. Over broken stone and twisted rock she ran, past fallen soldiers and the four plain-clothed bodies of the other Elysian, she ran. The air thrummed with power, but it was only a dull echo of what she'd felt earlier—when the world had tilted and broke beneath the weight of Kaila's magic.

*Remember what I told you.*

Eliza's boots skidded across the dirt.

Ahead, her friend lay in a shallow crater of melted rock, her limbs limp, the dark crystal still clutched in her hand.

And there—black sword raised to strike—stood the prince.

Rohan.

*"Stop!"*

---

Ambrose watched Eliza flee from the corner of his eye. Even as he kept the majority of his power focused on the Warden, he diverted a portion towards the former Daughter. Any soldier that looked her way would see only swirling dust and empty rock. It was the best he could do for her now.

His heart hurt as he concentrated on the Warden. He had already woven a net of illusions about her, trapping her in place, distorting reality, assailing her with visions of terror and darkness in the hope of cracking open that wicked mind.

She stood calmly through all of it, arms crossed against her chest, refusing to be drawn into the illusion. His most terrible manifestations could not budge her, and as he finally saw Eliza disappear amongst the rocks, Ambrose let them fade with a sigh. Using a weaving against a Warden in that black armour was like waves upon the Fresian coast. He would burn through all the *atar* in his possession long before he made an impression.

Cold laughter echoed from the dark helmet. "So, you're *that* variety of rat," she rasped in that terrible voice. "Truly, did you think to destroy a Warden of the Nameless with *illusions.*"

Ambrose grimaced but did not respond. His gaze darted to where Garrick lay. The man was still unconscious, but his power had at least troubled the Warden until his agimet ran out. Ambrose still had three left. If he could get a crystal to his friend, they might theoretically stand a chance.

The Warden seemed to realise his intention, however, for as he took a step towards the large Elysian, she shifted quickly to bar his path. Heart sinking, Ambrose cast around him and spied a fallen soldier nearby. Quickly, he darted to the body and retrieved the sword lying nearby.

The laughter chased him again as he spun, raising the blade to fend off a blow. His adversary was no fool, however, and she advanced cautiously. She held no weapon—Rohan still had her sword. The Trickster-cursed-prince had used it to break the illusion he and Macy had cast over the soldiers. Between his weaving and her Psionic manipulation, they'd almost sent the Magisterium's servants fleeing for the hills.

Instead, they'd burnt through two crystals and still ended up trapped.

Poor Macy. She'd still been reeling from the Psionic backlash when the first soldiers had reached them. Her horse had been downed and her throat sliced opened before Ambrose could reach them. Omar, his only Mover other than Kaila, had been the next to fall. He hadn't seen what had become of the siblings Pete and Maya, the youngest on his crew. Perhaps the Trickster had smiled on them and they'd slipped away in the chaos.

"Come then, little rat, why don't you try your luck?" the Warden mocked as she approached.

Ambrose grimaced. Even without a weapon, a Warden's touch alone could kill an Elysian. If she got her hands on him, this creature would drain every drop of *atar* from his blood— and then begin on his *soullight*. His only chance was to find a way through that armour of hers, but he was no swordsman. Unless he got *incredibly lucky*, that was no chance at all.

He darted backwards as the woman lunged, iron fingers grasping for his throat. Sparks flew as he struck back, his blade clanging from her helm. Thankfully, without her blade, he could at least counter. Theron had told Ambrose of his own counter with one of their kind. Within a few exchanges, Theron's iron blade had been spotted with rust.

"Typical rats," the Warden mocked, her advance pressing him back. "Always trying to flee instead of fight. Tell me, Elysian, is there not a single daring soul amongst your kind?"

Ambrose bared his teeth. "It is not *my* kind who hide behind cowardly armour."

A growl rumbled from the black visor. She charged at him again and once more Ambrose hurled himself aside to avoid her grasp. Something in his shoulder screamed as he struck the ground, but clenching his teeth, he recovered and spun. Thankfully, the Warden took her time to recover. He used the opportunity to spin another weaving, then glanced over his shoulder. Thirty feet away, Garrick looked to be stirring.

"I'm over here, Elysian!"

Ambrose swung his sword as the black-garbed monster closed on him. His arm *jarred* as the weapon struck her outstretched hand. Gasping, he stumbled back, but before he could withdraw the weapon, black-steel fingers wrapped around the blade. Metallic laughter echoed from behind the visor as lines of copper rust spread through the weapon. In horror, Ambrose released the blade and leapt back.

Iron screeched as the Warden took the sword in both hands and tore it in two. He stumbled backwards as the remaining iron crumbled to dust, his own strength failing.

The Warden continued her advance. "Pitiful," she mocked. "I thought I might actually have to use my armour's Gift today. Truly, I am disappointed."

His stomach twisted and glancing at the crystals in her

chest, Ambrose saw that it was true. There were five in all, each still glinting with the full force of the *atar* within. This woman had manhandled Garrick and withstood Ambrose's most powerful illusions—*all without using any atar of her own.*

How in the cursed name of T'iana had Theron and Kaila ever defeated one of these things?

"Come then," the Warden mocked, "let's not draw this out. Allow me to send you to meet the Nameless. Do not expect him to be merciful when he cleanses your foul soul."

Trembling, Ambrose allowed his shoulders to droop. The dark creature advanced, sunlight glinting from her armour, the black armour carrying her forward with the irresistible force of a landslide. Crystals burned in her chest as she reached for him…

…only for Ambrose to hurl himself backwards. The Warden snarled as her fingers found empty air, then enraged, she swiped at him again. He ducked, ignoring the screaming from his shoulder and the fire in his lungs. Pain no longer mattered—only keeping out of reach of the killing machine. Stones crunched and snapped as a fist smashed into the ground, then struck a boulder, and still he managed to evade her.

Until his back touched stone.

Ambrose froze. Panting, he lifted his head to stare at the woman in the nightmarish armour. She had come to a pause as well, seemingly as surprised as the tailor to find her quarry cornered. His heart pounded in his chest as he looked into the black visor, seeking some hint of humanity inside.

He found none.

"And so the chase comes to an end, little rat," she laughed—and then lunged.

Ambrose smiled.

As her fingers found his throat, the weaving cracked and

shattered. His laughter was the last thing the Warden heard as she plunged through his dissipating body and the cliff-face that wasn't really there—right over the precipice he had steered the fight towards while she'd been distracted.

Thirty yards away, Ambrose watched the Warden plummet into the abyss. He couldn't celebrate, not yet. The fall might not kill her—but it would buy them time to deal with the other soldiers and make good their escape. He had used the distraction to reach Garrick, and now he knelt beside his stirring friend and slipped a crystal into the man's fingers. A groan rasped from the Bruiser's lips as *atar* seeped into his body. His Gift would help him to regain consciousness—

Ambrose felt the magic touch his *soullight* a second before it took hold. But even as he summoned a weaving, he knew it would do him no good. Not this time. Not against this Gift.

The Warden was a Mover, like Kaila.

With a *yank*, Ambrose was ripped away from the giant Elysian and tossed across the broken ground. He caught a glimpse of a dark shadow at the cliff's edge—where the Warden had somehow used her power to haul herself back up —and then he *slammed* into a boulder.

*Crack!*

Ambrose heard his outstretched arm break before he felt it. *Then* he felt it. A scream tore from his lips, but he couldn't even right himself before that *yanking* sensation came again. Desperately, he clutched his agimet and channelled *atar* into his soullight, trying to dislodge the connection. Unfortunately, he knew how a Mover's power worked well enough to know that was futile.

Stones and rocks and dirt tore his skin as the Warden dragged him bodily across the ground towards her. The treatment was pure spite. She could have just have easily lifted Ambrose clear of the rubble and landed him directly into her corrosive grasp—but the creature obviously wanted to make a point.

It gave him a chance.

Not for himself, but for the others.

His soul full of *atar*, he spun out one final weaving. Not directed at the Warden this time. Not even towards the battle or his poor, lost Eliza.

He sent it to Garrick. In the distance, the Bruiser stirred and sat up…

…and found the tailor standing over him, offering a hand.

"Quickly then," Ambrose said, the words tumbling from him in a rush. The weaving was a poor one and would not last—especially as each rock he struck tore yet more strips from his life. "While she's distracted."

Blinking, Garrick looked around, but he wouldn't see the Warden or Ambrose's half lifeless body being dragged across the broken ground.

He only saw what the tailor wanted.

Grimacing, the Bruiser clenched the crystal Ambrose had given him. *Atar* blazed in his eyes, and then he was on his feet again.

"Where is she then?" he growled.

"Never mind that," Ambrose hissed. If the woman possessed the Gift of a Mover, she had only ever been toying with them. "Quickly, Garrick. My leg is hurt. I need you to carry me out of here."

Surprise showed on the Bruiser's face. Garrick was not the kind of man who ever ran from a fight. But to his credit, he was a soldier first and after only a second's hesitation, he nodded and swept the spectre of Ambrose over his shoulder. The Bruiser's own mind completed the illusion, telling him he now carried the tailor's weight.

It broke Ambrose's heart, knowing what he was doing as

the Bruiser started scrambling up the scree into the mountains. But this was one battle the giant Elysian couldn't win. And even in his beaten, disembodied state, Ambrose knew what was at stake. He would try and prevent it, but if the Warden took him alive…

…someone had to survive and carry a warning to the rest of his organization. Garrick was that man.

He held the weaving together as long as he could. The Warden seemed to be taking great pleasure drawing out her victory. She'd stopped dragging her victim, and now approached his motionless body with slow, measured footsteps.

"I can feel you working your magic, Weaver," she said as her shadow fell across him. "You won't fool me again." Laughter rang in his ears as she crouched beside him.

Ambrose closed his eyes. "I'm sorry, Garrick."

"Sir, what was that?" He felt the Bruiser begin to slow.

"You know what you have to do, soldier," Ambrose whispered.

Then he severed the weaving. A hiss of breath rattled from his throat as he found himself fully back in his broken body—just in time to feel the iron fingers close around his throat.

"Come, rat, no more tricks."

# 17

"Stop!"

Eliza's shout cracked across the canyon like a whip. Rohan froze, the dark blade inches above Kaila's chest. It hung there, trembling. His shoulders rose and fell, his breath rasping on the chill air. Eliza stumbled forward, breathless. Maybe she should have fled. She had no Gift or talent with weapons like Kaila. But she had already turned her back on Ambrose. She couldn't do the same to Kaila.

And so she approached, heart thundering in her ears, arm aching where she had landed on it earlier, determined to save her friend.

"Please…Rohan, don't hurt her."

She could see the effect her voice had on the prince, the way he flinched, almost as if he'd been struck. Stones crunched as he shifted his weight, though he didn't turn his back on Kaila.

"Eliza…is that you?"

Perhaps she shouldn't have been surprised to hear the emotion in Rohan's words, the way his voice cracked and broke. She was like a ghost to him. Her voice, her face, they belonged to the woman he had fallen in love with all those months ago. The woman he had lost.

In his pain, Eliza saw her opportunity.

"Rohan," she whispered.

Now he turned. As their eyes met, the colour drained slowly from his face. She took a step towards him and he staggered back, the dark sword coming up. The point quivered as it pointed at her chest.

"Back!" he cried. "You're not her, you can't be!"

Trembling, Eliza raised her hands. "It's me, Rohan," she said. Shame welled inside her as she saw the agony play across his face, but she crushed it down. Rohan was their only chance of surviving this disaster. "Please…"

The black blade wavered as she narrowed the gap, until the deadly point rested against her chest. Eliza shuddered as she felt its icy touch. Steeling herself, she raised a finger and moved it aside, then stepped in close. Rohan's mouth opened, his lips moving as if to speak a command, but no words emerged.

And then Eliza was standing before him, looking up into that face filled with pain, and she said the words she imagined he wanted her to say.

"It's me, Rohan. It's Eliza."

"No," he spoke the word like it was a ward against evil, "no, no, you *died.*"

Eliza winced at the force in his voice. Terror fluttered in her heart. It took all her strength not to glance at that deadly blade. She could feel his anger, and yet, beneath it, she saw a spark of something else, that familiar, fickle thing that every human clung to in their darkest days.

*Hope.*

Guilt churned in Eliza's gut. This man had already

suffered so much. Using his hope against him would be another betrayal. But it was all they had.

"No, Rohan," he whispered, the lie burning in her chest. "They hid me away. Made me their prisoner—so they could get to you."

"It's…it can't be…it's not…" He closed his eyes, his entire body trembling. "You're just another illusion."

"I'm not," she whispered, raising a hand to his cheek. He flinched, but did not move away this time. His skin was cold as she cupped his cheek. "I'm really here, Rohan. It's really me."

For a second, she thought he would deny it. Then, like a dam bursting beneath the weight of its dike, he seemed to shatter. His face broke and crying out, he swept her up in his arms, holding her tight.

"Eliza," he gasped. "It's really you. I thought I lost you."

Eliza closed her eyes and steeled her soul against the shame. "I'm here, Rohan," she whispered, hugging him back. "I'm here and I can explain everything."

"I know…" the prince began, when a voice interrupted their reunion.

"Well, well, well, what do we have here?"

A chill spread to Eliza's stomach as she looked around. The Warden approached. She carried a body over her shoulder, and Eliza's fear turned to terror as she recognised Ambrose's cloak. There was no sign of Garrick.

"Warden Laura," Rohan was the first to speak. He turned to the black-garbed Warden, though his hand remained around her waist. "Daughter Eliza has returned to us."

Darkness glinted behind the Warden's visor. "Is that so?" she murmured, her voice cold and distorted. "How fortunate for us."

"Warden—" Eliza began, but her words turned to a cry as the Warden tossed Ambrose's limp body to the ground.

He struck with a heavy *thump* and did not move. Eliza's heart was racing so fast she feared it would burst from her chest, but to her pride, her face remained calm as she met the Warden's empty gaze—until the woman stretched out a gauntleted fist and pressed an icy finger against her throat. A cold burning began in her scar, almost like a remembered pain. A squawking noise escaped Eliza's lips as she inhaled, but somehow, she managed not to flinch away.

"You removed your collar," the Warden said calmly. "That is a crime punishable by death."

A trembling spread down her spine, but still Eliza held her nerve. "They would have killed me if I refused."

"Then you should have died," the Warden grunted. "Because of your failure, an Elysian was able to access the Sanctum."

Closing her eyes, Eliza bowed her head. "I will accept whatever penance the Magisterium deems necessary."

"*No,*" Rohan interrupted. He had remained silent during the exchange, but now he stepped forward to confront the Warden. "Eliza Wrenn has suffered at the hands of our enemy and returned to us whole. Let that be enough."

To her surprise, the Warden actually seemed to consider his words. "You led the soldiers against the Elysian's spell, Prince Rohan. If not for your bravery, this day may have been lost," she paused, regarding the prince. "So I will allow the Daughter a chance to prove her devotion, if that is truly what you wish."

"*Yes!*" Rohan gasped. His hand tightened around Eliza's waist as he turned to her. "Eliza will do whatever you require, Warden Laura."

Meeting the prince's eyes, Eliza nodded and attempted a smile, even as an icy pool of terror gathered in her gut.

"Good." The Warden extended her hand. Darkness gathered there, forming into a dagger. The slits in the black visor regarded her. "Take it." She held it out to Eliza.

Trembling, Eliza's hand rose almost of its own accord. As her fingers closed around the hilt, she felt something brush against her soul.

"Kill the girl."

Eliza stood fixed in place, frozen by her own terror. Her eyes darted to where Kaila lay, and to her shock, she realised her friend was awake. Kaila had pushed herself to her knees, but apparently that was the limits of her strength. Pale faced, she met Eliza's gaze—and gave the slightest nod.

*No, no, no!*

Rohan tried to come to her rescue. "The general said the Elysian was mine," he said, his voice low as he challenged the Warden. "I was promised."

"That was before the Daughter lived," the Warden replied. "This creature took everything from her, prince Rohan. Would you deny her right to vengeance?"

"Please, Rohan," Eliza whispered. "I owe her my life. The others would have killed me, but Ka—this Elysian—argued to let me live." She tore her eyes from Kaila and fixed them on Rohan. "Please, none of this is her fault."

She felt the arm he still held around her waist trembling, shaking, though she didn't know now whether it came from sorrow or rage. His own gaze bored into Kaila with an intensity that frightened her.

"Is it true?" he demanded.

On her knees, Kaila flinched from the rage his voice. Eliza could see the pain behind her friend's eyes. Despite all the lies, she had loved Rohan.

"It is, Rohan," she whispered, and Kaila heard her friend's heart breaking.

Rohan offered a curt nod. "Then you deserve a quick death."

Eliza gasped and tried to pull away from him, but his hand closed around her fist, holding the dagger in place.

"My love, I understand your hesitation," he whispered, "but now you must trust me. There is no good in these creatures. If you knew what I have seen." His eyes fluttered closed as a long, shuddering breath escaped him. Then he looked to the Warden. "Must she be the one to do this?"

"She has been months with the enemy." The Warden's voice was flat, pitiless. "If she is to return, her loyalty to the Magisterium must be beyond doubt."

Rohan's fingers tightened around her own. "I believe in you, Eliza," he rasped. "It will be a mercy, for a creature such as her."

Looking into the prince's soft blue eyes, Eliza found herself nodding. The dagger was heavy in her hand as she stepped away from him. Her feet, as if by a will of their own, carried her towards the broken girl swaying on her knees.

*Whatever else happens here today, do not let Kaila touch agimet again.*

Shards of glass twisted in Eliza's chest as she remembered Ambrose's words just a few moments ago. He was *afraid* of her, had even contemplated leaving her to die. This was the same, wasn't it? Kaila was dangerous…

Numb, Eliza knelt beside Kaila Dwyn. Her oldest friend. The only other person in this world who understood what they had suffered in Elgoss. Who understood the sheer evil the Magisterium was capable of—the lies it would tell to keep humanity under its thumb.

Reaching out a trembling hand, Eliza brushed the raven locks from Kaila's face. She blinked, and her head tipped towards Eliza, as if in acceptance. As if she understood this was the only way. Swallowing, Eliza leaned in, so the others wouldn't hear her words.

"I'm sorry, Kaila."

---

KAILA COULD BARELY LIFT HER HEAD. HER BODY SCREAMED and her vision was a blur of amber haze. Somewhere nearby, she sensed Eliza leaning close, felt her friend trembling. Her eyes slid closed. It was time. She could accept this. She had already lost everything; her father, Theron, and now Rohan. She had seen the loathing in his eyes. It didn't matter how many times she told him the truth; he would never believe it. Better if she died, so Eliza had a chance to live.

"I'm sorry, Kaila."

Something in her friend's voice made Kaila's eyes snap open. She felt a hand brush her side, a weight in her jacket pocket, then Eliza was rising, dagger still clutched tight in her hand, turning to face the others.

"I can't. I won't." Eliza's voice rung out across the broken plateau.

Kaila swayed. The drums pounding in her skull made it difficult to concentrate. What was she doing?

"Eliza, please," Rohan stepped forward. Not *her* Rohan. Not the man she loved, but someone else, someone consumed by hatred. "You must."

"I'm not Eliza," Eliza whispered. "At least, not the one you knew. The only time we ever met, you barely looked at me. That first dinner." Her voice was soft, but there was a power behind it now. "The one you knew *is* here though, if you have the courage to believe. Kaila is the one who stole your food. Who listened to you. Who loved you. It was always her."

Eliza looked back to where Kaila knelt. Her heart caught in her throat as she saw the fear in her friend's eyes.

"Don't you see, Rohan?" Eliza continued. "What you had, it was real. They're not the monsters the Magisterium wants us to believe. They're just people. Desperate, maybe, driven to do terrible things, but they're human like you and me."

Rohan's face was pale. "Eliza…" he breathed. "Eliza, please, no…"

Heavy footsteps approached. A shadow fell across the pair. The Warden looked from Eliza to the prince, before the iron voice rasped from inside the visor.

"Prince Rohan, if the Daughter will not complete her task, you know what you must do."

"No…" he whispered, head bowed, shaking. "Please, Warden, there must be another way…"

"There is not."

"Leave her alone," Kaila growled.

Her fingers tightened against the earth. Every movement sent agony searing through her body, but somehow she managed to pull herself to her feet. Swaying, she glared at the Warden—and wished that alone was enough to defy its power. But her crystal was dead and there was no nexus to charge its power. All she had left was her will and…

…a frown touched Kaila's lips as her fingers brushed something in her pocket. *What?*

Ignoring Kaila, the Warden's attention remained on Rohan.

"I don't know if I can," he whispered.

"You must."

"Rohan," Eliza tried again, lifting her hand towards him. "Don't listen to her—"

For a heartbeat, Kaila didn't understand what had happened.

One minute, Eliza had been reaching for the prince—the next, he had stepped towards her, so quickly neither Kaila nor the Daughter from Elgoss had a chance to react.

The black sword made no sound as it cleaved Eliza's chest.

*No, no, no!*

Blood pulsed in Kaila's skull. She watched was Eliza's lips parted, trying to form a word, but only a little *oh* rattled from her throat. Her hand, still stretched towards Rohan, fell to the blade, clutching it as if to pull it free, before her strength failed. Her knees buckled. As she crumpled to the ground, her glassy eyes found Kalia's.

*"NO!"*

Kaila started towards them, but a blast of unseen forced hurled her backwards. She hit the ground hard, pain flashing through her ribs.

Across the broken ground, she saw Ambrose struggle to his feet. Blood streaming down his temple, he stumbled towards where Eliza had fallen. He didn't make it two steps before the Warden struck him in the back of the head. He landed beside Eliza, unmoving.

The Warden turned to Rohan.

"Finish the job."

Kaila choked on her sobs, struggling to regain her feet, but her legs gave way beneath her. All she could do was watch. Eliza's body jerked as Rohan tore the blade from her chest. Blood pulsed from the wound, spreading across the dirt, then slowed. And stopped.

Stones crunched as Rohan started towards Kaila, the black blade clenched in his hand.

"Rohan," she gasped. "Don't—please—"

His eyes found hers—and Kaila saw none of the man she had once loved. There was only hatred in those sapphire depths. Blood dripped from the blade as he approached.

Despair swelled in Kaila's throat. Why had Eliza done that! She had thrown her life away, and for what? Even if she'd had a crystal, her magic didn't work anymore. Not against him, of all people. She had nothing left—

Kaila froze as her hand brushed the object Eliza had slipped into her pocket. She felt a tingling, and suddenly, she knew what it was. *Eliza's wristwatch.* She could sense the outer agimet, cut and broken, deadly to an Elysian. But hidden inside was the second crystal, the raw gem that fuelled Ambrose's weaving. Tiny, barely enough *atar* for a single thread, but *full.*

It wasn't enough to fight the Warden. Even if her magic was working, she had seen it defeat both Garrick and Ambrose.

A chill crept across her skin as she saw again Eliza on the ground, her lips moving, trying to speak. And she thought she knew what her friend had been trying to say.

*Jump!*

Her fingers closed around the tiny device. *Atar* hissed, crackling as it raced through her veins, filling her *soullight.* She closed her eyes to hide its glow, listening to Rohan's approach. She stood on the trail, just a few feet from the cliff's edge. She had to time it right. Had to make them believe. He was close now, *so close.* What had happened to the young man she had loved?

The footsteps came to a halt.

"Was it really you?"

Her skin crawled. Kaila trembled. "It was," she whispered.

She waited, wanting to believe it would make a difference, that the truth would finally cut through all the lies and betrayal, that he would see she was still the woman he had fallen in love with back in the capital.

Then she sensed it—the *hunger* in the dark blade is it rose, the *shriek* as it plunged for her flesh. For a second, the world stood still.

Kaila Dwyn hesitated no longer. The blade fell—and found only empty air as she turned and leapt.

Rohan and the Warden and the world fell away as she plummeted into the abyss.

*Atar* surged from her, grasping at something, anything that could hold her.

A boulder groaned, then tore from the cliff. She grasped at it, desperate to halt her plunge.

Abruptly, the *atar* in the crystal gave out. Her Gift spluttered and died.

And she fell into the darkness.

# 18

In the heart of the Sanctum, there stood a statue of the First Matron. Carved entirely from marble, it was perhaps the most stunning piece of stonework Jenna Frye had ever seen. Robed in a flowing dress, the First Matron stood twice the height of a man. One arm reached skyward, palm open to the heavens, while on each wrist she wore the twin armlets of the Aegis. Her face was ageless, her jaw set with quiet resolve, and her eyes—none who passed beneath that stone gaze could deny this had been a woman of power.

Jenna had stood beneath this statue a hundred times—but only now did she stop to think about the woman who had worn the crown.

T'iana, the First Matron of Fresia—sworn enemy of the Elysian—had been Elysian herself.

Now Jenna stood in her place, the first Elysian in a thousand years to become Matron of the Magisterium.

Her hands trembled at her sides. If only she could be like her predecessor, wielding both halves of the Aegis against her enemies, a force that would be remembered a thousand years later.

Instead, Jenna found herself entirely powerless. She couldn't even command the half of the Aegis she had taken from her mother.

At least Rohan was alive.

The news had arrived this morning. Apparently, he'd won a great victory in the Iron Pinnacles, even killing the creature that had called itself Kaila Dwyn. Jenna's stomach twisted as she remembered the young woman from that night atop the Sanctum. Could she really now be dead?

Could Rohan truly have been the one to have cut her down?

Unfortunately, her relief for her brother's safety was short lived. Because Rohan was now on his way back to the capital.

She was out of time.

Footsteps echoed through the concrete chamber. Jenna didn't turn. She already knew who it was.

"Matron," General Falkenrath greeted, his voice soft as velvet.

She turned slowly, her expression hard. "General."

He grinned. "You've heard the news, then?"

"My brother lives," she said simply.

"It would seem I have lived up to my side of our bargain," as he spoke, the smile slid from his lips. "I hope that does not mean you are second guessing your own part of our agreement."

Jenna stared into his empty eyes. "I would hardly call it an agreement," she said, her voice flat. "You threatened my only family."

"I did offer you my aid in good faith, Jenna," the general grunted. "Indeed, one could argue my actions have *saved* your brother."

"I would beg to differ," she hissed.

"Then you are a fool," the general snapped. "I spoke with the men who guarded his apartment. Rohan invited that creature into his home and bed. And then, the greatest crime of all, he *swore a vow of marriage to it*." His eyes bored into hers. "Do you really believe the Magisterium, *the people of Fresia*, could forgive such crimes?" He shook his head. "Only by slaying that creature Rohan Frye earn his redemption."

"And I suppose it was just happy coincidence that his peril gave you everything you needed to blackmail me?"

The general regarded her for a long moment. Then, with a grunt, he clasped his hands behind his back and looked up at the statue of the First Matron.

"Ah, to have lived in her time, don't you think?" he said quietly. "When the Elysian fought with honour—man against beast, steel against magic. Sometime in this last century, our people forgot who their true enemy is."

Jenna swallowed. "And who is our true enemy, General Falkenrath?"

"Chaos. Disorder. Weakness." He turned to Jenna. "We fight amongst ourselves, distract ourselves with pretty toys and grow weak relying on your father's machines—and all the while, the Elysian bide their time, waiting for their opportunity to take back this world." He advanced, looming over her. "When I am king, I will make us strong again. I will need a strong Matron at my side." Reaching out a massive hand, he cupped her cheek. "We do not have to be enemies, Jenna."

A tremor ran down Jenna's spine. Her skin crawled where his fingers touched cheek. She held her breath, waiting for the Aegis to strike, but whatever magic had risen inside it before, it did not react this time. Instead, she lifted her eyes to meet his gaze.

"I would rather burn with my city than see it fall into your hands."

For a heartbeat, there was silence. Then Falkenrath's hand dropped away, his face hardening. Whatever warmth had coloured his tone fled, replaced with cold iron.

"We could have been allies," he said quietly. "Now…" He shook his head. "You will learn your place soon enough, Jenna Frye."

With that, he turned and strode back down the hall, boots thudding against the concrete floor. Jenna held herself together until he was gone, then sank to her knees at the feet of the great statue and put her head in her hands. Rohan would be back within days, and the Sisters were already pushing for their union to be completed.

The moment she spoke those vows and the general took up the Aegis of the king, he would know Jenna couldn't control her piece. She would be powerless against him. Her life would be forfeit.

What was she going to do?

# 19

The battlefield was quiet now. No more clashing weapons. No voices. Nothing but the wind and the sickly stench of blood. The living had departed hours ago, leaving only the dead—and the condemned.

Quintin had watched the struggle unfold from behind a fallen pillar. He had wanted to help. When Kaila and Eliza had surged ahead, he'd followed, albeit at a more cautious pace. His magic relied on remaining unseen, after all, and he could already sense a Psionic working their Gift ahead, tugging on the soldiers' fears. Together, they should be able to send the prince and his soldiers scurrying…

Then he'd felt it. A void amidst the mass of *soullights,* a black mass that repelled all attempt to influence its soul. A Warden had entered the battle. Quintin sensed the moment it reached the Psionic and cut his fellow down. The other souls wavered a moment longer, still caught by the tailor's illusion, until another advanced into the fury—and that too broke.

By the time he reached the bend and saw the chaos that filled the canyon, Quintin's courage had fled. In truth, he'd surrendered it months ago, when he'd handed his children over to the Magisterium rather than face the possibility that one day he might have to bury them.

So instead, he'd hidden behind a pillar of stone and watched as his friends fought the might of the Magisterium—and lost. One by one, they were cut down. Ambrose was first, his body flung like a ragdoll across the broken ground. Then Eliza, standing tall against the prince and his black-garbed bodyguard.

Finally, they came for Kaila. Whatever unnatural force the girl had channelled earlier, it failed her now. Bloodied and broken, she had defied the man she'd loved—only to be tossed from the cliffside, down into the darkness.

Quintin had shut his eyes rather than watch her fall.

There had been no way to block out the harsh laughter of the Warden, however. The sound was soon be joined by the soldiers—those who'd survived at least—as they cheered their victory.

When Quintin finally opened his eyes again, however, he saw there was one who did not celebrate. Rohan knelt at the cliffside, his head bowed, Eliza's body clutched in his arms. He stayed that way long after the laughter and the jeering had ceased.

Once, Quintin would have tried to understand the boy's pain, to know what emotion could have driven him to such a terrible act. He could still remember the man who had cared, who had believed that every act of hatred was born of fear.

But that part of him had died the night he'd given up his girls to the Magisterium. Now, he no longer cared whether it was true. Because he had been forced to confront reality: the Elysian could never defeat the Magisterium. They would always be humanity's scapegoat—the monster in the dark they united to defeat.

For the Elysian, this world would never offer anything more than the promise death.

And so, as Quintin watched the prince grieve, he didn't care whether fear or pain or hatred had lead him to his choices—he just wished the boy would hurl himself into the ravine and save them all the hassle of killing him.

Finally though, the Warden approached the prince. Words must have passed between them, for shortly after, Rohan took the Warden's hand and rose. Shortly afterwards, the group started back down the road in the direction of distant Tah'raus. Quintin shrank into the shadows as they passed his hiding place. His horse had run off at the start of the battle and he prayed it didn't choose now to return.

Within minutes, the sound of their boots faded into the whispers of the ravine. Then he was alone again. Even then, he'd waited, crouched in the dark, unmoving, in case it was all a trap and they had spies watching for survivors.

Eventually though, he could take it no more. Rising, he stepped into the sunlight. Darkness was creeping across the sky, but a sliver of light remained from the scarlet horizon. No shouts went up at his appearance, and so he started across the battlefield, taking care to avoid the dark stains left by the fallen soldiers. The Magisterium still had enough honour to return the fallen to their families—the bodies of their enemies they left to rot where they fell.

The first body was an Elysian he did not know. He thought it was the Mover he'd glimpsed briefly, before Kaila had intervened. Apparently, the girl's sacrifice hadn't been enough to save the poor man. He looked to have been stabbed a dozen times. Given his crystal was dead, the butchery had been unnecessary, but after watching dozens of their comrades fall, the soldiers had obviously not been inclined towards the mercy.

Three other Elysian had fallen in the same way. His stomach churned, however, when he realised the body of Ambrose was absent. It meant the worst had happened; Ambrose was prisoner. The tailor was a hard man, but the inquisitors in the Sanctum would break him eventually. When that happened, the underground, the resistance—all semblance of order amongst the Elysian—would evaporate like morning dew on the streets of the capital.

There was also no sign of Garrick. Ambrose had seen the man flee the battlefield. Hopefully the Bruiser had the good sense to keep going until he reached the frontier.

Finally, his path carried him to the body of Eliza. There was surprisingly little blood on the ground around the girl. Rohan had left his jacket draped across her midriff, hiding the wound that had ended her life. The expression she wore in death was strangely peaceful, as though some part of her had accepted this at the end.

Quintin knelt beside her, his hands trembling as he reached out—but couldn't quite bring himself to touch her. Anger welled inside him and he clenched his fists instead. *We don't kill the innocent.* That was their rule, his and Theron's and even Ambrose. But not the Magisterium. Eliza hadn't been Elysian. She wasn't a soldier. She was just a girl trying to make the best of a difficult life. And now she was gone, another life snuffed out as though it held no more value than the vermin in a farmer's field.

Guilt followed hot on the heels of his anger. It should have been him lying there. Instead, Quintin had proven his cowardice, freezing when his friends needed him most. Now Eliza would never have her chance to live, to laugh and love in the sun.

All because he had failed.

"I'm sorry," he whispered, before he rose and looked to the cliff.

If his grief had carved out a hollow for Eliza, the thought of Kaila was acid poured into his naked wound. At every step of her journey, he had failed her. First, when he'd allowed her to enter the Sanctum, alone and without her Gift—then again when he had revealed Theron's plan to the old Matron. And last and worst of all, today, when he should have stopped her from confronting the Warden.

Now she was gone, another young Elysian, so like his daughters, snuffed out by the insurmountable power of the Magisterium.

Night was falling now, the sun dipping below the ridgeline. As the shadows stretched across the road, Quintin clutched his crystal and allowed its light to bathe the battlefield. He closed his eyes as *atar* flowed through his veins, awakening his Gift. He feared to use it in Tah'raus now. Too much noise. Too much *pain*. He couldn't bear to feel all that emotion. But tonight, the silence was almost reassuring. A reminder that even as the Magisterium's fingers closed around the continent, these ancient stones remained untouched—

*Ring!*

Quintin froze as a distant chime carried to his ears. A tingling spread across his scalp. Trembling, he clutched the crystal to his chest and closed his eyes. It couldn't be. He wanted to close himself off again, to silence that faint ringing. Instead, he drew more power from the crystal and opened his soul to the music of the world.

From somewhere far below cam the quick, high-pitched notes of fear. A chill spread down his spine as he recognised the soul. *Kaila.* Her *soullight* was faint, flickering like a lantern on its last drops of oil, *but she was alive.* As his power connected with hers, the sound of her soul changed. Fear gave way to a sharp, almost shrieking blast of emotion. It washed through him—surprise, excitement, *hope*.

Opening his eyes, Quintin stumbled to the edge. The cold hand of fear closed around his heart. Darkness clung to the mountains now, growing with each passing moment. The cliff plunged into shadows. Somewhere far, far below, he heard the faint murmur of a stream.

*Don't think, Quintin.*

Clenching his agimet in one hand for light, he slid over the edge before his courage failed him. Shadows swirled around him as he searched for somewhere to place his feet. Eventually finding solid footing, he stretched out for the next hold—only for his stomach to lurch as the gravel slipped beneath his boots. Desperately, he grasped at the ledge, managing to catch himself before he plunged into the dark.

Heart pounding, he rested his head against the cold stone. His entire body was shaking. He couldn't do this. Maybe when he'd been a young man. Maybe before he'd betrayed his only friend and become this hollowed out husk of a man…

*Ring!*

From far below, he sensed a pulse, not of fear, but the warm embrace of hope. Almost like a message—*I believe in you!*

Gritting his teeth, Quintin searched with his foot for a fresh hold. This time, he checked that it took his weight before continuing.

Step by step, inch by careful inch, he worked his way down the cliff. In the shadows, it was impossible to tell how far it was until the bottom—and as the last light faded from the sky, impossible to know how far he had come. Down he continued, back upright, blood pounding, lungs burning. Several other times he slipped—and each time, he clung with all his strength to the rockface until he regained his purchase.

His fingers were soon bloody and his eyes burned with grit and dust, but he didn't stop.

Below, the music of Kaila's soul drew him on, each passing moment fluttering, like an ember burning against the storm.

When his feet finally touched the bottom, he didn't allow himself to believe it. Carefully clutching at the cliff with one hand, he raised the crystal. Its glow reflected off a thin stream of water threading its way amongst the boulders that filled the base of the gully.

And there she was. Kaila Dwyn. Thin trees—little more than bushes—grew from the cliff-face close to the ground, branches stretching towards the water as if to drink. She had landed amongst a cluster of the stark vegetation. The thin branches had broken her fall; but even then, it was a miracle she had survived. By the light of his crystal, he saw the lacerations on her face and arms. It would be an outright miracle if she hadn't sustained any permanent damage.

Her eyes were closed, but they fluttered as he approached.

"Quintin," she whispered, her voice slurred, as if she wasn't entirely conscious. "I…heard you."

"Don't move," he murmured. "You fell a long way."

"Half…a long way," she croaked, but after that she obeyed and did not elaborate further.

Quintin drew a knife from his belt and set to work, sawing through the branches that had caught Kaila on her descent. It was slow going. The blade slipped more than once, biting into the already torn flesh of his hands, but he didn't stop. Not until the final limb snapped and he could reach her.

With the last of his strength, he lifted her down from the twisted mass of roots and bramble.

Once she was on the ground, he pulled a flask from his pack and offered her water, followed by a strip of jerky. She chewed slowly, eyes closed, while he ran his hands gently over her limbs, checking for damage. The miracle was complete: no broken bones. Just several deep cuts and scrapes, and bruises already darkening from purple to black.

Sitting back on his haunches, he shook his head. "I think you're going to be alright."

"Told you." Reaching into her pocket, she removed a wristwatch. "Caught a rock halfway down."

Quintin lifted his eyes as he took it from her fingers and sensed the empty crystal inside. It was one of Ambrose's. His stomach twisted at the realisation these devices would soon be useless with the tailor in custody.

A cold breeze blew through the gully. He sat back, the faint hope he'd felt at finding Kaila alive crumbling to ash. Because Ambrose was already lost. Once the Sanctum swallowed him up, there would be no escape. Just a slow, inexorable unravelling, until all the most precious secrets of the Elysian were given over to the enemy.

Then they were all as good as dead.

# 20

The morning light was a pale glow, filtering down between the steep canyon walls and the thin veil of mist that hung about the stream. Kaila stirred, then groaned as she found her entire body one large bruise. Every breath pulled at her ribs and it took a moment just to remember where she was—then it all came back to her in a rush: the fall, the impact, the music from above…

She opened her eyes. Quintin was already awake. Crouched a few paces away, he'd lit a small fire. He had his hands held out to the flames. A shiver ran through Kaila as the cold finally filtered its way through the pain. She tried to sit up, then cursed through her teeth as pain seared through her muscles.

Quintin turned at the sound. "Don't move too fast," he said. "It's a miracle you're alive at all."

"Eliza…" Trembling, Kaila tried moving again, and this time managed to drag herself a few feet closer to the fire. "She…she gave me her wristwatch, before…"

She couldn't say it. The scene played out again and again

in her mind, her friend confronting Rohan, and the black blade striking, the surprise in her eyes as she fell, the dark blood staining her dress…

"I know," Quintin interrupted her waking nightmare. "I saw."

Her head jerked up. "You saw?" she hissed. "*Then where were you?*" This time she barely felt the agony as she clambered to her feet.

Quintin flinched at the question. "I couldn't…" he croaked. "I should have…but…" He bowed his head. "I'm sorry, Kaila. I was a coward."

Kaila stared at him, blood pulsing in her skull, an ache twisting in her chest. She wanted to lash out at him. To scream and rage at the Psionic for standing by while Rohan and the Warden slaughtered Eliza and took their friend hostage.

But even as she felt that heat within, she couldn't ignore the truth. The Psionic hadn't come out of the encounter unscathed. His hands were raw and red, scraped bare by the climb down the cliffs, and there was a nasty bruise decorating his lip. Quintin might be a Psionic, but he was no warrior. The Warden would have shrugged off his powers like a hog would a gnat.

"There was nothing you could have done," she rasped at last, slumping back to the ground as a fresh bout of pain stole her strength. "Without the nexus, there was nothing *I* could do."

Quintin's eyebrows lifted. He seemed taken aback for a moment, then offered her the waterskin. "What…did happen back there?" he said as she drank.

The void in her soul trembled. "I don't know," she whispered. "Ever since that night on the rooftop of the Sanctum, my Gift has been…broken."

"That didn't feel broken, Kaila," he replied. "It felt like…" he trailed off, pursing his lips as if he wasn't sure exactly what to say.

Kaila swallowed. "I should have stopped Rohan," she rasped. "If I'd just thrown him off the cliff, maybe Eliza…" Her voice cracked and she felt tears threatening. "The Warden offered her a chance to live if she killed me…"

Hot tears spilt down her face. Why had Eliza done it? She could have *survived!* Gone back to Tah'raus and lived out the rest of her days as a princess of the Magisterium—maybe even become Matron one day, if Jenna produced no children.

Instead, Eliza had met her end in the same cold, dead mountains as her parents. And for what? So, Kaila could continue this painful existence, unable to make a difference, to save even a single one of her friends?

"The Warden would have killed her anyway," Quintin rasped. "The moment that thing saw Eliza's scars, it knew what she was, what she'd done to survive. The Magisterium doesn't tolerate oath breakers."

"It doesn't matter," Kaila whispered. "None of it matters. I give up. They've won."

Quintin kept his silence. Kaila wasn't surprised. What *could* he say? They both knew she was right. That was why he'd given up after Theron had been killed, why he'd turned his back on Ambrose and his plans and drowned himself in drink. The Magisterium had ruled this world for a thousand years—and nothing any of them did was ever going to change that.

"You know, sometimes I wonder if he was right."

Kaila's head jerked up at the words. "Who?"

Quintin sat watching the stream. "Theron," he said. "The night I found out about his lies, I confronted him. Accused him of being willing to burn it all down to get his revenge."

"What did he say?"

"He didn't deny it," Quintin murmured, his eyes never leaving the stream. "But he said it didn't matter. That the Magisterium needed to be destroyed, even if all that remained in the aftermath was ashes."

A lump lodged in Kaila's throat. That certainly sounded like Theron.

"I should have listened to him," the Psionic continued, "then maybe all of this…"

"What do you mean?"

Finally, the man met her eyes, and for a second she saw his pain, a hurt she'd never seen on the Psionic's face before. For a moment, it seemed like he would say something. Then he pursed his lips and looked away again.

"He said it needed to be destroyed because people like his father and the Matron and that Warden will never let go of what they have," he continued. "And so long as they rule, the people will never be able to hope for something more." He bowed his head. "They could have had that hope, maybe, if I hadn't ruined it."

Kaila's heart ached at the pain in his voice. "Quintin," she rasped, swallowing the lump in her throat. "No one blames you for what happened. Even if you'd been there that night…" She glanced away, remembering hers and Theron's struggle beneath the twin moons. "You couldn't have changed things. Just like you couldn't have saved Eliza."

A choking noise came from Quintin and when she glanced his way again, she glimpsed the shimmer of tears in his eyes. They didn't fall, however, as gathered himself and pushed himself to his feet. He offered his hand.

"Come on," he whispered. "I think I found a path up the cliff, if you've the strength to stand."

She wasn't sure she did, but the Trickster knew no one was

coming to help them. So gritting her teeth, Kaila accepted his help and rose to her feet. Half a dozen muscles immediately locked up in a searing cramp. She barely stifled her scream. Eyes watering, she gripped Quintin's shoulder and turned towards the cliff.

His path was little better than a goat track, but it was better than climbing out. Looking at the stark cliffs, she couldn't believe Quintin had managed it in the dark. Thank the First Matron he had—injured and without supplies, she wouldn't have survived the cold mountain night alone.

Kaila limped on. Her body had stopped screaming, but her muscles still shook and trembled like frayed rope suspended above a mineshaft. And that wasn't even the worst of it. There was a deeper pain inside her, like she'd torn something vital when she'd used her power. Her skull ached like the village blacksmith had been pounding it all morning, and with every step, her vision spun, the meagre contents of her stomach attempting to rearrange themselves with a better view of the river.

Eventually, she lost that battle too.

The sun rose above the canyon rim as they wound their slow way upward, catching them in its rays. Its heat soon had sweat streaming down her face, mixing with the blood and dust. They didn't speak, for which Kaila was grateful—all her breath was needed for the climb. Though she did catch Quintin glancing at her on occasion, that strange look on his face.

Was he thinking about her Gift? It had failed again— worse than ever this time. It had to be Rohan. For one singular moment, she had felt him, felt his soul and his pain, even greater than her own. It had overwhelmed her, sent her Gift spasming out of control.

The stones themselves had warped and twisted at the

energy streaming from her soul, and those men and women closest to her had been torn apart. Others had turned on one another, hacking and swinging at friend and foe alike, and all the while they screamed.

*Whoever said a Gift must work the way we want?*

Cassandra's words seemed a mockery now. What could she do with a power that didn't obey her command—a Gift that, if she lost control, everyone around her suffered and died?

By the time they crested the ridge and Kaila found herself looking down at Eliza's body, her despair had returned. Why had Eliza given up her life for Kaila? She had failed as a human, then again as a Daughter—and now she had even failed as an Elysian. Better that Eliza had lived, that she returned to the Sanctum with Rohan. Then maybe one day *she* would have been Matron, might have made a difference.

Instead, Eliza was dead and all that remained was a pitiful, broken excuse for an Elysian.

Legs trembling, Kaila slumped to ground. There were no more tears as she took her friend's hand, though a moan rasped from her throat when she felt the icy cold of Eliza's flesh.

"We should bury her," Quintin said quietly.

Kaila nodded, though she didn't move. After a moment, Quintin wandered away, and she heard the sound of metal breaking hard ground. Closing her eyes, she tried to ignore the sound, to pretend the hand in hers was warm and full of life, that the nightmare of yesterday had never happened. If only her Gift gave her that power, to restore her lost friend to life, to banish death.

But not even the Oberon or T'iana had possessed that power.

She didn't know how many minutes or hours passed, but

eventually Quintin returned. He rested a hand on Kaila's shoulder.

"It's time."

A trembling began in her chest, but she nodded. Rising, she ignored the growing void inside and took her friends legs, while Quintin gripped her carefully beneath the arms. The hole he'd prepared dug out with a discarded sword was only a few yards away. It felt like an eternity as Kaila's body screamed every step of the way. Finally, though, they lowered her into the grave. It was shallow, barely a few feet, but given the rocky ground, Quintin had done well.

"Would you like to say something?" Quintin asked.

Swallowing, Kaila looked at her friend. Eliza seemed almost peaceful as she lay amongst the stones, if not for the blood that stained her dress. The trembling had spread to Kaila's entire body now. She opened her mouth, but found the words would not come. So instead, she crouched and gently began to place rocks from the nearby pile into the grave.

She felt Quintin's eyes on her as she worked, but he said nothing, and after a few minutes he knelt and leant his aid. Together, it didn't take long to build the cairn over Eliza. When it was done, they both stood back, covered in dust and sweat from the midday heat. Kaila felt Quintin's eyes on her again. It seemed like the time to speak, that she should have found the words by now to farewell her friend.

Instead, she turned towards the distant capital. A piece of her still longed to complete the journey to Elgoss, to look upon the walls of her hometown and know once and for all whether the people there had survived. But it was a small piece. They were not her people—she didn't *have* people anymore. She was an Elysian without a Gift, a human hated by all. Alone.

Pulling up her hood to shield her face from the sun, Kaila

started walking. Somewhere in the distance, Tah'raus and the Sanctum waited. Her enemies thought she was dead. They had cast her aside, dismissed her.

It would be their undoing.

Kaila Dwyn was alive—and the next time she faced Rohan and his pet Warden, she would have the power of the nexus to fuel her Gift.

And broken or not, Kaila was going to use it to kill them all.

# 21

Jenna had to run. It was her only choice—to take Theron and run to his friends, and pray to the First Matron they gave her sanctuary. Though she'd better not mention *that* particular name to any of them, she supposed, given what she now knew about T'iana.

There was just one hitch to her plan.

Rohan. She couldn't leave without him.

*He'll come. He loves me. He'll come.*

So why was she standing frozen outside the door to his quarters, too afraid to raise her hand and knock?

Probably because Theron had warned her against this plan. When Jenna had told him she would take him and the Aegis to his friends, he'd been excited at first—ecstatic even. But then she'd mentioned bringing Rohan along, and his eagerness had quickly turned to concern.

*Are you sure you can trust him, Jen?*

His warnings echoed in her mind as she lingered outside the heavy oak door, about the prejudice the Magisterium sowed in the minds of its people from the time they could first speak. But this wasn't just anybody; this was *Rohan*. The brother that had stood with her against the cruelty of their mother. He *knew* her, loved her. He would understand, once she explained what the general was doing.

*No more delaying. It's time.*

Stealing herself, Jenna raised her hand and banged it against the door. A moment of silence was followed by the rattle of the bolt being drawn back. Her heart pulsed as the door swung open.

And there he was, Rohan, her brother. He stood with a weary look on his face, but as he saw her, his face lit up.

"Jenna," he exclaimed, a smile spreading across his lips. "You're here!"

"Of course I'm here, you idiot," she said, grinning despite herself. Stepping forward, she embraced him. "You're the one who went scampering halfway across the country without telling me!"

"I'm sorry," he replied somewhat sheepishly as they broke apart. Stepping aside, he gestured for her to enter. "I wasn't sure you would approve though," he added softly.

"Of course I wouldn't have approved," Jenna muttered, though her heart warmed as she stepped inside. The living quarters was much as she'd seen it last—a mess—but now there was a fire burning in the hearth. Ignoring the armchairs, she crossed to the fireplace and extended the hands towards its warmth. "You could have been killed."

"Warden Laura was there to protect me," Rohan said hesitantly, before he straightened. "But even if she wasn't, Jenna, it was something I *had* to do."

"Why, Rohan?" she said softly. "If you were worried about the Magisterium, you know I would have protected you…"

"It wasn't that. It was…" he trailed off.

For the first time, Jenna saw the tension in her brother.

The way he clenched his fists, how his body trembled, the fury that burned in his eyes as he glared at the fire, as if the dancing flames were the woman that had betrayed him.

"Rohan—"

"Eliza never existed," he interrupted her. "I didn't want to believe it, but that's the truth. That creature, Kaila or Eliza or whatever her real name was, she made a fool of me." He drew in a breath. "If I was ever to restore my pride, if I was to be a man worthy of my title..." His voice cracked. "I had to, Jenna," he croaked. "It hurt so much, but I had to…"

Turning, he met her gaze, and in that moment she saw the hurt beneath the anger, the sorrow as it leaked from his eyes

"Oh, brother." Stepping forward, she enfolded him in her embrace. "It's okay, Rohan. It's not your fault. It's theirs. It's all of them, Falkenrath and the Sisters and the Wardens, this is what they want."

At those words, however, Jenna felt Rohan tense and pull back from her.

"What do you mean?"

Drawing in a breath, she placed a hand on his shoulder. "Leonardo Falkenrath wasn't trying to help you, Rohan," she said quietly. "He sent you away so I couldn't protect you. He wanted to use your life as a bargaining chip to blackmail me."

"Blackmail you?" he frowned. "He told me he wanted to redeem himself for the crimes of his son."

Jenna snorted. "He wants to be *king*, Rohan," she replied. "The Wardens are in league with him. They put you in danger so I would have no choice but to swear a vow to the Sisters."

"A vow?" Rohan seemed genuinely confused.

"That I would wed the General," Jenna murmured. Drawing in a breath, she released him and slumped into a chair. "They only care about power, Rohan."

"Jenna, what are you *talking about?*"

Her heart twisted in her chest. Looking up at him, she saw the confusion in her brother's face, the doubt. He had wanted to believe in something greater than himself, someone that could protect him from the darkness and the pain. But the truth was, they only had each other.

"They *used you*, Rohan," she replied. "The truth is, they're no better than Kaila. The rest of us are just pawns to use in their games."

"That's not true," Rohan whispered. "The Wardens protect us, and General Falkenrath…he helped me." He hesitated. "Maybe…maybe you should listen to him."

"What?" she asked, stunned.

He nodded. Crossing to the chair, he sank to his knees beside her. "He's a good man, Jenna. Can't you see? He's just trying to fix what his son broke."

Jenna felt her hope shrivel. Where had this devotion come from, this zealous faith in the general and the Wardens? A tremor began in her stomach. She couldn't lose Rohan as well. She wouldn't. Reaching out, she took his hands in hers.

"Rohan, he's going to kill us both," she whispered. "You have to come with me, please."

His eyes widened. "Go with you where, Jenna?"

"I have some…friends who are going to help us," she said quickly. "Please, you have to trust me. We're not safe here, not once Leonardo gets what he wants from me…"

She trailed off, staring into her brothers eyes, pleading for him to see the truth, to understand.

Instead, he rose, shaking his head. "No, no, I can't," he whispered. "Warden Laura, she saved me in the Pinnacles. And General Falkenrath, you're wrong about him, Jenna."

She rose, reaching for him. "You don't know what he's like—"

"*Stop!*" the word burst from Rohan with such violence that Jenna froze, hand still outstretched. Chest heaving, Rohan sucked in a great breath and stilled. "Just stop, Jenna. Don't say anything more. I'm not going anywhere with you."

"Rohan, please, it's always been us against the world," Jenna whispered. She stood trembling in the middle of the room, fists clenched, refusing to look away. "You always trusted me before. Why won't you now?"

For just a second, she thought he wavered. Then his jaw clenched and he lifted his head to meet her gaze. "I…I think you should leave, Jenna."

She stood there a moment, searching hopelessly for something else she could say, some way to convince him not to do this. But she had nothing.

"Okay, Rohan," she said at last. Turning, she made to leave, but paused in the doorway. "I'm sorry," she whispered, glancing over her shoulder.

He stood by the flickering hearth, his eyes on the flames, but with her words he looked up. "For what?

"I should have done better, protecting you from them."

He stared at her for the longest time, the firelight flickering in the darkness of his eyes. She waited, holding her breath, hoping against hope he might see reason…

"Go, Jenna," he whispered.

Swallowing her grief, she nodded. "Goodbye, Rohan."

And she went.

# 22

It took Quintin and Kaila a week to complete the journey back to Tah'raus. Thankfully, they didn't have to make the journey on foot, as Quintin had been able to track his mare into a crag where it must have fled the sounds of battle. Given Kaila's condition, however, he'd had her ride most of the way.

They'd briefly discussed—then discarded the idea—of investigating Elgoss before they returned. The town was the reason they had come, the juicy prize the Magisterium had used to lure the tailor all this way. But their crystals were spent and not even Kaila could recharge them without a nexus nearby. Without agimet, they were just a pair of injured mortals against whatever perils the Magisterium might have left in Elgoss to trap them. And however slow their return, the news they carried of Ambrose's capture might still save lives. If the tailor didn't break first…

For the first day of their journey, Kaila had said little. Quintin recognised the emotion written on her face, however, even without the use of his Gift. He'd seen that look in many young Elysian—right before they went and did something stupid. Thankfully, neither of them were in any condition to take the shortcut through Iselador, so they'd taken the longer route along the main road that connected the Iron Pinnacles to the Cascades and capital lands.

And as the days crept into nights, he saw the rage fade from her eyes. What replaced it was almost as bad, however, as Quintin watched a terrible despondency take over his friend. He made a few poor attempts at lifting her mood, but it was a hopeless cause. Kaila had suffered more than most endured in a lifetime—what right did he have to ask anything more of her?

Especially after what he'd done.

Guilt churned in his stomach. After his failure in the canyon, he'd wanted to tell her the truth. That his betrayal was the real reason Theron had met his end that night. But how would the truth help her now? Quintin would only be serving himself, unburdening his guilt and hurting the girl further.

And so day had become night, then day again. They rested frequently, and even when they travelled, their pace was sluggish, slowed by the aging mare and their injuries.

So it was that, almost a week later, Quintin and Kaila entered the capital smuggled in the back of a wagon. They'd abandoned the mare in an old farmstead, then hidden themselves amidst the cargo of an unwitting merchant, allowing them to enter unseen.

Inside the walls, surrounded by the harsh glare of cut agimet crystal, Kaila finally seemed to regain some of her life. Feeling his own crystals come alive, Quintin had the presence of mind to tuck them deep into his pockets, least their *atar* fill his eyes and alert those around them to his true identity.

Speaking of which, they needed to decide their next move carefully. Rohan and that Warden had probably reached the capital a few days ahead of them. Would that be enough to crack the tailor? Quintin's old friend was undoubtedly tough, but even Ambrose couldn't withstand the Sanctum's questioning forever.

They certainly couldn't risk any of the tailor's front-facing businesses. Even if Ambrose still held out, chances are someone in the Magisterium would have recognised such a prominent citizen of Tah'raus. He was surprised the prince hadn't—then again, the lad wasn't exactly the most sociable of the noble class.

And if Ambrose *had* broken…he knew about the clocktower. It might not be safe to return to his own home…

…so focused on his thoughts, it was a few blocks before Quintin realised Kaila was no longer at his side. Blood rushed to his skull, he quickly retraced his steps. He found her standing in the middle of the main avenue, staring at the black concrete dome rising above the rooftops.

*The Sanctum.*

Quintin shivered, looking from the terrible building to Kaila. She had recovered somewhat from her injuries, but the dust of the road coated her clothing and her raven locks were a matted mess.

"Kaila, what is it?"

Blinking, she looked around—as if surprised to find him standing there.

"What was the point, Quintin?" she whispered. "She died for me, but they won anyway. And now…now we're here, and I have *nothing!*" As she went on, her voice rose in pitch, drawing glances from passersby. She gestured wildly at the Sanctum. "I can't even avenge her!"

Cursing beneath his breath, Quintin grasped Kaila by the arm and dragged her into a nearby alleyway.

"Is that why you think Eliza sacrificed herself??" he hissed once they were safely in the shadows. Glancing over his shoulder, he studied the crowd, trying to assess whether they'd attracted anything more than a passing curiosity.

"Why else?"

"So you could *live*, Kaila," he said. "So you would have a future."

"A future?" Kaila's words dripped bitterness. She gestured at the people in the street. "Can you honestly say you or I have a future after this, Quintin? *Do any of them?* We both know the Magisterium has won. That's why you disappeared last time, wasn't it? Because you knew—"

"Why do you think they've won?" he interrupted her, surprising himself at the intensity in his voice.

Why did he care whether she gave up? Because Kaila was right—he already had. All those months ago, when confronted with Theron's lies, and the power they faced, the chances of it all falling to pieces and him losing everything, he had made his choice. He had given up.

And he was realising just now what a terrible choice that had been. Because he hadn't saved his daughters, not really. All he'd done was condemn them to a different kind of misfortune. Maybe not the kind that sent them to an early death like so many other Elysian.

But Eliza had lived that life, and she had chosen to give up her own life rather than return to it.

"Because they're too powerful," Kaila said. She was staring at him like he'd gone mad. Maybe he had. "If even Ambrose, with all his wealth and influence, couldn't stop them, what chance do we have? They control everything."

"That's what they want you to believe, because that's the only way they can truly win." Quintin gestured to the crowd in the street. "Do they control what these people will do if the food runs out?" He turned to look at her. "Do they control you, Kaila—the Elysian whose Gift doesn't even obey its own laws." He took a breath, letting those words sit with her, before he continued. "Did they control Eliza, when she defied a Warden and chose to save your life instead of killing you?"

Kaila swallowed. "No," she rasped, "but what does any of that matter? They still won."

"That's just it, Kaila," Quintin hissed. "The Magisterium doesn't win when they *kill* us. They only win when young men and women speak like you. When despair is so engrained in our people that we believe there's no hope of victory, so that we no longer fight."

"I…" Kaila trailed off. He could see the doubt in her eyes as she looked away. "It's just…so hard."

"Nothing of value in this world was ever won easily," Quintin said quietly. He bowed his head, that familiar guilt swelling in his chest. How could he have allowed himself to be led so astray?

"There's so many more who suffer under the Magisterium's rule than there are of them. Do you *really* think they can survive if the people of this city turn on them?" He regarded Kaila with a grimace. "*That* was Theron and Ambrose's final plan. Not that we would win some great battle, but that we would win a thousand small battles in the hearts of the people. That's how *we* win. We show them the Magisterium isn't invincible. That they can fight back. Even if it costs us our lives."

Kaila's lip quivered, before her jaw hardened and she offered a curt nod. Drawing a breath, Quintin returned the gesture. There was a strange sensation in his chest, a warmth he hadn't felt in the longest time.

*Hope.*

By the Trickster, that was foolish. By any sane judgement,

Kaila was right. The Magisterium had managed a crushing victory in the mountains. And yet…

He didn't have any of Ambrose's contact lenses, so he didn't risk his power, but even without it a Psionic learned to read the atmosphere in the streets. And there was a tension about the capital. He felt it in the way passersby kept their heads down and went quickly about their business, in the boarded-up shop fronts and the groups of men and women gathered on the street corners.

Yes, the Magisterium may have supressed the Elysian resistance, but Ambrose's plan was working. The city was a tinderbox—all it would take to set alight was the right strike of a match.

"Let's go by The *Rusty Gull*," Quintin announced as they set off again.

"What about Ambrose?"

"The tailor is a hell of a lot tougher than he looks," Quinton replied. "And even *if* they've broken him, there are plenty of higher priority targets than an empty tavern in the port sector." When Kaila still looked doubtful, he chuckled. "We'll be careful, but we need supplies. Lenses, coin. And it's our only contact with Ambrose's network. Maybe we can still send out a warning."

That finally drew a nod from the girl. After that, they completed the rest of the journey in silence. Despite his earlier words, Quintin wasn't sure on their next moves. His clock-tower was probably safe for another day or two, but after that…

They approached *The Rusty Gull* from the rear, weaving through a cluttered alley that stank of rotting fish and seawater. The tavern's back door was unmarked, its windows sealed with rusted iron bars. A crate shifted under Quintin's boot, sending a stray cat hissing into the shadows. He froze, breath held, watching the empty windows for signs of inhabitants. Nothing moved, and after a moment, he a glanced at Kaila and shrugged.

Moving to the backdoor, he carefully turned the handle and was surprised to find it unlocked. That gave him pause. If the place hadn't been raided already, why would it be unlocked? And if it had, surely there would be more sign of an attack. The Magisterium wasn't exactly known for its subtly when dealing with enemies of Fresia.

Unfortunately, there were no answers for them in the stinking alleyway, so first Quintin reached into his pocket and drew out his agimet. He had their only decent crystal—Kaila's had shattered in the fall. However, now Kaila was within the influence of a nexus, the tiny crystal inside Eliza's wristwatch was all she needed. Hopefully, that would help to level the playing field if they encountered someone within.

Feeling the *atar* creeping through his veins, Quintin extended his senses. A Psionic's *atarsight* worked differently from a Movers. Instead of *seeing* nearby *soullights,* he *heard* them. Each emotion sung with a distinct music. He wasn't surprised to find the tavern silent. Unfortunately, that didn't tell him much. The Magisterium would have sent Wardens if they were expecting Elysian, and the black armour of those monstrosities muted the sound of their *soullights.*

Well, that was all the precautions they could manage. No choice now but to go in. Gathering himself, he exchanged a glance with Kaila, who nodded back. Then taking a firmer grip of the handle, he shoved the door open and charged inside. *Atarlight* spilt across the dark interior as Kaila followed him, wristwatch gripped in one hand and her eyes aglow.

Inside, the tavern was silent. Quintin had only ever been here once, and so he knew the place wasn't exactly known for its bustling clientele, but as they stepped through the back door into the kitchens, there was an emptiness to the place that was telling. Pots had been left out, food half congealed in the bottom and a half drunken glass sat on the bar.

Kaila brushed past him, eyes wide as she cast them about the room. Several of the stools had fallen to the floor. Someone had obviously left in a rush. But otherwise, the place seemed undisturbed. He ran a finger along the benchtop. It came away clean—no dust. So it had been recent. Had someone been able to warn Ambrose's network after all?

A floorboard squeaked as Kaila moved into the dining hall. There she turned, looking at him across the bar with a frown on her brow. "How?"

"I don't—"

*Crash!*

The pair spun as the front door of the tavern tore from its hinges and flew across the room, crashing into the ground before Kaila. She already had a hand up as a hulking silhouette filled the doorway. Quintin went for his knife, even as he struck a chord with his Gift—not that it would do any good against a Warden's armour…

His eyes widened as he felt the sharp *trumpeting* of anger ring through the tavern.

"Kaila, wait—" he started, but she was already moving.

The door flew backwards, slamming into the newcomer— who caught it with a massive fist and *wrenched* it from control of Kaila's Gift. Tossing it aside, the silhouette advanced…

"*Garrick, stop!*" Quintin bellowed. He combined the shout with a tolling of peace against the man's *soullight*.

That brought the Bruiser to a halt long enough to notice it was Kaila's skull he was about to cave in—and not someone in the black armour of a Warden.

"Kaila?" he whispered. Blinking in the harsh *atarlight*, he slowly lowered his fist. "What are you doing here?"

"Garrick!" Kaila seemed as surprised as the Bruiser. "I…I don't…"

She trailed off as Garrick blinked, finally seeming to notice Kaila was not alone. His face darkened as his eyes found Quintin.

"*You*," he hissed.

# 23

Jenna couldn't leave. She couldn't abandon Rohan, not now, when doing so would leave him powerless to the whims of General Iron Hands. Nor could she stay and marry that foul man and become his play toy, to beat and abuse as he pleased.

Which left one last, desperate plan.

And if she was going to have any chance of pulling it off, she needed Theron.

She found him where he always was—sitting on that stone bed, watching her with those eyes of his. Her stomach twisted, thinking of the night they'd fallen asleep together. He could have killed her, stolen her agimet and broken his chains, escaped.

But he hadn't. He'd stayed. Tied his future to hers. It was almost enough to make her believe…

"What is it?"

She swallowed. Those eyes saw more than they should. Letting out a long breath, she stepped into the room.

"Rohan is back," she said quietly. "He won't come with me."

Concern showed on Theron's face. "I warned you, Jenna…"

"I know," she sighed. Slipping across the room, she sank onto the bed and placed her head in her hands. "But what else could I do? What would *you* have done in my place? Flee, and leave him to his fate?"

Silence. She shouldn't have been surprised. What would a man like Theron know about family…

"I had a sister, you know," he said, interrupting her thoughts. "That was how he learned about the Elysian blood. She failed her Trial of Agimet." He turned to look at her, and in his eyes, she saw the pain that had haunted him all these years. "My father had his soldiers string her from an oak tree."

"Theron, I'm so sorry, I didn't know…"

He shook his head. "She's the only reason I escaped," he continued. "The first and only time she used her Gift. She sent me a warning, told me to run." He swallowed. "I have regretted that day ever since."

A tingling spread across Jenna's scalp as she met those haunted eyes. "What are you saying, Theron?"

"That maybe you're right. Maybe you should stay and fight for him."

The words hung between them like a blade ready to fall. Jenna searched his face for some hint of betrayal, for something, anything of the duplicitous man she had dragged into this prison all those weeks ago. But if he was there, Theron hid him well.

"Can I trust you, Theron?" she asked at last.

His jaw clenched and she saw the tension in his muscles, before suddenly he relaxed. "Until death do us part, right?"

She snorted. "Let's hope it doesn't come to that." Rising,

she looked down at him. With a flourish, the key to his chains appeared in her hand. "Alright then, let's go and steal the Aegis of the King."

Theron blinked. "You want to *what?*" he exclaimed, sitting bolt upright in bed.

"It was your idea, remember?"

"I didn't think you'd ever actually *go for it!*"

"Well, now it's our only chance."

With that, she knelt to unlock his shackles. The iron made a harsh *clunk* as it struck the ground. Surprise showed on his face as he flexed his ankle, still watching her.

"My mother was *convinced* that two people were needed to wield the Aegis," Jenna said. "That's why she set up that whole test between me and Rohan. So…maybe you were right, and the longer they've been apart, the weaker they've become. But that means I need someone else to wield my father's piece—and you're all I have."

Theron sighed. "That's all well and good, Jenna, but didn't you say the Wardens were guarding it?"

"Yes," Jenna started, "but with my Gift—"

But Theron was already shaking his head. "As soon as you step into the same sphere of influence as a Warden, you'll burn through your *atar* like grass on a campfire."

Jenna muttered a curse beneath her breath. She'd forgotten that lesson. Her eyes were drawn to the soft glow of the Aegis on her wrist.

"It will protect me," she said quietly. "It did as much against the General. And they fear it. Maybe I can use that against them."

"More likely, they'll call your bluff, Jenna."

Silence fell between them. Jenna's mind raced, trying to find a better way, a plan that didn't have so many variables that could go wrong. But if there was a solution, it refused to gift her with its knowledge.

"What other choice do I have, Theron?" she whispered at last.

He sighed. "None."

She met his eyes. "Then you'll help me?"

He gave her a long, unreadable look, then nodded. "My plan to steal the Aegis started this mess in the first place," he said. "Might as well see it through. Who knows, maybe the stories are true and returning the Aegis to the Elysian will finally turn the tide against the Magisterium."

Jenna smiled, but there was no joy in it. "Let's hope we live long enough to find out."

---

THE CITY WAS QUIET. ROHAN STOOD ALONE ON THE ROOF OF the Sanctum, the cold wind cutting through his clothes. Below, the black dome sloped away into the night, while the rooftops of the capital rose to meet it.

Somewhere down there, his sister was preparing to betray the Magisterium.

He pressed his hands against the stone plinth, struggling to breathe, to gather his mind into something resembling a rational thought.

Could he trust no one in this foul world? First it had been Eliza. They had stood together in this very spot and sworn vows to one another, to guard and protect Fresia. He knew now the girl he'd loved had never existed, that she had been in collusion with the Elysian all along. Why else would she hesitate to slay the creature that had stolen her life?

It hurt, what he'd had to do in the Iron Pinnacles. But he had done it for his kingdom, for the future of humanity itself.

In the face of their monstrous enemy, the Magisterium could afford no traitors.

*They used you, Rohan. The rest of us are just pawns to use in their games.*

Could Jenna be telling the truth? Was the general yet another traitor to the memory of the First Matron and the Nameless Warden? His knuckles pressed deeper into the altar, as if he could break stone itself with only his mortal strength.

It seemed almost the way of the world. His mother had killed their father because she thought him weak, while Eliza had never been what she pretended. Now Jenna sought to flee the power of the Magisterium, and the man who'd dragged Rohan from the depths of his despair had only ever been working towards his own betterment.

Who was left to care for Fresia? For the citizens of this poor city? Every day was a struggle for the people of the capital, toiling away for a cause that grew dimmer by the day. Food and supplies vanished and soldiers were slaughtered in the streets, and not one of their leaders had the fortitude to step forward, to fight back.

He stared down at the city, remembering his desperation that night. Theron, Jenna's cursed husband, had almost killed them all. The others had stood and watched in horror, unable to act. But Rohan hadn't frozen. He had taken up the fallen dagger and plunged it into the creature, interrupting its magic, saving them.

Then again in the Pinnacles, when others had faltered before the Elysian magic, Rohan had defied them.

The wind howled around him as he rose. The roof sloped away, the darkness of the edge concealed by the size of the dome. He'd been a coward once, fleeing from the responsibilities of his birth. It shamed him, thinking of what he'd once been. That man would have fled now; betrayed everything he had known and run with Jenna.

But Rohan Frye was no longer that man. Forged in the flames of pain and betrayal, he would not flinch from his duty now.

The sound of boots on stone steps snapped him from his thoughts. Turning, he found the general climbing the stairs to the roof. Reaching the platform, he came to a stop, regarding Rohan with those cold eyes of his.

"Welcome home, my prince," he said. "I understand congratulations are in order?"

Exhaling, Rohan nodded. "I thank you for the opportunity, General."

The man inclined his head. "I understand you have spoken with your sister?"

"I have."

"She told you of our…arrangement."

"She did." Rohan stared into the general's eyes and wished there was a way he could know the truth inside this man's soul.

And then, with a start, he realised there was.

Leonardo Falkenrath called himself a loyal citizen of Fresia. His greatest shame was his wife's betrayal. She had born not just one, but two foul Elysian children.

"I fear I was not the most diplomatic in my request," the general said, joining Rohan by the ledge. "However, I trust I have your support, Prince Rohan."

Turning from the city, Rohan regarded the general with cold eyes. "I would give it gladly, General," he said quietly, "but first, there is something I require of you."

"Something more than the life of Kaila Dwyn, prince?"

He pursed his lips. "It is a small thing."

"Then speak it."

"I would have you confess the sins of your son to the Sisters of the Magisterium."

The General's eyes widened. "What? Why?"

"How else could you earn the forgiveness of the Nameless?"

"My prince, you must understand…" The general's lips pressed into a thin line. "This is a shame I must bear alone. The sisters would not understand—but I swear, when I am king, I will ensure no other man suffers the deceit we have endured."

Rohan's heart sank as he finally saw behind the man's mask. There was no change to his expression, no shift in his tone, but Rohan knew. He should have seen it before, but he saw it now. No true believer would hesitate to confess such a crime before the servants of the Nameless. Rohan had done so himself, after his return from the Pinnacles. That Falkenrath hesitated…

…it meant Jenna was right. This man served only himself.

"Very good," Rohan said, keeping his true thoughts silent.

"I heard a prisoner was brought back. Not the girl, I assume…"

*Eliza.*

Rohan shook his head. "No, you were right. She had been…corrupted," he said quietly. "One of the Elysian. Warden Laura believes him to be some kind of leader amongst their kind."

"It has not spoken yet?"

Frowning, Rohan turned his gaze on the man. Was the general worried about something the captive might say?

"Not to my knowledge," he replied, "but I am told the Wardens have their methods. Whatever knowledge is in this Elysian's possession will soon be ours."

"Good," Falkenrath grunted. He stood there a moment,

looking out over the city. Far out across the harbour, lightning flashed above the swirling sea. Abruptly, the General nodded. "If you'll excuse me, Prince Rohan, I must make my preparations. Now you have returned to grant your support, the Sisters are pushing for a union as soon as possible."

Rohan watched the man descend back into the darkness of the Sanctum, wondering. The general's duplicity was clear, but could it go further than that? He had raised not just one, but two Elysian children. And when their heritage had been uncovered, instead of declaring it to the Magisterium, he'd handled it in secret. Why?

His frown deepened, thinking back to the young Elysian that had wedded his sister. There had certainly been a resemblance to the general, now he thought about it. Then again, he also knew the eyes could not be trusted when it came to these creatures.

He clenched his teeth, anger building within. Was there no one he could trust in this foul house of wolves? No one he could turn to in this moment of need, someone who would place the needs of their kingdom and its people ahead of their own selfish desires…

Rohan's blood pulsed as he realised there *was* someone he could trust. Someone who would *always* put the needs of the Magisterium ahead of themselves—because they had sworn oaths to a force far greater than themselves to do so.

*Warden Laura.*

# 24

"**Y**ou!"

Kaila leapt back, surprised at the sudden return of Garrick's fury. Afraid they were under attack after all, she spun around, expecting to see a Warden advancing on them, but there was only Quintin, looking as shocked as she was to see the Bruiser standing there in Tah'raus—alive.

"It's only Quintin," Kaila started, "he's been helping me…"

She trailed off as Garrick strode past. "I know *exactly* who it is." His fist snaked out, catching the Psionic by the shirt and dragging him bodily across the bar. "What are you doing here, traitor?" he spat. "Come to sell another of us out for a pretty title from the Magisterium?"

Kaila was halfway across the room, intent on putting a stop to the violence, but those words brought her to a halt as surely as a fist to her stomach. Suddenly, she couldn't breathe, couldn't…couldn't think.

"What?" Speaking was like squeezing a dead rabbit from a

drainage pipe. Her heart pounded in her chest, as she looked from Garrick to Quintin, then back again.

"Kaila, I—" Quintin started, but he broke off as Garrick lifted him bodily into the air and slammed him against the wall.

"Ambrose didn't want to tell you," he growled. Holding the Psionic pinned, he ruffled through the man's pockets until he came up with his agimet crystal. That he tossed to Kaila. She caught it wordlessly, lips parted, still struggling…struggling to understand.

"Who?" she rasped.

The grief on the Bruiser's face told Kaila the truth even before he spoke. "Theron."

*No! No, no, no!*

That couldn't be true. Theron had been Quintin's best friend. The Psionic would never have betrayed him. Not unless…

Her skin crawled as she remembered what he'd said earlier, about despair being the Magisterium's true weapon. Kaila turned to him, and the roaring in her ears was so loud she hardly heard her own words.

"Tell me it's not true," she whispered.

The sight of her friend looking anywhere but at her was like a knife tearing into her heart. "I'm so sorry, Kaila," Quintin choked. "I…I let the despair consume me."

The sorrow in his voice made her angry. How dare he? *How dare he? Atar* pulsed in her veins, a burning flame fuelled by the crystal Garrick had taken from their friend. She struggled to keep it contained as she advanced on him.

"*Why?*" she demanded, and felt the *soullights* in the room tremble, the world shake.

She saw the way Quintin's face changed, how the blood

drained from his cheeks, the fear that suddenly permeated the room.

"I thought…I thought protecting my daughters was the best I could hope for. That the Magisterium was invincible. So I did the only logical thing and gave up." He hesitated, watching her with that familiar fear in his eyes. "But I was wrong."

Kaila shook her head. Wrong didn't begin to explain what he had done. She wanted to lash out. To grasp his *soullight* and crush this man for everything he had done. His betrayal hadn't just cost Theron his life, it had forced Kaila to reveal herself to the Matron and Jenna, destroyed any chance she'd had of a happy ending with Rohan. He had taken *everything* from her.

"Kaila…"

She started at Garrick's voice. The Bruiser was staring at her…was that fear in his eyes? Blinking, she looked around and saw the tavern *moving*. Everything from the fallen barstools to the tables to the unfinished drink, it was all vibrating, trembling, as if connected to her power.

Except she hadn't created a single thread of *atar*.

*What's happening to me?*

Her eyes fell to the agimet in her hand. Swallowing her own doubts, she crossed to the bar and carefully placed the crystal on the countertop. The power flowing through her veins cut off immediately. At the same time, the room stilled. The rattle of wood and metal fell silent.

"Kaila…" Quintin began.

"No," she snarled, turning on the man again. "I don't want to hear any more of what you've got to say, Quintin."

Teeth bared, fists clenched, she came to a halt beside the pair. Trembling, she glared at him, daring him to disobey the command. To his credit, the Psionic pressed his lips in a thin line and held his tongue.

She swallowed. A piece of her wanted to kill him. To draw the dagger from her belt and plunge it through his chest. For Theron, and Rohan, and her own bruised heart. But she didn't.

Instead, she gestured to Garrick.

"Let him go."

"What?" the Bruiser frowned. "You heard what he said…"

"I know," she whispered. Crossing to a nearby table, she slumped into the chair. "And you're right. He deserves to die."

The Bruiser's frown deepened. "Then why…"

"I don't know," she said honestly.

"He'll betray us again, Kaila. They always do."

She shrugged. "Maybe. But he had every chance to betray us in the Iron Pinnacles and he didn't." She swallowed. "Just…let him go, Garrick. Please. For me."

The Bruiser hesitated a moment longer, then did as she said. Releasing the Psionic, he stepped back. Quintin frowned at him, then looked at Kaila. His lips parted and it seemed he would speak, before he thought better of it. His shoulders slumped and bowing his head, he started for the door.

"Take it," Kaila said before he could make it outside.

He paused, glancing at her. She gestured to the crystal on the countertop. Without it, Quintin would have no access to his Gift. He would be as good as helpless when the Magisterium's hunters inevitably came looking for him. After a moment's hesitation, he pocketed it.

Then he was gone, and Kaila was alone with the massive Elysian.

"What happened in the mountains?" she whispered, staring at the floor between her legs, not looking at the man.

She heard the floorboards creak as he shifted on his feet. "Ambrose tricked me," he whispered, and she heard the pain in his voice. "Made me think I was carrying him to safety. By the time the weaving dissolved and I realised what he'd done, it was too late. They already had him. And…" she heard the pause there. "I thought you were dead."

"I survived."

Another pause. "And Eliza?"

She shook her head, unable to speak the words. After a moment, however, she recovered her voice. "You warned the others in Ambrose's network."

It was a statement rather than a question. That was obviously why *The Rusty Gull* was empty.

"His ghost protocol," Garrick replied. "In case he was ever taken, there are backup safehouses, ones kept off the books, known only to his lieutenants. I returned over the Iselador pass. We had a day before they reached the city. This was one of the last places we cleared, in case…" he trailed off with a glance in her direction.

"Has he broken yet?"

"We don't think so," Garrick whispered. "That's why when I thought someone was in here…"

Pinpricks danced across Kaila's scalp. "You were waiting to see if the Wardens came."

Garrick shrugged. "Instead, I found you."

"And Quintin."

Lips pursed in a thin line, he nodded.

Kaila gripped the lip of the table until she felt the splinters cutting into her flesh. Quintin had betrayed them. Theron and Eliza and her father were all dead. And now Ambrose was a prisoner. What hope did any of them have…

*The Magisterium only wins when young men and women speak like you. When we no longer fight.*

Her skin crawled as she remembered Quintin's words. Tainted now as they were, there was still a ring of truth to them. The Magisterium had Ambrose, but…

"What if we rescue him?"

"What?"

Her heart pulsed as she rose and turned to Garrick. "Ambrose is tough. If he hasn't broken yet, maybe we can get to him."

"Kaila, the Sanctum is *impregnable*."

"Except it's not!" she countered. "I was able to move in and out of its gates for months." Stomach twisted in a ball, her entire body trembling, she faced the Bruiser. "If we could fool them once, why not again?"

He seemed to actually consider it, but finally he just sighed. "I can't, Kaila," he said quietly. "Ambrose kept things compartmentalised—other than himself, no one knew every piece of the organisation. They need me."

"Then send someone else!" Kaila hissed. "What about Cassandra? She had power. With her help I *know* we could save him!"

"Cassandra? Kaila, I don't know any Elysian by the name of Cassandra?"

"She was a Mover…or maybe a Weaver? Ambrose sent her to help me, the night you left for the Iron Pinnacles."

The frown on the Bruiser's face deepened. "Ambrose didn't send anyone that night, Kaila."

"Then who…" she trailed off, thinking back over the conversation.

A chill spread through her stomach. The woman had never actually confirmed she was working with the tailor.

But if she wasn't a part of Ambrose's organisation, just who the hell *was* she?

Garrick was still watching her with concern in his eyes.

"I'm sorry, Kaila," he said softly. "I can't help you. I won't let Ambrose down with this. I can't."

Her shoulders fell. She knew when she was defeated. The big man approached, laying a hand on her shoulder.

"I know you want to help," he said softly, "but by the looks of it, you didn't exactly escape the Pinnacles in one piece. Come on, I'll take you to the new safehouse. You can rest there." He paused, looking around at the silent tavern. "Then we can figure out what comes next."

Closing her eyes rather than let him see her grief, Kaila allowed herself to be lead away. They left behind the tavern and the docks, moving through the back alleys and slums of the capital. As she walked, the faces of everyone Kaila had lost ran through her mind.

Her father, all those months ago now, as he was cut down by the Warden.

Theron as he sacrificed himself to stop the Matron.

Rohan atop that towering dome as he turned from her.

Eliza, smiling as the blade tore through her stomach.

And now Quintin, head hung in shame as he walked away.

The worst part, Quintin had been right in the end. She saw it now. Not despair, but the cold, terrible truth. They had nothing left. Garrick and the scant remnants of Ambrose's organisation would continue for a while, but ultimately, they too would fail. It was inevitable.

Because the Magisterium had already won.

# 25

Creeping through the dim corridors with Theron at her side, Jenna couldn't help but wonder how it had all fallen apart so quickly. She was Matron of the Magisterium and all who roamed these halls must bow to her authority. She should have no need to sneak in this place.

But without the Aegis, her authority was all but non-existent.

And so they slipped in silence through the deepest levels of the Sanctum, where the Wardens had dwelled since the days of the First Matron. She had expected movement, the flickering of old torches and lanterns, even a challenge.

Instead, they found darkness and silence.

"Where are they all?" Theron whispered.

The still air felt wrong, stale, as if it had not been stirred in an age. Their only light was the dim glow of the Aegis on her wrist.

"I don't know."

It *all* felt wrong. Like she was missing something terrible.

Her heart thundered in her chest, but they couldn't turn back now. She had come too far.

She had come this way only a few times, in the company of her father or mother, and then once more after her coronation, when the Wardens had invited her to lay her blessings on the Aegis of the King. Until she took a husband, their order was charged with its protection—just as the Sisters would guard the Aegis of the Matron, should she pass without a successor.

With only her memory to guide them, it took a long time to finally reach the nave at the heart of those strange corridors. It was as she remembered it—a vast, circular chamber with strong concrete walls soaring up three storeys to an empty dome. Again, there was no light but for a dim glow that came from the altar at the centre. The breath caught in Jenna's throat as they stepped towards it.

There it was.

*The Aegis of the King.*

The twin of the device on her arm, it rested on a low marble pedestal, its crystals strangely dim, as though their power had faded after so long without an owner. Could it really be this easy? Jenna cast an eye around the nave, suspicious, but nothing moved. Clenching her fists, she glanced at Theron.

"Quickly," she gasped. "Before someone comes."

Theron didn't need telling twice. Nodding, he darted for the pedestal.

But before he could reach the device, an invisible force slammed into him. His body lifted from the ground and smashed against the wall with a sickening crack. A cry tore from his throat, but it turned into a strangled gasp as something pressed against his windpipe.

"Theron!" Jenna screamed, rushing forward.

"Do not take another step, Matron." A voice stopped her cold.

A Warden stepped into the chamber, dark armour glimmering in the light of its own agimet. Behind came others—three more Wardens. And Rohan. He was wearing a sword. Since when did her brother carry a blade?

"Rohan—" she choked.

"I didn't want to believe it," he said quietly, coming to a stop beside the first Warden.

"It's not what you think," Jenna said, eyes darting to Theron as he struggled for breath.

"No?" Rohan stepped closer. "Then you're not betraying the Magisterium? You haven't keep this monster alive, in secret, all this time?"

"I—I can explain—please—"

Rohan shook his head, a sad expression on his lips. "Warden Laura will wring a confession from you. Then the Nameless can judge whether your life was worthy of the gifts he granted."

Trembling, Jenna looked into the eyes of her brother and saw no mercy in their depths—only that terrible hatred.

*First Matron, don't let it end like this*, she whispered a silent prayer.

She tried to retreat, but footsteps behind her announced the arrival of more backup. She had walked herself and Theron right into a trap. Her fingers twitched towards the crystal in her pocket. Theron said the agimet would be drained in seconds if she used her Gift against the Wardens. Carefully, her eyes shifted to the pedestal where the Aegis rested.

Maybe she only needed seconds.

Drawing in a breath, she looked her brother in the eye—then closed her fingers around the crystal.

Immediately, the Wardens shouted a warning. Their leader raised a hand.

*Atar* flooded Jenna's veins.

And the world fell silent.

*Quickly*, she urged herself, looking at the frozen soldiers.

Already, she could feel the *atar* draining from her veins, consumed at a terrible rate by the effort of holding time still in the presence of so many Wardens. She darted forward, sliding between Rohan and the Warden he'd called Laura. The Aegis of the King waited for her, its glow dimmed. No time for hesitation now; she snatched it up and turned to go…

…and paused.

Theron was still pinned against the wall by the Warden's power. For a second, she considered leaving him. That had been his plan for her after all, hadn't it? Steal half of the Aegis and flee, leaving her to look like a traitor to her own people.

But that wasn't the man she had worked alongside these past few weeks. Something had changed. Grown between them. Something that might even be real.

She couldn't leave him.

Only sparks remained in her soul, but she forced her limbs to move, darting across the chamber to where he was pinned against the wall. As the last of her *atar* flickered and died, she slid the Aegis onto his wrist.

The power vanished. Movement resumed. A moment later, the force holding Theron disappeared. He collapsed to the ground, gasping and clutching at his throat, while murmurs spread through the nave.

Jenna turned to face her brother and the Wardens. A hush fell over the chamber, and she imagined the last glimmer of *atar* vanishing from her eyes. Rohan was the one to finally break the silence.

"So, you're one of them," Rohan whispered. His voice was hollow, as though something inside him had broken. He bowed his head. "All this time…tell me, did our mother know? Is that why you killed her?"

A lump lodged in Jenna's throat. "Rohan, I didn't even know myself. Not until Mother died. She hid it from all of us. I never wanted this. I swear it."

He looked at her, eyes gleaming. "I wish I could believe you, sister. Truly, I do." He glanced at Theron, and the Aegis now blazing on his wrist. "But you seek to wield the power of our First Matron against our people." Steel hissed against leather as he drew his sword. "I will not allow it."

Jenna's heart twisted, but she didn't move. Couldn't. The man before her was still her brother.

Then Theron was at her side, face set.

"I suggest you stand down, Prince Rohan," he said, his voice low. "I do not wish to harm you."

Several of the Wardens flinched as the Aegis lit up on his wrist. Its burning glow chased the darkness from the chamber, making even the power of their own agimet seem dim. Even Warden Laura took half a step back.

But Rohan stood firm, blade steady. "Do your worst, Elysian."

And then he charged.

Theron raised the Aegis with a grimace.

And the chamber exploded with light.

# 26

Darkness. Then…

…*the creaking of wood beneath boots. A noose, swaying in the breeze. A crowd, screaming its rage…*

Kaila gasped awake. Slowly, the room resolved, the dream fading back into the dark where it belonged. Heart hammering, she clutched at her chest. It had been days since she'd had the dream. Not since the night before she'd faced Rohan in the canyon.

Why had it returned now?

Kaila could hear several others in the room, speaking in hushed voices, so letting out a breath, she pushed herself up. She'd fallen asleep on the sofa in the new hideout. They still didn't have room for her—Ambrose's failsafe's apparently hadn't put much stock in things like 'comfort' or 'personal space'.

The half-light of dawn filtered through a crack in the wall, catching in the dim facets of a crystal lying on the table in front of her. She'd been toying with it before she slept, running it through her fingers, wondering whether she should use her Warden's Gift to restore its power, or allow the natural process to occur while she slept.

In the end, she had left it empty. It was safer that way. What she had done in the Iron Pinnacles—what she had *almost* done at *The Rusty Gull*, it wasn't natural. She had seen the way Garrick looked at her, the fear in his eyes. She didn't blame him.

Outside, the sounds of the city were slowly gathering pace; the ring of a hammer, the shout of a merchant, the rumble of steel wheels on concrete. The new safehouse was close to Soul Square, inside the largest slum in the city. The Magisterium's guards had recently abandoned this part of the city, after a food riot had cornered several of their fellows and torn them to pieces.

Frustration bubbled in her stomach. She could *see* the beginnings of Ambrose's plan coming to fruition. But it was too little, too late. Without his organization disrupting the Magisterium's shipments, the resources from the Dominances would soon flow into the city again. The mob would be appeased.

And everything they'd lost—everything they'd sacrificed— would be for nothing.

A noise outside made her flinch. Low voices were followed by boots scraping against stone. She turned as the door burst open and Garrick stumbled in. The others in the living room turned at his arrival, surprise showing on their faces.

Breathless, the Bruiser gestured for the others to join him. Kaila recognised only a few of the faces—Sonya was another Bruiser, while Jack was a Binder who seemed to style himself after the tailor, since she'd never seen him without a suit. Unfortunately, given his talent for blowing things up, she'd also never seen him in clothing at least partially singed. The last, Dalen, was a young man with a sword on his belt. Kaila wasn't sure of his Gift.

She'd done her best to avoid the others since her arrival in the safehouse. It was better that way. She'd already surrendered to her despair. If even someone like Quintin, who'd given his entire life to the cause, had given up, what reason did she have to continue?

*Soldiers…Soul Square…coming…*

Sadly, given the rather public nature of the gathering—and that the weren't particularly discrete—it was difficult to ignore their conversation. The tension in their voices burrowed under her skin, until at last she swept the crystal off the table and rose with a growl.

"Well, what is it?" she snapped, stomping over to join them.

"Something's happening," Garrick replied. "Soldiers are on the march. Wardens as well; the first we've seen on the streets in months, if the reports are right."

"What are they doing?" Kaila frowned.

"Marching on Soul Square."

Silence fell over the room as the five Elysian regarded one another.

Kaila was the one to finally break it. "Do you think they're planning to crack down on the district?"

Jack grimaced. "The girl could be onto something."

Garrick pursed his lips, but before he could reply, a fresh face entered the safehouse. This one Kaila didn't recognise—which meant it was probably one of Ambrose's informants.

"Garrick, sir?" he asked, eyes darting over the five of them before settling on the big Bruiser. "You asked for an update if anything new came of light?"

Five heads turned as one to stare at the man. He took a

moment to realise that the attention of everyone in the room was on him.

"Go on then, man," Garrick rumbled. "Out with it."

The man shifted nervously on his feet. "Word on the street..." he said, "they're saying there's going to be some kind of execution."

Kaila's mouth went dry. She barely heard the rest of the man's words over the pulsing of blood in her ears.

*Ambrose.*

"They're calling out the entire city," the messenger continued awkwardly. "There are Wardens in the streets. And soldiers. Everyone's being herded towards Soul Square, like..." he trailed off.

"Like they're going to make a spectacle of it," Garrick muttered. Stumbling to the sofa, he slumped into its cushions while the others watched on.

"What do we do?" Sonya whispered.

"They're going to use the tailor's death to send a message," Dalen replied.

Silence. Kaila looked around the room, waiting for someone to speak, to announce a plan of action, a rescue. *Something. Anything.*

No one moved. Garrick didn't even lift his head. He just sat, staring at his massive hands.

"So that's it then?" she found herself speaking. Her gaze passed over each of them. "We're just going to sit here and wait until its done?"

Garrick looked up. "They have Wardens, Kaila. A lot of them. What else can we do?"

She drew in a breath. "We can be there," she said quietly. "We can make sure he's not alone."

The room remained silent. The others stared at her, but no one spoke. No one moved.

In the end, Kaila didn't wait for their answer. She turned on her heel and stalked out the front door. The moment she stepped outside, however, she found herself swept up in a crowd. Panic clawed at her chest as the weight of bodies pushed her towards the plaza—and then Garrick was there. The mass parted before the Bruiser as he shoved past, forging a path. The others followed, forming a protective guard around Kaila.

Her heart thundered as they neared Soul Square. A piece of her already knew what they would find, even before the crowd parted and she saw the gallows rising above the empty fountain. This was the scene from her nightmare, brought to life. Wardens in their black armour flanked the platform and soldiers ringed the perimeter, spears extended like teeth towards the crowd. They were taking no chances.

Men and women dressed in the clothing of nobles had gathered atop the platform and were chattering amongst themselves, as if this was nothing more than a day at the market for them. From the distance, she couldn't make out their faces. Nodding to Garrick, they pushed their way closer to the gallows.

Abruptly, a stillness came over the crowd. For a second, Kaila thought they had been spotted. Then movement came from the stage. She craned her head, trying to catch a better glimpse.

As if by the will of the Trickster, the crowd parted and the breath caught in her throat. She recognised the man approaching the front of the stage, arms spread as if to embrace the crowd.

It was Rohan.

Kaila froze. A chill danced across her skin. Something was wrong.

"What's happening?" she whispered.

Rohan began to speak. "You know me, people of Tah'raus," his voice rung across the square, supernaturally enhanced by a crystal powered device alongside him. "I am Rohan Frye, son of our slain king and Matron. For months, I have struggled with my part in that tragedy, with the knowledge I allowed one of the enemy to deceive me. My mistake cost the lives of my parents, and our kingdom their monarchs."

A ripple spread through the crowd with those words, a rumble of discontent, but Rohan forged on.

"However, never in my darkest days could I imagine the depths of our enemy's treachery. The rot of their evil has spread to our every institution, infected even the heart of this great nation."

A tingling began in Kaila's scalp as Rohan turned. A pair of hooded prisoners were led up the stairs, their arms bound behind their backs. As they reached the platform, Rohan made a gesture. Immediately, a Warden stepped forward and kicked the feet out from beneath the prisoners. They fell to their knees with cries of fear. The first hood was torn from the woman's head.

Kaila's knees nearly buckled.

It wasn't Ambrose.

It was Jenna Frye.

Matron of Fresia, wielder of the Aegis and the most powerful individual in all of the Magisterium. There she knelt, eyes wide, mascara running down her cheeks and hair in disarray. Her lips moved as she tried to speak, but the Warden backhanded her across the face, sending her sprawling.

"The daughter of our beloved Matron," Rohan cried, while the Warden removed a crystal from his belt. "My own sister—is one of the enemy. An Elysian, parading itself as one of us."

As the crystal was pressed to Jenna's flesh, her whole body jerked as if struck by lightning.

And her eyes glowed silver.

Unfortunately, whatever Gift she possessed was countered by the black fingers of the Warden closing around her throat. A scream tore from Jenna's lips as the *atar* was drawn from her like blood from a wound. Kaila trembled. She knew well that burning touch, the feeling of *atar*—and a piece of her soul— being scraped from inside of her by a rusted blade.

The Warden didn't stop until the light died from Jenna's eyes. When he finally released her, she crumpled, coughing and heaving on the boards of the stage.

Lightning flashed across the sky. Rain began to fall.

"And this sorry creature here…"

Silence came over the crowd as the prince turned to the second prisoner. This had to be Ambrose, the poor, iron willed tailor. Kaila trembled as the Warden ripped the hood loose. "Was her paramour."

This time, Kaila's knees really did give in.

It wasn't Ambrose.

There, knelt on the stage, blinking in the dawn light, was Theron.

"No," Kaila whispered.

*No, no, no, no!*

It couldn't be true. Theron was dead. She had seen it. Seen him dying. The cruel Matron standing over him, Aegis in hand. And Jenna had said…

She closed her eyes, her entire being shaking, breaking.

"Kaila, get up," a voice called to her. Firm hands gripped her beneath the arms and lifted her. "We have to go. They're searching the crowd."

She swayed on her feet, staring up at the stage. The twin

nooses swirled in the flickering light as the crowd roared. Theron and Jenna were on their feet now. This was what she had been seeing. What strange ability had shown her this? She had no idea how, or why? Guarded by half a dozen Wardens, there could be no saving either of them. They were already being lead towards the gallows.

*No, no, no!*

Her vision blurred. It wasn't fair. Theron was *alive*—but doomed. All this power at her fingertips, and there was nothing Kaila could do to save him.

Garrick tugged at her arm again, insistent. "Come on, there's nothing we can do."

Her whole body shook. "No," she whispered, and tore away from him.

The crowd surged around her, jeering for blood. She stumbled, then righted herself and pushed forward. She couldn't stop this. But she couldn't just stand by and let it happen. Not this time.

Her fingers found the crystal in her pocket. The nexus swirled all around, through the crowd and Rohan and Jenna and Theron, its energy just out of reach. But not to Kaila. She caught a loop of its terrible power and threaded it through the crystal, where several had already begun to gather. She became the catalyst, and a second later, Kaila felt the burning of *atar* fill the piece of agimet.

She couldn't save them. She had already lost. She knew that. But it didn't matter. Theron was alive.

She couldn't lose him again.

*The Magisterium only wins when young men and women no longer fight back.*

Atar flooded through her veins.

And a single, tolling bell rang out across the plaza.

QUINTIN SAT SLUMPED OVER THE BAR, CHEEK PRESSED TO THE rim of a half-empty glass of warm ale. The tavern buzzed with the low hum of conversation and the scraping of cutlery against ceramic plates as the clientele broke their fast. Someone near the hearth was laughing too loudly. Despite all its recent hardships, life in the capital went on.

But not for him.

He hadn't slept. How could he, after what he'd done? *Traitor, worthless, coward!* The words chased themselves around his mind, robbing him of any hope for peace. Even the refuge of his daughters safety was denied to him now, after Eliza's sacrifice.

Exhaling through his nose, he reached for his glass and downed the remaining drink. The sour ale was almost as bad warm as it had been freshly poured. Still better than he deserved, however. Maybe if he had another, it might finally finish him off.

As he looked around for the bartender, however, he noticed a change had come over the room. The gentle hum of noise had fallen silent. The attention of the other diners had turned towards a shadow in the doorway.

Quintin almost toppled from his stool when he saw the black armour of a Warden.

"There is to be an execution," the creature announced into the terrified silence. "In Soul Square. The king demands your attendance."

It was gone again before anyone had a chance to speak, the double doors squealing as they rocked back and forth from his departure. Not that anyone would dare question a Warden of the Magisterium.

"King?" someone whispered.

"Who are they executing?" Another added.

For a few seconds, the occupants of the bar looked at one another. Then, with a slow reticence, they began to file outside Within a few minutes, Quintin was left alone in the tavern.

The bartender slid his glass from the benchtop and placed it in the sink.

"Come on then," he grunted, jerking a meaty chin toward the street. "Best not dally."

Quintin grimaced but obeyed, stumbling out into the blazing daylight. He knew who it would be—the Magisterium had obviously decided Ambrose would be more valuable to them as a spectacle than any information they could wring from him. He had no wish to watch his friend's execution, however the tavern wasn't far from the plaza and a crowd was already streaming through the streets, making it all but impossible to move in any direction *but* Soul Square.

Grudgingly, he allowed himself to be swept up in the human tide. The crowd was strangely quiet, hushed, as though every soul in the city was waiting. Clouds were gathering and the air was heavy with anticipation for the coming storm.

He reached the edge of the plaza just as voice rang out from the stage.

"You know me, people of Tah'raus!"

Quintin's heart twisted in his chest. Rohan. He came to a stop, allowing the crowd to sweep around him. On the stage, the prince of Fresia wore a purple tunic and sleek black pants. He strode up and down the platform, gesturing to the crowd, and then at a pair of prisoners. A Warden stepped up to the first and removed her hood.

Quintin didn't recognise the woman, but from the reaction of the crowd, he knew who she was. Jenna Frye. Matron of Fresia—and Rohan's sister.

She was also Elysian.

*What's going on?*

He swung around, searching the crowd for sign of Kaila or Garrick. So it was that he wasn't watching at the stage when the second of the prisoners was revealed.

He heard the prince speak the name though.

"Theron Falkenrath."

The blood froze in Quintin's veins, the breath catching in his throat. Unable to bring himself to turn, his eyes remained locked on the crowd as they jeered and raised their fists. It couldn't be. He would have known if Theron lived. He would have sensed him…

A flicker passed across the sky. A few seconds later, thunder crashed over the rooftops. The crowd flinched and Quintin took the chance to reach for the crystal in his pocket. He had no lenses to cover the glow of *atar*. Hopefully those nearby would think it lightning reflected in his eyes.

As his fingers touched the crystal, however, he felt something shift. A pulsing in the air, powerful, growing louder, more shrill. At first, it was mindless, without rhythm or reason, a lost soul screaming into the void. Clutching his crystal, Quintin reached for it—

Screams interrupted his concentration. Blinking, he tore himself from his *atarsight*, expecting to find the crowd turned against him. Instead, he saw a commotion nearby; men and women scrambling back from a shimmering light…

His heart plummeted into his stomach as he recognised Kaila. Eyes blazing with all the fury of an Elysian, she stood staring at the figures on the stage. The crowd pulled back in a ring around her, leaving her standing alone. Quintin watched in horror as soldiers in black armour began to shove their way through the crowd towards her.

It was over. Kaila was powerful. She might even be able to

go toe to toe with a Warden here in Tah'raus, with the nexus to draw on. But against so many…all it would take was for one to get its hands on her, and her power would be drained away, her crystal broken. Quintin had failed her again…

…so why was he charging through the crowd towards her?

Heart hammering in his chest, he burst through the ring of bystanders. As he did so, he felt that pulse again. There was a nervousness to it, almost hesitant, like a calf taking its first steps. Some part of his power responded to it, but he drew it back. Kaila stood frozen, her eyes burning, wind swirling about her. In despair, he realised it was happening again.

The air trembled as he approached, his clothes tugging at his skin, twisting, burning. Hooks twisted inside him, drawing a hiss from his teeth. Whatever was happening to Kaila, he couldn't begin to explain it. But after witnessing it in the canyon, and now again in the square, he knew it came from her soul, from that terrible agony she had buried inside.

Maybe, just maybe, he could help her.

The crowd was thickest around the stage, hindering the passage of the Wardens, and so Quintin reached the girl first. His hand snatched out, catching her arm in his fingers. Through his Gift, he felt her pain, the screeching, discordant notes within her soul, locked so tightly inside their energy had gathered into a storm rivalling the one overhead.

As lightning clashed and the air vibrated, Quintin reached for Kaila's *soullight*, strumming a counter to her pain, a song of peace and love and redemption. The notes twisted between them, trembling as they met the jagged edges of Kaila's song. For a moment, they hung between them, mixing, swirling— discordant rather than in harmony.

Then he felt Kaila's fingers tighten around his own. She stiffened, a shudder running through her body, before she blinked and turned towards him.

"Quintin?" she whispered.

"I'm here," he gasped, struggling to maintain the melody. He sensed that pulse again, the power beneath it, and the pieces of the puzzle clicked into place. "Kaila, you have to stop…"

"I see it now," she replied. To his alarm, Quintin saw a tear streak her cheek. "Thank you,."

"Kaila?" He screamed her name as the song built between them. The shrieking, wrenching pain of Kaila's *soullight* somehow seemed to be gathering force, as if it was being fed…

"For showing me the path," she replied, and her voice was sharp, almost metallic. "Finally, I can make them all feel the way we do."

"No, Kaila—"

It was too late. With a wrench, Kaila tore her hand from his.

And a final pulse burst across the plaza.

---

Rohan stood on the wooden platform as the rain began to fall. Within seconds, the planks were slick beneath his boots. The wind whipped water into their faces, forcing many of the nobles and Sisters who accompanied him on the stage to raise their arms to protect against it.

Rohan only lifted his face to the sky and let the rain pour down. Above the rooftops, lightning danced and thunder cracked. The Nameless showed his approval.

His throat was tight. What had he done to deserve such pain? He had suffered and suffered and still more was demanded of him. It was a test, he knew. To decide his worthiness for the days to come, the burdens of the crown.

It did not make this task any easier.

As another flash lit the sky, he turned and the prisoners were brought to the gallows. First was the Elysian man. Theron Falkenrath. His appearance betrayed his father's true allegiance. General Iron Hands was yet another traitor in their midst. No wonder the Nameless had invoked its wrath—the Magisterium had allowed the tainted blood of the enemy to walk their halls, lead their men, even sit upon the First Matron's throne.

Rohan's heart pulsed as he turned his gaze to the other.

Jenna Frye. His sister—and the last of the Elysian spies to ever besmirch the sacred grounds of the Sanctum.

Her eyes were soft as they gazed up at him, pleading. "Brother," she rasped, "please, don't do this—"

He cuffed her across the face with the back of his hand, sending her sprawling to the ground. A cry tore from her lips and the device she wore upon her arm flashed brightly, casting its glow over the platform. Rohan didn't flinch. The Nameless had already proven its power—the filthy creature that wore his sister's face could not wield the Aegis.

Behind him, the crowd roared for the blood of the Elysian. At a gesture from Rohan, soldiers dragged the prisoners to their feet. Jenna fought and struggled, spitting curses at her captors—until Warden Laura stepped forward and caught her by the arm. Her expletives turned to shrieks as the black armour seared her skin. Laura ignored her pain, yanking Jenna's arms behind her back so her wrists could be bound. When it was done, she retreated, the black slit of her helm turning in Rohan's direction.

He nodded his thanks. The Warden had been his guiding light these past weeks, the only stable force in a world that threatened each day to upended itself.

The other Elysian, Theron, offered no resistance as he was

lifted to his feet. All signs of fight had left him since the crystal had been pressed to his skin and his eyes had glowed bright—before Laura had drawn the magic back out of him. He didn't even struggle as the noose was looped over his neck.

"Please don't do this, Rohan," Jenna begged as the soldiers drew aside her scarlet hair and tightened the noose around her throat. "Please, it's me, Jenna. Your sister! You've known me your entire life. *Please!*"

His soul trembled, the rage at her insolence burning through him. This creature had murdered his sister—and now it had been discovered, *still* it had the gall to pretend it was her.

"I don't know who you are," he said, turning cold eyes on the creature, "but you are *not* my sister."

All his life, he'd run from power. From responsibility. Now, finally, he saw how wrong that had been. He'd been selfish, abdicating power to others, believing they were better fit to rule. But that had only ever been an excuse. He needed to be more like his parents, serving a greater cause rather than his own selfish needs. Only then would this world be safe.

"You need not fear any longer!" he shouted to the crowd. "Today, we reclaim our kingdom. Today, the power of the enemy is claimed by the Magisterium—and made our own!"

Then he turned to Warden Laura and extended his hand. She advanced, placing an object around his wrist. Silver and gold and platinum threads spun strange patterns around a dozen tiny crystals of agimet. His skin tingled as the clasps closed around his arm. Light flickered, catching in his eyes, and a warmth appeared in his chest, spreading slowly to fill him.

It was a mirror of the device worn by his sister. The other half of the Aegis of T'iana, the most sacred artefact in all of this world. The Elysian, Theron had tried to claim it—but by the power of the Nameless, had been rejected.

Now, as its power flowed into his veins, it marked Rohan as the one true King of Fresia.

Turning, he met Jenna's eyes. Even now, after everything he had learned, a piece of him still yearned to believe her. That she was truly his sister. Empathy was the curse of humanity, the weapon the Elysian wielded against them. Looking into Jenna's eyes, he saw again Eliza in the canyon, heard her pleas for him to listen, to *trust* the foul creatures. It had almost broken him. How close he'd been to surrendering to that weakness.

But the Nameless had given him strength that day. Now he must find it again. This final trial would expunge the last of his weakness and cast him anew, ready to lead Fresia to a final victory against the Elysian.

Drawing a breath, he tore his eyes from the monster that had stolen his sister and turned to Warden Laura.

"Do it."

The Warden inclined her head. "As you command, Your Majesty." He thought he sensed a note of pride in her voice as she turned to the gallows.

At that moment, however, a single voice rose above the shouts of the crowd and crackling of thunder.

"*No!*"

Rohan froze, his head whipping around. Amidst the press of bodies, a brilliant, burning light pressed back the darkness of the storm. A young woman stood haloed amidst the brilliance, and it seemed for a second the glow came not from a crystal or her eyes, but her skin itself, as if her entire body had been infused with the power of the enemy.

It was Kaila Dwyn.

"Impossible," he whispered.

His heart pulsed, even as his mind froze. He was looking at a ghost. He had seen her die in the Iron Pinnacles, stabbed with the Warden's blade and hurled into the twisted canyon.

Yet there she was, alive, without so much as a scratch on her.

Another beat of his heart, and finally his mind caught up with him. A dangerous Elysian stood in the heart of Tah'raus, daring to defy the might of the Magisterium. It could not be allowed to stand. Gritting his teeth, he drew his sword and pointed across the heads of the crowd towards the creature.

Before he could speak, however, the energy swirling around the Elysian *pulsed* and a wave of light spread from her. It passed through the crowd like a ripple upon the water, leaving no trace of its passage. For a moment, the people stood frozen, unmoved by the dark magics, and Rohan allowed himself to hope the devotion of his citizens had made them impervious.

Then, like a scrap of meat thrown into shark infested waters, the stillness shattered.

And all hell broke loose.

# 27

I*t was Theron.*

No matter how many times her mind repeated it, Kaila still couldn't comprehend the truth before her eyes. Theron was alive. Theron, who had taken her from that terrible place, who had opened her eyes to the cold cruelty of the Magisterium. Who had shown her how to use her Gift to fight back. The man she had loved, and then lost, was alive.

And now they were going to kill him all over again.

He looked almost at peace, as if these past few months had somehow heeled him from the broken, twisted creature he had become that night atop the Sanctum, consumed by addiction and withdrawal. His eyes gazed out over the crowd, as if they were searching for someone, and as Kaila grasped the agimet tight in her hand, they found her. A smile touched his lips, gentle, as if to say to her this was okay, that this had to happen.

*No. No, no, no!*

*"No!"*

With a scream, the last sliver of sanity and rational

thought shattered inside Kaila. She couldn't take it, couldn't let this happen. Not now. Not after all this time thinking she'd lost him and now discovering he lived. Never. *Never!*

First she needed power. She had already recharged her crystal, but as she drew on its *atar*, its glow diminished. She needed more. Loops of the nexus swirled all about the plaza and these she grasped, drawing them to the crystal, so that it brightened once again, its power renewing even as she drew more of it into her veins.

A hiss escaped her throat. The rush of that energy was beyond anything she'd felt before. It filled her up, the energy pulsing in her ears, her veins. It screamed to be used, and so her eyes shifted once more to the stage. To Rohan.

She had never loved him. You couldn't betray someone you loved the way she had done. She saw that now. It had only ever been the idea of what they could have created together.

She had hurt him, torn him apart with her betrayal. This was the monster she had created. But she had never harmed him. Not like this. He had already killed her friend in cold blood and stolen her hope. Now he wanted to take Theron as well.

*Atar* filled her soul, flooding from the crystal, and then pulsed from her in a wave. Not the Gift of Movement, but a sound. Harsh and shrill, it spilled through the plaza—and wherever it touched, the *soullights* of the crowd changed. Before they had been soft and muted, unsure at the sight of their Matron standing before the hangman's noose. But as that sound filled their souls…

Kaila gasped as a hand closed around her wrist. Immediately, the sound wavered, and she felt a peace replacing the cold rage. She blinked, as if coming up from a long dip in a mountain stream, and looked around.

Quintin stood beside her. She spoke his name. But something was wrong. He had betrayed her as well. Where was her rage?

"I'm here," he seemed to be struggling with his words. "Kaila, you have to stop…"

Stop? She frowned. It was him, wasn't it? This strange peace. A part of her wanted to embrace it. To imagine a world without the hurt and the anger and the rage.

Her eyes shifted from Quintin to the stage. Black armoured Wardens struggled through the crowd towards them, while beside the gallows, Rohan watched her with that odd frown she knew so well. Yes, she could stop, turn and flee this place.

Then she saw Rohan's hand reaching for the lever that would drop the trapdoors.

The harmony in her soul flickered, like a candle short of wax. The sharp notes of her rage cut through. The pain returned.

"I see it now," she whispered, turning to Quintin. "Thank you."

There was only one way to make things right. To make them all see what it was like to live her life, to understand the Elysian. She would share it with them all.

"For what, Kaila?" Quintin was shouting. She barely heard him over the pulsing in her soul, the wrenching, the tearing pain in her heart.

"For showing me the path," she replied. "Finally, I can make them all feel the way we do."

"No, Kaila—"

She felt his Gift again, understood it as he tried to restore the harmony. But his peace was just as much a lie as Ambrose's Weavings. Her hatred tore through it like a blade through paper. He had told her once that these people drew their hatred from their fears. Not Kaila. Hers had been earned by the cruelty of her people when they'd discovered her true nature, from the murder of her father and Caellum and Eliza.

She hated this world, this kingdom, this city. The Magisterium and its Wardens and its Sisters and Daughters.

And she hated Rohan Frye.

All of it, it built within her, a burning, crackling force, and then burst forth, and once more that terrible tolling rung through the square, carried by a wave of *atar* that pulsed from her soul.

It was time the people of Tah'raus understood.

For generations, Soul Square had been a place of judgment, a stage to judge murderers and traitors and criminals, to watch them meet their end.

Today, it was the turn of the people to be judged.

Eyes wide, they turned to one another. Jaws clenched. Fists trembled. A hush filled the plaza as Kaila's music stirred the darkness hidden within every man's soul.

Silence.

And then, a man moved. A knife flashed. A scream broke the stillness, as sharp as the distant thunder.

The dam broke.

And the slaughter began.

***

*RAGE!*

It was all he knew. Even his own name had been consumed by it, by the need to destroy, to lash out, to kill the ones that had caused this pain. The blade in his hand was slick with blood, his cuff soaked with it. And still he fought, still he needed to fill that void, to silence the hatred that demanded more and more and—

*This is not you, Quintin…*

The thought rose from deep within, cutting through the *buzzing* in his mind. For a second, he stilled, and he realised his hand had brushed against his pocket. There was something there, something that tingled with a familiar energy…

*Agimet.*

The rush of *atar* in his veins was like a mug of cold water in the depths of a raging fever. Quintin had gulped down half the crystal before he regained enough sense to pause. Reason returned and carefully, he used the *atar* to build a shrine in his soul. Inside it, he placed every good memory of his daughters, and Claire that he could summon.

It was the only thing that might hold against the pure hatred Kaila had cast upon the square.

He still didn't know how she was doing this. It was impossible for an Elysian to possess two Gifts. And yet he could not deny the bloody truth of his own eyes.

Just minutes ago, a hundreds of men and women had packed Soul Square. Already, dozens were dead. And the rest…

…the rest fought with a terrible, awful violence. With knife or sword or their bare hands, they set upon one another. Not even the Wardens had been spared, for while their armour resisted Elysian magic, the sheer weight of the crowd had pulled down those who'd been trying to reach Kaila.

His soul trembled as another wave washed through him. The light in his crystal flickered. His blood chilled. It wouldn't last—whereas Kaila could replenish her crystal from the nexus at a whim. He needed to reach her, to stop her before it died…

…but one glimpse of those burning eyes, and Quintin knew it was hopeless. So much *atar*…trying to stop her with his Gift would be like gnat biting a bison.

He jumped as overhead, thunder *cracked*. The rain poured down, mixing with the blood that filled the plaza. Rivulets of red ran through the gutters into the drains. A whimper slipped from Quintin's lips, and he closed his eyes—but he couldn't escape the sounds of the dying, nor the stench of all that blood.

His panic swelled as another pulse hit. He felt the anger rising in his soul again. What could he do? He was no one, *nothing*. He'd failed everyone he'd ever loved. He couldn't save these people. And why should he be the one to save them anyway? They hated him…

*Their hatred comes from fear…*

A shiver ran across his skin as he steadied his soul. Even with his Gift, it was difficult to resist Kaila's call. He had to stop her. Or find someone who could.

Then—he heard it. A roar. More beast than man. It was followed by the sound of flesh tearing like wet parchment.

---

THERON WATCHED THE CHAOS ENVELOPE THE PLAZA WITH A mix of dread and horrified curiosity. He had seen just about every one of the Elysian Gifts—even the fabled powers of a Wraith—but he'd never seen anything like what he witnessed now.

A piece of him knew this was only the power of a Psionic. He knew their Gift well enough from his training with Quintin to resist it—almost. But knowing something like this was *possible* was entirely different than seeing the reality.

Tah'raus had always been a raging pit of suffering and hatred. Kaila had simply pulled the cork from the bottle and set it loose upon itself. But as he stood balanced above the trap door, hands bound and a noose around his neck, he just couldn't understand *how* she was doing it.

Elysian couldn't have more than one Gift, and she was a Mover. He had witnessed it himself, the first time they'd met.

It wasn't possible.

Yet there she stood, eyes ablaze amidst the slaughter, more powerful than any Psionic he'd ever met. He doubted even his practice resisting Quintin's influence would have been enough to save him if he was any closer. The other nobles on the stage certainly hadn't been saved from its effects—they were currently occupied trying to tear themselves to pieces.

The only others who seemed unaffected were the remaining Wardens, and Jenna and Rohan.

The two wielders of the Aegis.

His stomach twisted as he met Jenna's eyes and saw her fear. They'd been *so close*. Why hadn't it worked? *It should have worked!* The legends said if the device was reclaimed by its makers, they would be freed. They should have had the power to stop Rohan, to crush the Wardens and free this city from the Magisterium.

Instead, Theron had found a cold, impenetrable barrier between himself and its power. They'd failed. And now they would hang. Whatever power Kaila might hold over those below, Theron knew well enough the limits of the human body—especially when it came to the Gift of the Elysian. She was using her Warden's Gift to replicate the properties of a broken crystal, giving her endless *atar*. But channelling all that energy still took its toll. She couldn't keep at it forever. And when her body gave out, Rohan and his Wardens would be waiting.

For now, the Wardens were keeping their new king safe on the other side of the stage. If only he and Jenna weren't bound, they might have slipped away into the crowd—though given the current agitation, that would be almost as dangerous as hanging around with the prince. His one good hand was slick with blood from trying to free himself, but however hard he pulled, the rough cords just dug deeper into his flesh.

Theron flinched as a *roar* sounded from the crowd. His breath caught as he saw a man bashing through people like they were made of straw. His eyes shone like the burning moons.

*Garrick.*

Theron's attempt to free himself abruptly turned from calculated to desperate. A regular man enraged by Kaila's power was dangerous, but a Bruiser would be death incarnate. Blood already coated Garrick's sleeves and chest and matted in his beard. Roaring, he batted aside another man in the crowd and grasped at the edges of the stage.

Almost sobbing, Theron tore at the bindings, and finally— slickened by his own blood—his hand slipped free. Crying with relief, he struggled to remove the noose, but with only one hand, the slipperiness worked against him. His fingers couldn't get a grasp on the slipknot.

He sensed Garrick's presence even before the shadow fell across him. The Bruiser's massive frame blotted out the burning sky and his chest rose and fell with the exertion below. Blood dripped from his beard and ran down his chest. Eyes burning, he stretched out one massive hand towards Theron's throat...

...and removed the rope with a flick of his powerful fingers.

Theron blinked, looking from the noose to the Bruiser's face—who grinned back. "Quintin helped me out," he said, before turning to Jenna.

Theron watched as the Bruiser freed Jenna from her bindings. They shared a glance as she rose. Quintin. So, the man was alive. Well, Theron's grudge would have to wait—they had to get out of here before Rohan noticed—

"Come for another round, Bruiser?" a metallic voice interrupted his thoughts.

Theron's stomach dropped into his breeches as he turned and found a Warden approaching. Four fully charged crystals shone on her chest, and she carried a sword almost as large as Theron.

"You again," Garrick grunted. His eyes darkened as he met the Warden's iron gaze. Apparently these two had a history. "Theron, you should go talk to Kaila. Quintin thinks you're the only one that can get through to her."

The rock in Theron's stomach did a little backflip. "Garrick…"

"Go, Theron," he growled. "Before Quintin runs out of *atar* and we all succumb to this madness."

Theron grimaced, but he gave a quick nod and grasped Jenna's hand. The Warden growled and advanced on them, but before she could engage, Garrick slammed into her with the force of a small avalanche, driving her backwards across the stage.

They took that as their opportunity to depart. Scrambling down the makeshift scaffolding, Theron looked around, but all was chaos. There'd been hundreds of people in Soul Square when this had started. Now there were…less. They had gathered to watch his execution, so Theron struggled to feel much empathy for them…

…except he knew the innocent were always swept up with the guilty. They had to stop this.

As if summoned by his thoughts, the mob around them stilled, then parted.

Quintin appeared. Advancing through the crowd, he came to a stop before Theron. They stood staring at one another for what felt like an age, though it was probably only a few seconds.

"Theron, I'm sorry—"

"It's forgotten, old friend," Theron said softly. The words surprised even himself, but he realised they were true. Seeing the slaughter in the square, he finally realised he wanted nothing more to do with anger and hatred.

Quintin's brows lifted, clearly surprised. Then his eyes were drawn to the burning glow at the centre of the square. "I'm almost out of *atar*, Theron."

"Then I'd better see what I can do." He hesitated, glancing at Jenna. "Will the Aegis…"

She grimaced. "It's protecting me," she replied, "but it still won't work for me."

"Then you'd better stay out of sight."

"What about you?"

It was a good point. Just standing on ground level, he could feel the song Kaila was singing in his heart. It raged against his wall of calm, battling to overwhelm him. He was struggling to maintain control as it was, and if he got any closer…

"Do you have enough *atar* left to keep me sane?" he asked, glancing at Quintin.

The Psionic's lips thinned. "I can maybe give you a minute, at best."

Theron grimaced. "That'll have to be enough."

---

*The world was chaos. The void in her soul swirled about the square, its emptiness made music, filling the people with the truth. That there was no future, no love, no hope. Only despair.*

*And so the people raged.*

*Finally, they could all feel what she felt, could understand what it was to be Elysian. To be hunted—hated—for something you couldn't control. To have everything you held precious snuffed out or taken away, turned against you, as if you were no better than dung beneath their feet.*

*Finally, they could see.*

"Kaila!"

*A voice. It rang through the power, the white-hot heat that burned within her. It almost fooled her, almost made her open herself again. As if she was still that person. Weak, able to be fooled, tricked into giving a piece of herself away, so they could hurt her again, and again, and again…*

"Kaila, it's me, *Theron!*"

*Theron…*

*That name. That name had started all this, hadn't it? The pain. She reached for the voice, to rend and break it, to make it* see, *but the song didn't take hold. The hatred only swirled around that soul, and passed on to others more susceptible.*

"Kaila, please, you have to stop this."

*Kaila. She knew that name as well. The fool that had allowed herself to be hurt. For them to stab and cut and rend until there was nothing left but a void…*

"They're dying, Kaila. Innocent people."

*A piece of her trembled. No, no, there were no innocents. Not anymore. They wanted to hurt her…*

*…and yet even as she thought it, she heard a scream. High-pitched, in pain. It cut through the rage, gave her pause.*

Blinking, Kaila rose slowly from the dark. Or rather, the light that had filled her. As she had drawn more and more power from the nexus to fill her crystal, to fuel her Gift, it had swollen within her, washed away all thought and reason, until there was only that fury, only all the hatred.

But something had interrupted it. The voice. She was

afraid to look, in case it was another trick. But she had to know. So gritting her teeth, she forced her eyes to open.

And found Theron standing before her.

*Theron.*

A part of her still didn't believe he could truly be alive. But she reached for him, and her hand brushed his cheek. It was warm to her touch.

"It's really you," she whispered.

A hint of that familiar smile touched his lips. "It's really me, kid," he whispered. Then he extended his hand. "Now, how about you hand over the agimet, and I get us out of here?"

She swayed on her feet, looking from him to the crystal she held. Hand it over? But it was…hers. She needed it, needed its power…

"Please, Kaila…" there was a note in Theron's voice that made her glance back at him. "Before anyone else gets hurt."

*Anyone else?*

She frowned, her eyes moving beyond Theron to the crowd…

Bodies covered the ground of *Soul Square.* All around her, twisted and torn and bloodied, they lay amongst the swirling rain, some with eyes closed, others still staring at her, accusing. She staggered back a step and almost tripped over a leg.

*No, no, no.*

This wasn't what she'd wanted. She hadn't done this, had she? She'd only wanted them to know what she felt inside, the darkness, the anger…

*The hatred.*

"No…" she whispered.

Her fist closed around the crystal, feeling the pulse of energy within…

…and then she released it.

The moment it left her fingers, the flow of *atar* cut off. Without it, the aftereffects of using so much *atar* in so little time struck her with the force of a runaway carriage. A gasp hissed from her lips as her knees buckled, every muscle in her body suddenly screaming out in agony. The darkness was already rising to swallow her up as she fell.

The last thing she knew was firm hands catching her before she could strike the pavement, and a voice in her ear.

"I've got you, Kaila. Everything's going to be alright."

THERON CAUGHT KAILA AS SHE FELL. HER BODY WAS LIMP, HER breath shallow, her skin hot to the touch. *What the hell are you, kid?* That kind of power, even a Psionic with a broken crystal couldn't have controlled so many people. And they certainly wouldn't have *survived* using that much *atar*.

He swallowed and held her tighter, his heart pounding. There would be time for questions later. His soul still felt taut, squeezed by the pressure of all that rage and loss and pain. Theron had played a part in that, he knew. He should have told her about the broken crystal and his addiction back in Iselador. Instead, he'd pushed her away. Ignored her warnings when she'd tried to tell him the Matron was plotting something.

A flicker of movement caught in the corner of his eye. He turned as Quintin lifted the crystal Kaila had dropped. It was still fully charged, and as the Psionic's fingers closed around the crystal, his eyes glowed afresh.

"Is she alive?" he asked, not looking at Theron. His gaze swept the plaza, taking in the remnants of the battle.

"She'll live, I think."

A frown came to Theron's lips as he heard the distant

clash of weapons. Following the Psionic's gaze, his heart quickened. Of the initial crowd, a few near the exits had managed to flee before Kaila's Gift got its hooks in them, but many more lay twisted and broken on the pavement. The fortunate had died quickly, while others struggled to drag themselves through the dirt and the blood to safety. Yet others were still on their feet, a hundred or more…

"Why are they still killing each other?" Theron croaked, his heart clenching.

"They're too far gone," Quintin whispered. "By the time the effects fully wear off…"

Theron glanced at Kaila, then at the Psionic. Laying her down, he rose and extended his hand. "Give me the crystal," he said softly. "I'll shake them until they regain their senses."

"There's too many for that," Quintin replied, still not looking at Theron. "Do you remember what you said that last night by the pool?"

"About…my father?"

"About burning it all down." Finally, the Psionic turned to him. "You were right, Theron. So long as the Magisterium rules, no one in this Trickster forsaken land will ever know hope."

Theron frowned. "What are you saying, Quintin?"

Quintin's eyes travelled past Theron to where Kaila lay. "I don't know *what* she is," he said softly, "but she's your fire, Theron. Just…" He paused, eyes lifting to meet Theron's. "When it's all over, just make sure there's someone left to help rebuild." With that, he turned towards crowd.

"Quintin, wait!" Theron cried, starting after his friend. "What are you doing?"

"You should go, Theron," Quintin called back. "Look after our people. You're all they've got now."

"Quintin, I'm not—"

*Fear. Terror. Unthinkable dread. It filled him from the depths of his soul, unmanned him. He barely paused to lift the girl before he fled from that terror, from the terrible unspeakable danger, until…*

"Theron…Theron, what's happening? Why did you stop?"

Gasping, Theron blinked and looked around, surprised to find himself in the main street. He carried Kaila over his shoulder and Jenna was beside him, her brow wrinkled with concern. Heart pounding, he looked back. They were already half a mile from Soul Square.

Quintin had used his Gift on him. That wasn't supposed to be possible. He'd trained himself to resist a Psionic's abilities, been trained by Quintin himself…

*Trickster curse you, Quintin!*

Snarling, he made to go back, but Jenna caught him by the hand. "Theron, stop," she whispered. "You can't. The Warden's…"

Even as she spoke, bells began to toll from the direction of the plaza.

***

QUINTIN'S HEART TWISTED AS HE WATCHED THERON FLEE. A piece of him felt guilty. When he'd taught the man how to defend himself from a Psionic, Quintin had been sure to leave a little chink he could exploit if the need ever arose. Theron would never forgive him for the betrayal—but it had been worth it to save his friend's life.

Besides, he couldn't stay angry at Quintin for long. It was hard to stay angry at a dead man.

*First, however, you've got work to do.*

Drawing in a breath, he pulled *atar* from the crystal Kaila had dropped. It *burned* with so much power, Quintin wasn't sure how it hadn't shattered. It was just as well, however, as even with a fully charged crystal his task would be nigh impossible.

The fighting was concentrated around the stage now, as the surviving citizens tried to reach the noblemen taking shelter atop gallows. Kaila's influence over their souls might have ended, but all this hatred and anger was their own. The strange young Elysian had only brought it to the fore.

Now, even without her power influencing them, those emotions were still far more powerful than their better counterparts. Someone had to reverse what she had done, to bring back the love and warmth inside these people.

A shiver ran through Quintin as he opened his soul and heard their collective song. It was awful, sharp and grating, discordant as it filled the air, inviting each of them to greater and greater acts of violence.

He swallowed. It would be so easy to walk away. To leave these people to suffer the hatred they had invited into their hearts. Most would have done just that—especially with the prince and his Wardens still lurking atop that stage.

*Their hatred comes from fear.*

Maybe Quintin could make them fear the Elysian just a little less.

Gritting his teeth, he strode towards the mob, extending his Gift as he did so. He didn't have unlimited power like Kaila, so he spun out threads of *atar*, inviting in the music of each *soullight* he encountered. Even in this manner, the strain quickly grew as first dozens—then hundreds—weighed on his soul.

He played his own song to counter it. A music of life and beauty. Of his, Claire, who had been the love of his life, and his children Max and Jasmine, the warmth of their smiles, the wonder in their eyes as they looked upon this city, the beauty of their Gift as they held a piece of agimet for the first time.

These people and their fear had taken them from Quintin, but he refused to let that pain fester into hate, to be consumed by those emotions again.

Instead, he strode through their ranks, the music of his *soullight* spreading to those connected souls. And as they heard its warmth, the people paused—and the madness left their eyes. A stillness passed through the crowd, followed by a sorrow. Some only stood, staring into the distance, while others sank to their knees and began to softly sob. A few turned and fled, desperate to escape the horror their own hatred had wrought.

And still Quintin advanced, until the last of the survivors had fallen silent, until the fighting and the bloodshed and the death had stopped.

Until he reached the stage.

There, at last, he stopped and looked up to those above. Here, too, he tried to extend his love—but at last his Gift met a power it could not match. The Aegis protected the prince, and the black armour of the Warden's consumed the last threads of his *atar*. In his hand, the crystal spluttered, its light dying. A sharp *crack* echoed through the square as it crumbled to dust.

The music in his soul fell silent. But it had done its task, lifting the survivors from the all-encompassing darkness. Smiling, Quintin turned to the survivors. There were tears in the eyes of many as they looked back, and more than a few were unable to meet his gaze. They knew what he had done. They had heard his music in their very souls.

His eyes continued though, eventually returning the stage and the eyes of the prince.

"We are not all evil, Prince Rohan," he said softly. "Some of us have only ever wanted peace."

Whispers spread through the crowd, while beside the gallows, the young prince stood frozen, his eyes wide, lips parted. Quintin couldn't hear his soul, but he knew that look of sudden uncertainty, the internal crisis of doubt.

Then a snarl broke through the silence.

"Do not let this creature fool you, my king," a Warden strode across the stage. Blood streaked her black armour and her sword shimmered in the gloom. Behind her, Quintin glimpsed a massive body. His stomach twisted as he recognised Garrick.

"This creature wrought this evil," the Warden continued, her voice rising so the crowd could hear her words, "now it seeks to gain from bringing it to an end."

A ripple went through the survivors. Some glanced again at Quintin, while others wavered. He didn't need a crystal to sense the change in mood, the way their faces hardened, their posture stiffening. So much blood had already been spilt this day—it would not take much for them to resume the slaughter.

Extending his arms, Quintin bowed his head. "I would not wish this darkness upon my worst enemies."

"Lower the stairs."

His heart began to thunder as the prince's words cut through the tension. There was a buzz of whispers as the crowd drew back, followed by a *thud* as a set of wooden stairs were drawn out and lowered from the stage.

Heavy boots sounded on wood, then splashed into the mud.

Quintin lifted his head as the prince approached. Light shimmered from the crystals embedded in the Aegis on his wrist. The old king had worn it as a bracelet similar to the Matron's—but as Rohan neared, the device changed. Silver metal flowed like liquid, forming into a blade in Rohan's hand.

He came to a stop before Quintin. The pair stood for a moment, staring into one another's eyes. A part of Quintin pitied this man. All his life, Rohan had been little more than a pawn—first to his parents, and later in Theron and Kaila's plan to steal the Aegis. Little wonder there was such hatred in his heart now.

"Did you truly stop the killing, Elysian?" Rohan spoke suddenly.

"Your Majesty—" the Warden started, but Rohan held up his hand—the one holding the Aegis—and she fell silent.

Quintin met the young man's eyes. "You have my word, Rohan," he said quietly. "I did all in my power to stop this."

"Then I thank you, Elysian," Rohan said softly. "For your service to the Magisterium, I grant you a quick death."

Quintin flinched at the words, but he was already too late. The prince moved faster than he would have believed possible for a human, the silver blade in his hand blurring as it lanced out. It caught Quintin in the chest before he could take a single step.

Strangely, there was no pain as he stood there. His eyes fell slowly to the blade, and he watched with a disjointed fascination as the crystals within the metal flickered and darkened, almost taking on a scarlet colour.

*Thump, thump, thump…*

Quintin felt the pounding of his heart slow, sensed the flickering of his soul.

His knees buckled and the world tilted. He sank to the ground, the breath catching in his throat. His vision blurred. The square, the stage, Rohan—all dissolved, their colours bleeding into one another like the coming of dawn.

*Thump, thump…*

How he wanted to hear that music one last time, to feel the city awakening. He tried to draw on his Gift, to find some remnant of that music—but there was nothing. Instead, the silence was growing, the sounds of the world retreating before the dark. Then…

Claire's smile.

Max's laughter.

Jasmine's hand in his.

He heard the music one last time, the souls he had loved throughout his long life. Men and women he had loved and lost, and those who marched on, who would fight the good fight after he was gone, the ones who would build a new world, one his children could be proud of. It was a gentle song, wistful, filled with love and loss, and the hope of peace.

*Thump…*

And then there was silence.

# EPILOGUE

For days, Kaila drifted in and out of a haze. Whether it was sleep, a coma, or something in between, she didn't know, but when she finally woke almost a week after the incident in Soul Square, her body no longer hurt. That should have been a relief, but instead, she felt worse than ever. Her mind was filled with images of the aftermath, the bloodshed and the death her power had left in its wake.

When she finally felt strong enough to rise, Kaila went looking for Theron. The others in the hideout had filled her in on events since she'd lost consciousness. Theron and Jenna had escaped, carrying her to safety. But they'd lost others. Eliza and Garrick and Quintin. And of course, Ambrose was still missing. In their absence, Theron was doing his best to salvage what he could of the tailor's organisation. Thankfully, the underground remembered him, and after coming back from the Sanctum—from death itself—his status had been elevated to almost god like.

She found him in the study, hunched over a desk covered in papers and scrolls. Her heart pulsed in her ears as she watched him, still hardly able to believe it was really him. All this time, she'd thought him dead; now for him to just *be there*, missing a hand albeit, but scratching notes on a stack of papers…it felt unreal.

"Kaila," he said without looking up, surprising her. "How are you feeling?"

She hesitated in the doorway. "Can we talk?"

Setting down his quill, he looked up with a smile. It was forced, but after all this time, it was a relief just to look into those emerald eyes again.

"Of course," he said, gesturing for her to close the door. "I think it's past time."

Kaila swallowed. That was…ominous. She closed the door anyway and sat in the chair opposite him. Clasping her hands in her lap, she stared at them as if they were suddenly the most interesting things in the world.

"What am I?" she said at last, the words bursting from her lips in a rush.

A pause. "I was hoping you might be able tell me."

Her eyes slid closed. "I'm not a Mover."

"We both know that's not true," Theron said gently. "I've seen you use that Gift."

She shook her head, eyes lifting to meet his gaze. "I mean, I'm not *just* a Mover." A deep breath. "You remember how I passed the Test of the Aegis?"

He nodded. "We never could explain it."

"I can now," she replied. "Until I met you in the mines, I didn't have any power. Or at least," she continued when Theron opened his mouth to speak, "I didn't understand how to use it."

Theron frowned. "Understand?"

She looked away, out the tall window to where the

Sanctum rose, black and gleaming against the sky. Her throat tightened at the memory of the square.

"That day, when I was holding the crystal, I *saw* you use your Gift and…I understood. I knew how it worked."

"I'm not sure I'm following. That's how the Gift works."

Kaila swallowed. "Except it happened again, when Quintin used his power on me the first time."

"What?"

"You remember that night I brought Eliza to the shop. I was…agitated. Quintin used his Gift to calm me. I wanted to see what he was doing, so I used my *atar sense* to watch and… something happened."

Theron's eyes widened. "I remember…" he trailed off.

"I didn't realise it, but I understood then how his Psionic Gift worked," she swallowed, looking down at her hands as tears formed in her eyes. "But then I put on Eliza's collar and my powers were muted. We all forgot what had happened…"

"Until you escaped," Theron surmised, "but then Quintin and I were gone, and your power…it just seemed to be acting strangely."

"Because I wasn't just moving things anymore," Kaila whispered. "I was feeling them. Altering their soul's song—"

Her voice cracked and she squeezed her eyes closed. It didn't make any sense. An Elysian couldn't have more than one Gift—that was the first thing Theron had taught her. And yet…the rules had never truly applied to her. Because she wasn't *just* an Elysian. She had the powers of a Warden as well.

Not that her Gifts had ever done her any good. All she'd ever done was get the people she loved killed.

The silence stretched out between them, the pressure in Kaila's chest building, until she couldn't take it any longer.

"*I'm so sorry!*" she gasped, "I didn't mean—"

Theron was there in an instant, his arms wrapping around her, holding her tight. "It's not your fault, Kaila," he murmured. "You didn't know."

"I saw them, Theron," she sobbed, tears streaming down her face and dampening Theron's shirt. "I felt them all." She clung to him like he was the last real thing in the world, and he hugged her back, his strength reassuring, promising her everything would be okay, that she was safe…

…Kaila didn't know how it happened, but suddenly she was kissing him.

And the cold was gone, the heat of his presence filling her up, chasing away the pain. For one moment, one singular heartbeat, she felt she could escape the terrible knowledge of what had happened, what she'd done…

But then he pulled away. "Kaila…" Theron whispered, and his eyes were filled with apology.

"What is it?"

"I'm sorry." His eyes flicked past her.

She turned.

Jenna stood in the doorway. She wore a plain emerald dress—nothing like the kind she'd worn in the Sanctum, but her auburn hair was the same, tumbling in silky waves around her shoulders. There was an expression of regret in her gaze as their eyes met.

And Kaila knew.

It shouldn't have hurt. Not after everything else that had happened. Somehow, it did.

She nodded curtly, unable to keep the pain from her voice. "I see. I'm sorry too." She rose and strode to the doorway, until she stood face to face with the former Matron. Jenna was the first to look away. Kaila swept past without a backwards glance.

Her feet carried her back to her bedroom. She had her

own now. No bunks to share, no Eliza to whisper midnight secrets with or drag her away in the mornings to pore over endless records from Ambrose's spies. Just her.

Alone.

Tonight, however, the world refused to leave her alone. Kaila's head had barely touched the pillow when a tap came from the door. She didn't answer. Hopefully they would take the hint and go away.

Instead, it opened with a soft creak. Snarling, Kaila lifted her head to send the intruder fleeing with a curse—and froze when she found Jenna standing in the doorway.

"I'm sorry you had to find out that way," the former Matron said softly.

Kaila struggled to swallow the curse she wanted to spit at the woman. "What do you want?" she asked instead.

Jenna opened her mouth, as if to apologise again, then closed it. She crossed the room instead, coming to a stop over Kaila's bed. Then reaching to her arm, she grasped the shimmering light that was the Aegis and slipped it from her wrist.

"This should have been yours," she said. "You should have it."

For a second, all Kaila could do was gape at the device. "You won," she managed at last. "It's yours."

"Except I can't use it," Jenna replied. "If you're really going to fight Rohan and the Magisterium, this is the best chance any of you have."

"Then Theron should take it."

"Theron doesn't want anything more to do with agimet and the Elysian Gift."

Kaila's eyes widened at that. She'd been so consumed by her own pain and what she'd done, she hadn't even asked about Theron's addiction. A tremor shook her soul, and a piece of her was forced to admit that maybe Theron had made the right decision, picking someone that wasn't as… broken as her.

"Take it, Kaila."

Kaila swallowed. She had once dreamed of wielding this artefact—had sacrificed everything to steal it from people like Jenna.

So why did she hesitate now?

Slowly, cautiously, she reached for it. Even before her fingers met that strange, ethereal metal, she could feel the energy building, like a charge between two magnets. Trembling, she closed her hand around the device.

Immediately, light burst from every crystal in the Aegis— as well as every piece of agimet in the room—brighter than she had ever seen it burn for Jenna or the old Matron. And as she slid it onto her wrist, she felt something inside her responding to it, a flicker of power, a warmth that burst to life and grew, swelling, filling her like the first breath of a newborn.

She clenched her fist, and the entire world seemed to tremble.

And then, a voice in her mind:

*Hello, little lamb. I thought you'd never call.*

---

**Enjoyed Warrior's Redemption? Don't forget to leave a review!**

# A NOTE FROM THE AUTHOR

So turns out this isn't a trilogy! Who knew? Well, I might have figured it out in the last book when Kaila's little heist lasted 120k words and I didn't get to the point where things went wrong with her magic! The Daughter's collar really put a pause on that little plot point, but I'm quite happy that it let me put her struggle front and centre in this book—as well as introduce a couple of new characters who've been waiting in the shadows for some time.

As for future books, poor old Kaila just can't catch a break can she? Maybe she'll finally get one in book four now she has the Aegis? And a voice speaking in her mind? Yeahhhh, guess we'll find out soon enough. I'm already writing the outline for book four and have an ending in mind, so hopefully it'll all come together nice and tidy in time for Christmas!

For now, if this is my first series you've read, don't forget to check out my other series. You can even get a couple of my books for free by signing up to my newsletter. Hopefully you'll find them just as enjoyable as this one.

Write on!
Aaron

**FOLLOW AARON HODGES...**

And receive TWO FREE novels and a short story!
https://aaronhodgesauthor.com/newsletter

Book 1: Warbringer

Book 2: Wrath of the Forgotten

Book 3: Age of Gods

Book 4: Dreams of Fury

### *The Alfurian Chronicles*

Book 1: Defiant

Book 2: Guardian

Book 3: Conquest

### *The Swords of Heaven and Hell*

Book 1: Darkstrider

Book 2: Voidlight

### *The Four Circles*

Book 1: Help! My Wizard Mentor Had A Heart Attack And Now I'm Being Chased By A Horde Of Giant Spiders!

### *The Untamed Isles*

The Path Awakens

9 781991 018366